Cover to Covers

By

Alexandrea Weis

This is a work of fiction. Names, characters, places, and incidents are products of the author's imagination or are used fictitiously and are not to be construed as real. Any resemblance to actual events, locations, organizations, or person, living or dead, is entirely coincidental.

Copyright © Alexandrea Weis 2014
2nd Edition WEBA Publishing, LLC March 19, 2015

Licensing Notes

All rights reserved. No part of this book may be used or reproduced in any manner whatsoever without written permission, except in the case of brief quotations embodied in articles and reviews.

Editor: Maxine Bringenberg

Chapter 1

Veins of gold embedded in the onyx marble floor shimmered in the late afternoon sunlight that was sneaking in through the hotel's teak and glass entrance. Elegant arrangements of white orchids were strategically placed throughout the busy lobby, while women of all shapes and sizes, wearing skimpy fashions so common in the hot Dallas summer, were flitting about, carrying oversized suitcases and vying for the attention of anyone who would take the time to notice. Sharply dressed hotel staff politely scurried amid the guests, dutifully indulging the whims of their clientele. At the ornate teak-stained front desk, expensive leather luggage was piled atop several tall, gold racks, waiting to be delivered to rooms. Next to the bags, white-gloved porters stood at attention, demonstrating the renowned five-star service offered by the Ritz-Carlton Hotel.

"If I can be of any further assistance, Mr. Moore," a peppy blonde with too much black eyeliner said to the man in the impeccably tailored, dark blue Hugo Boss suit. "Please, let me know. I have your suite key." She pushed the white key-card over the surface of the front desk. "Your usual order of Veuve Clicquot and strawberries will be waiting in your room," she added with a welcoming smile.

The self-assured gentleman removed his dark Porsche sunglasses and let his deep-set dark brown eyes linger over the young woman's attractive face. "Afraid I won't be needing that this time, Missy," he murmured, getting a glimpse at her nametag.

"Oh, I'm sorry, Mr. Moore. I was informed you are always to have a bottle of Veuve Clicquot waiting in your room whenever you stay with us."

Wandering over Missy's stout figure, his eyes fixated on the way her blue blazer clung to her ample bosom. "I usually do when I'm staying here for a relaxing weekend. This time, however, is all business." He placed his sunglasses in his jacket pocket.

Missy leaned forward, revealing her cleavage as her blue eyes meandered up and down his body. "I am very sorry to hear that, Mr. Moore."

The flirtatious pout that puckered her red lips made Tyler Moore wipe his hand across his chin, attempting to hide his cocky grin. At six-foot-one, with black, wavy hair outlining his chiseled cheekbones and determined, square jaw, he was used to getting such suggestive looks from the opposite sex. But he knew that looks could only get you so far with a woman.

"How sorry are you?"

Missy's eyes popped with interest. "I…I'm not sure what you mean, Mr. Moore."

"How sorry are you that I won't be having any fun this weekend, Missy?"

She fingered the lapel on her blue blazer adjacent to her right breast. "I would hate to think your stay here would only be about business, Mr. Moore. If there was anything I could do to change that…."

He felt a kick of satisfaction as he gazed into her hopeful eyes. "Perhaps you might come up with a few suggestions of other ways I could spend my weekend in your wonderful hotel? We could go over them later…at the bar, after you get off work."

The pale blush blossoming on her cheeks was so becoming that Tyler almost began to believe their playful repartee had been worth the effort.

"I'll think about it, Mr. Moore."

"You do that, Missy. When you have an answer, you know where to find me." He motioned to his overnight bag and black suitcase by the desk. "Be a sweetheart, and have the porter take my bags to my room. I have to meet a client in the bar before I go up to my suite."

The flush on Missy's cheeks was positively radiant. "Yes, Mr. Moore. Right away."

Tyler turned from the polished reception desk, unable to hide his smug grin. No matter where he went, the lust in a woman's eyes never got old. The entire episode with the desk clerk had only reinforced his belief that it was his confidence, and not his looks, that always got a woman to give him what he wanted. He had learned long ago that his handsome face could only take him so far in life, and had made a concerted effort to take control of any situation. It was a philosophy he had incorporated into every arena of his life.

"I'll have to check back in with sweet little Missy. See how she looks without the blazer." He strutted across the lobby toward the arched entrance of the Rattlesnake Bar.

A warm glow of honey, onyx, and a contemporary Western-theme greeted him as he stepped into the cool bar. Perched on the brown leather barstools, an array of women sipped on a myriad of colorful alcoholic concoctions while trying to chase away the sweltering afternoon heat. Tyler noted how more than one set of eyes turned his way as he strolled up to the bar. He checked his confidence at the door and pushed all thoughts of possible late night hookups from his mind.

His flourishing oil and gas business was always more important than women. Besides, women were nothing more than a distraction at this point in his life. Having just passed the milestone of his fiftieth birthday, Tyler pondered that perhaps it was time for him to stop pursuing such meaningless liaisons and settle down with a tolerable woman who could cater to all of his needs.

"Two divorces is plenty," he reasoned as he arrived at the onyx marble and teak-topped bar. Lightly stroking the smooth surface of the marble, he remembered many of the encounters he had experienced in that very bar. Snapshots of blurred faces and forgettable names skipped across his mind. Some of the women had been exciting, a few horrific, but none had been…memorable.

You know who was memorable, don't you, Ty? *his inner voice taunted.* She was the one you let slip through your fingers.

Tyler snickered at his self-remonstrations. He hated to admit his inner demon was right, but it was. She had happened so long ago, but he found it funny how advancing age only seemed to make the memories of youth more poignant. It was as if growing older brought into focus the emotions that the impetuosity of youth seemed to blur.

"Mr. Moore," a gray-haired bartender in a red vest cheerfully greeted. "Welcome back to the Ritz-Carlton Hotel. Do you want your usual?"

"Yes, Mike." Tyler nodded. "Thanks for remembering."

"Of course, Mr. Moore." Mike reached for an old-fashioned glass and a carton of orange juice from the shelf below the bar. "You here for another weekend of…." Mike's dull gray eyes swerved to a group of women at the bar. "Your usual fun?"

"Strictly business this time around, Mike." Tyler grinned, looking amused. "I'm waiting on a client and will be tied up with meetings all weekend."

Mike finished pouring the orange juice. "What a shame. I've come to enjoy your weekends here, Mr. Moore. I live vicariously through your adventures at the Ritz-Carlton." He placed a napkin down on the polished marble before he set the glass of orange juice on top of it.

"Thank you, Mike. I'm flattered." Tyler scanned the crowded bar. "Is it my imagination, or are there a lot of women here for a Friday afternoon?"

"Not your imagination, Mr. Moore. There's some big romance convention in town." Mike waved casually to the barroom. "Several of the authors are staying here, along with their fans."

Tyler picked up his drink. "That would explain the women. Shame I have such a full agenda this weekend."

"Might not be your kind of crowd, Mr. Moore."

Tyler sipped his orange juice. "What makes you say that?"

Reaching for a towel, Mike chuckled. "Have you ever read a romance novel?"

"I can't say that I have."

Mike wiped away an unseen spot on the countertop. "My wife's addicted to them. I think most romance readers are the kind that only live vicariously through their steamy novels, and are not apt to fulfill those fantasies in real life."

"I guess it's sort of how you live vicariously through my adventures, eh Mike?"

"Safer that way, for everyone." Mike let his eyes take a turn of the room. "My wife has been talking about this convention for weeks; says she can't wait to meet all of her favorite authors."

"Really? Who are they?"

"A Penny Band or Brand, then Nigela Franklin…and of course, there is her absolute favorite, Monique…something."

A cold stab shot across Tyler's chest. He slowly put his drink down on the bar. "Monique?" His dark eyes never left his glass. "Do you happen to know her last name?"

"Not sure." Mike let out a short, snort-like laugh. "You would think after all the times my wife talked about her books I would remember. I know she's from New Orleans, though."

Tyler's stomach clenched. "Her name wouldn't happen to be Monique Delome, would it?"

"Yeah, that's it, Delome." Mike paused, observing Tyler with a renewed interest. "I thought you said you never read romance novels, Mr. Moore?"

"I haven't. I once knew a Monique Delome from New Orleans, but that was many years ago."

Mike dipped his head toward a section of brown leather booths at the other end of the bar. "Well, maybe she's the same woman you knew. She happens to be one of the writers staying at our hotel."

Tyler froze. "She's staying here?"

Mike's dull gray eyes twinkled with interest. "I take it she was a very good old friend."

Tyler got ahold of his emotions. What kind of man was he if he let the mention of her name get to him? "No, it's nothing like that. We were…." He shrugged.

"Yeah, I know what you mean. It's sort of like all those romance books my wife reads. She must go through a dozen or so a month, but when I ask her what they were about, she just shrugs. But when I ask her to tell me about her favorites, she can remember them like she just read them…even if she happened to read them a long time ago." The bartender slowly smiled. "The good ones always stay with you," he added.

Tyler lifted his drink from the bar. "Yes, they do."

A waiting customer momentarily distracted Mike. Standing just down from Tyler, a supercilious man was tapping his fingers impatiently on the bar. Tyler studied the stranger over the rim of his glass. His curly gray hair, lofty blue eyes, stoic features, and fitted gray suit reeked of irritation and arrogance. Tyler guessed that they were about the same age, but the world-weary essence in the man's eyes made him seem much older, but not very much wiser.

"I need a Dewar's and water, and a soda water with lemon," the haughty man ordered in a deep voice.

"Yes, sir." Mike nodded and turned away to make his drinks.

"You here for the convention?" the man inquired, his condescending eyes gliding up and down Tyler's figure.

"Me?" Tyler put his glass down. "No, I, ah…just heard about this romance thing." He curiously inspected the man. "You here with your wife?"

The man's hard features softened slightly. "No, I'm here with my client." He rested his elbow on the bar. "I manage a few writers and have to come to these things to make sure other agents and publishing houses don't steal them away. It's a real cutthroat business."

Tyler's eyebrows went up. "Cutthroat? Romance novels?" He suppressed an urge to break out in hysterical laugher. "I never realized it could be that way."

"I know, it sounds silly." The man's rigid posture relaxed as he moved closer to the bar. "But the women who work in this business are tougher than my male clients. The science fiction geeks have nothing on these romance writers."

Tyler rubbed his hand across his chin, hiding his grin. "I'll bet." He browsed the stranger's designer suit, posh Italian leather shoes, and the hint of the expensive steel watch under the sleeve of his jacket. Whatever he did for his writers, Tyler sensed he was good at it.

"So what does a manager do for a romance writer?"

The stranger pitched his head thoughtfully to the side. "Keeps the world at bay so they can write, would be the gist of it. I arrange their book signings, publicity tours, and attendance at these conventions, so they don't have to worry about it. Like many writers, they just want to stay at home and work on the next book. My job is to allow them to do exactly that. For some of my best writers, I do a hell of a lot more."

"Like what?" Tyler probed, intrigued.

The tall man cleared his throat as Mike returned with his drinks. "I become secretary, manager, friend, confidant, maid, and sometimes even a cook." He waved a tapering hand over the drinks on the bar. "Charge it to suite 831, will you?" he directed.

"Sure thing," Mike replied.

The gentleman pivoted his wary blue eyes back to Tyler. "I'm Chris, by the way. Chris Donovan." He held out his hand to Tyler.

Tyler nodded, giving him a firm handshake. "Tyler Moore."

Chris claimed his drinks from the bar. "Good to meet you, Tyler. You here long?"

"Just two days on business. I have a client coming in town from DC."

"Where are you from?"

"From here," Tyler asserted. "But I find it easier to stay in a hotel in town rather than driving back and forth from my home in North Dallas. The expressways are always packed."

"Yeah, I hear you. I live in Atlanta and the traffic there is getting ridiculous."

Tyler checked his pricey gold Italian watch that kept lousy time. "I suspect the traffic is probably why my client is twenty minutes late."

Chris let go a deep chuckle that belayed his suspicious eyes. "Sounds like one of my clients. They blame it on the traffic, but we know better." He turned to the booths against the wall. "Speaking of which, I'd better get back to mine. Good meeting you."

"You too, Chris."

Chris Donovan quickly maneuvered across the crowded bar to a corner brown leather booth. Tyler was interested to see who he was taking a drink to when a rolling lilt of laughter from further down the bar made him look away. That laugh sounded very familiar to Tyler. When he turned back, Chris was sitting at a booth across from a petite blonde with her back to him. The blonde stretched out a slender arm for the glass of soda water. Tyler waited to see her face. Then, she slowly eased around, and just as he caught a glimpse of her aquiline profile, a curvaceous brunette with perfect Barbie Doll features and dancing brown eyes hopped in front of Tyler.

"I thought that was you." The brunette's full lips curved into an alluring grin. "Happy to see me?" she added in a husky tone.

Tyler's heart sank. "Hadley, what are you doing here?" He peered down her snug green wrap dress to her black high heels.

"Janet Brubaker is meeting me for cocktails." Hadley ran her perfectly manicured hand along the sleeve of his blue suit jacket. "What? No kiss hello?"

Years ago Tyler had found her sultry voice to be seductive as hell. Now, it grated against his nerves like sandpaper on cement. Her smooth, creamy skin was still flawless, thanks to her plastic surgeon's expensive care, and her figure was still as firm as the day he had met her. But her sad brown eyes were the only true mirror to all the disappointment and ugliness that she hid behind her superficial façade.

"I'm here meeting a client, Hadley." Tyler grabbed for his orange juice. "Shouldn't you be out spending more of my monthly allowance?"

She tossed back her long, kinky brown hair. "Tyler, when are you going to forget about this silly divorce and let me come home?"

"It's not a silly divorce, Hadley. I've told you a hundred times, I'm done with you, your friends, and our marriage."

She seemed unflustered by his remarks. "I know better; that's why I've never signed the papers."

"After four years of living apart, I thought you wanted the divorce so you could marry your yoga instructor."

"You know Alfredo was only a fling. They all were." Her eyes came together, making her look much older than forty-one. "You were no saint yourself, Tyler. What about Maria, Belinda, and what was that chef's name?"

"Tammy," he admitted. "And you know I never started seeing anyone until you hooked up with that polo player."

She wistfully rolled her eyes. "Yes, Pierre was quite the charmer...not like you even cared who I slept with. You were always too busy with your stepfather's company."

Tyler tightly gripped his glass of orange juice as a knot pressed into the center of his chest. "It's my company now, Hadley, and somebody had to pay the bills."

"Have you told Barbara yet about the divorce?" Hadley smirked. "You know she will be furious."

"I could care less what my mother thinks."

"Oh, please. That heartless bitch has dictated every move you make for years, Tyler. You like to think that she has no control over you, but she does."

"My mother has got nothing to do with our marriage."

She rolled her head back and cackled. "Are you kidding? The woman damned near hand-picked me for you, just like your first wife, what's-her-name?"

The ringing of his cell phone made him put his glass down on the bar. When he pulled the iPhone from his trouser pocket, there was a text message waiting for him. After reading the brief text, he mumbled, "Shit."

Hadley leaned over and peeked at the screen on his phone. "Who is your newest flavor of the month? She got a name?"

Tyler yanked the phone out of her line of sight. "Grow up, Hadley. My client just bailed on me. His flight still hasn't arrived at DFW."

Hadley linked her arm around his. "Then you can buy me a drink. I'll blow off Janet, and you and I can spend some time together."

He pushed off her arm. "I don't think so."

"Are you staying at the hotel? You always preferred to stay in the city when you had weekend business meetings."

Tyler angrily shoved the phone into his trouser pocket. "Yes, I'm staying here for the weekend. Why?"

"Maybe we could go back to your room?" She brushed against him. "We can order room service and have a nice dinner together. Like old times."

He recoiled from her. "Sorry, Hadley, I have dinner plans."

"What about after dinner?"

He cocked an eyebrow at her. "What about Tessa? Shouldn't you be getting back home to your daughter?"

The edges of her mouth rose in a sardonic smile. "Your daughter, too, Tyler."

"Stepdaughter, Hadley. Stop using your kid against me. You know I care for her, but I'm not going to stay married to you to spare her another divorce." He went to take a step around her when Hadley blocked his way.

"So, who is she? Who's the woman you want to divorce me for?"

"There's no one, Hadley. Maybe I just want to be free of you and all of your bullshit."

Hadley fingered the lapel of his jacket. "Come on, Tyler, have dinner with me for old times' sake. We can discuss the divorce, if you like."

"There's nothing to discuss. Fred Bishop has already outlined the settlement for you. Don't suck up to me for more money. You're getting plenty."

She stood back from him. "I've told you and that idiot attorney of yours I will never agree to any terms. I like being Mrs. Tyler Moore. Your name opens a lot of doors for me in this city, and if we get divorced those doors are going to slam shut."

"You're a real piece of work, Hadley. We haven't been husband and wife for over four years, but you still want to keep me around, for what? So you can get into the best parties, dine at the best restaurants without a reservation, attend all of those social events you so desperately love to go to?"

"You know it. I like being Mrs. Moore, and I plan on being Mrs. Moore for a long time to come."

He angled closer and glared into her cold brown eyes. "Not if I can help it. You want me to keep paying for your Botox, plastic surgeries...." He motioned to her low-cut, green dress. "And all the fine clothes you like to buy, then you had better sign the goddamned papers and end this marriage, or I will cut you off."

Her smug grin stayed plastered on her perfectly made-up face. "You wouldn't dare. I could sue you for that."

"Sign the papers, Hadley. If you don't, I swear to God I will—"

"Excuse me," an airy, feminine voice cut in.

When Tyler turned to the woman standing next to them, his world came to a grinding halt.

The very petite, pale, dirty blonde had rosy cheeks, and sleek cheekbones that screamed of a Northern European ancestry, and also made her shady gray eyes appear a little distrustful. Her mouth was small, pink, and complemented her oval face. As his eyes drank in every feature from her slender nose to the wisp of bangs covering her smooth brow, Tyler was immediately transported back in time.

"Moe," he whispered.

She smiled, seeming pleased. "Hello, Ty."

As if suddenly remembering where he was, Tyler straightened up and cleared his throat. "Wow, Monique Delome, I would never have—"

"*The* Monique Delome?" Hadley quickly pushed her way in between Tyler and the attractive blonde. "I've read all of your books."

Tyler stared at his wife. "Since when can you read?"

"Ah, thank you," Monique mechanically responded, and then her eyes went back to Tyler. "I didn't think you still lived in Dallas, Ty."

"Never left. It's been what…twenty-one years?" He scrutinized every detail of her lovely face. "You look good, Moe."

She tucked her shoulder-length hair behind her right ear. "Thanks. So do you."

"How do you two know each other?" Hadley's irksome voice intruded.

Monique never turned away from him. "We met when I was going to SMU. Ty was a…friend."

Her penetrating eyes made him reflexively run his hand behind his neck. His gut was twisting tighter and beads of sweat were breaking out over his brow. "Ah, yeah, that's right." Tyler could see Hadley smirking out of the corner of his eye. "Hadley, why don't you give me a minute here?"

16

Hadley appeared bolstered by his obvious discomfort. "Why?"

He wheeled around to her. "Let me have a word with Moe, and then we can talk."

Hadley ignored him and stuck out her hand to Monique. "I'm Tyler's wife, Hadley Moore."

"Soon to be ex-wife," Tyler quickly interjected. "We're getting divorced."

Hadley flirtatiously elbowed her husband. "That is still open for debate."

"You two seem pretty friendly for a couple about to divorce," Monique commented.

"Not that friendly." Tyler placed his hand in the small of Hadley's back and pushed her away from his side. "We'll talk later, Hadley."

Hadley grinned at him. "At dinner, in The Gallery Restaurant just across the lobby. When you're done here, of course. I can get us a table while you two catch up."

Tyler gritted his teeth. "Fine."

Hadley veered her greedy brown eyes to Monique. "Ms. Delome, I love your books and it has been a real pleasure to meet you. I hope we meet again." She turned on her high heels and dashed toward the bar entrance.

Tyler breathed a sigh of relief when she was gone.

"How long have you been married?" Monique asked.

The unpleasant tension in Tyler's chest diminished to a tolerable twinge. "Six years, but we've been separated for four. I guess I'm improving, because my first marriage only lasted two years."

"I'm sorry, Ty. But I know you were never that crazy about marriage. You used to call it 'a medieval form of torture.'"

He shrugged. "Still do."

"So why do it twice?"

"You know me, Moe. I was always up for a challenge."

"Among other things." Monique nodded to the large entrance Hadley had just walked through. "Your wife seems like quite a character."

"On a good day, Hadley's impossible, on a bad day…well, it was pretty much doomed from the start."

"Any kids?"

"A stepdaughter. Tessa is from Hadley's second marriage."

Her eyebrows went up. "Her second marriage?"

"Yeah, I was number three." He snuck in closer. "Forget about her, tell me about you."

"Me?" Monique fiddled with her hair. "Not much to tell. I'm a writer and here for a convention."

"Since when did you write? I don't remember you ever talking about wanting to be a writer."

"That's because you never paid attention, Ty. You were always somewhere else when we were together."

"I paid attention, Moe. I always paid attention to you."

Her doubting eyes searched his. "Really? I remember one particular night, when we were at Laskey's Bar. You spent the entire night ignoring me and vying for the attentions of our well-endowed server. Mabel, I think her name was. "

"Forgive me. I was young and stupid, but I've grown up since then. Figured out what is important." He concentrated on her pert, pink mouth. "You know I never forgot about you. I always wondered how you were and where you ended up. Are you married?"

"Divorced."

"Have you got any kids?"

She took a wary step back from him. "No. Never found the time."

"Are you still living in New Orleans?"

Her lips twisted into a devastating grin. "You know I'll never leave my hometown. I love it there."

18

Tyler cleared a nervous lump from his throat. "Last time we spoke, you were returning home to care for your mother. You said she was quite ill. Did she recover?"

"No, ah...." Her grin retreated. "She died a year later."

"I'm so sorry, Moe." He wanted to kick himself for upsetting her. "What about your dad?"

"He's in Florida, enjoying his retirement with my stepmother, Meredith." Monique searched his eyes. "Did you ever go and work for your stepfather?"

He proudly held his head up. "I run Propel Oil and Gas. Gary retired a few years ago and left me as CEO of the company."

"That's really great, Ty. I know how hard you tried to prove to your stepfather that you were responsible." She touched the hint of gray hair along the edge of his left temple. "I like the gray. It makes you look...sophisticated."

He chuckled as a flare of desire sparked in his belly. "It makes me look old, is what you mean to say."

"You'll never be old, Ty. Not to me." She glanced over her shoulder to a booth in the corner where the sharp eyes of Chris Donovan were avidly taking in their every word. "I should get back," she whispered.

Tyler nodded to the booth. "So you're his client?"

"You know Chris?"

"We just met at the bar, but he never told me he was your manager."

"I have to go." She brushed the wisp of bangs from her eyes. "It was great to see you, Ty." She abruptly headed to her booth.

His heart plummeted to his knees as memories of a similar encounter twenty-one years prior flooded his mind. It was the last time he had seen her.

It had been raining in Dallas that spring day. Monique had met him outside of her dorm on Southern Methodist University campus. She had told him she was heading back to New Orleans to care for her sick mother. He had wanted her to stay,

19

but he never found the courage to say the words. Instead, Tyler let her walk away in the rain, and for years he had regretted that decision. He never saw her again…until today.

Picking up his glass of orange juice, he quickly downed the contents. God, he needed a drink. The forgotten impulse took him over, becoming almost overpowering. It had been so long since he had entertained the concept of alcohol that the sensation jarred his usually unflappable confidence.

"You want another orange juice, Mr. Moore?" Mike's mellow voice broke in from across the bar.

Shaken, Tyler turned to him. "No thanks, Mike. I think I'll get a bite to eat in the restaurant."

"You're not meeting your client?"

Tyler eyed Monique's booth. "No. It looks like my plans have changed."

Chapter 2

Hadley was waiting at a walnut table in a dark corner of The Gallery Restaurant. The sight of the empty gold-toned, plush chair across from her almost made Tyler turn from the restaurant and run. Grudgingly, he trudged across the dining room to her table.

After he had settled in his chair, Hadley's obnoxious brown eyes were all over him. "Are you going to tell me about her?"

Tyler arranged his long legs beneath the square table. "There is nothing to tell, Hadley."

"Bullshit!" Her voice carried to a few of the crowded tables close by. "I saw the way you looked at her. No one ever wipes that cocky grin off your face, but she did."

He removed the napkin shaped like a cone on the plate before him. Shaking it out, he then casually laid it across his lap. "You're exaggerating, as usual."

"Am I?" An amused titter escaped her lips. "She wasn't one of your usual bimbos. Tell me, did she come before your sobriety or after?"

"I met Moe before I gave up alcohol," he clarified, not hiding the aggravation in his voice.

"And you still remember who she was?" Hadley feigned a sarcastic look of shock by letting her jaw drop. "Wow, I find that hard to believe. From what I know about your life before sobriety, you couldn't remember your own name, let alone anyone else's."

A busboy in a white tunic came to the table and filled their water goblets. Tyler's eyes drifted to the tables nearby and the assorted groups of women daintily picking at their large plates of food. The air was heavy with the sickening smell of overly sweet perfume blended with the hearty aroma of broiled steak.

When the busboy left their table, Hadley leaned in closer. "She said you met at SMU." Hadley's brown eyes narrowed with doubt. "You never went to SMU."

He sat back in his chair and adjusted his jacket. "Moe went to SMU. I met her at a party one night and we became friends."

"Friends? Lovers, you mean," Hadley snorted. "You don't have friendships with women, Tyler."

He snapped up his water goblet as that awful yearning for a drink returned. "It was never like that with Moe. She was a real friend, in every sense of the word."

Hadley's perfectly tweezed eyebrows went up. "You never slept with her? Do you honestly expect me to buy that?" She waved her hand over his figure. "You sleep with every woman you meet."

He took a sip of water. "Not Moe. She was different."

Hadley sat back in her chair and folded her arms over her chest as her eyes registered with understanding. "I never thought I'd live to see the day when you were bothered by any woman. But this woman bothers you, doesn't she?"

He avoided her intrusive stare. Tyler could not let Hadley know just how disturbed he was by seeing Monique again. "She doesn't bother me. I'm just a bit put off by her success. I never thought she would become a romance writer. She always set loftier goals for herself."

Hadley shook her head. "That you even remember that she had loftier goals astounds me. You never listened to me when I talked about my goals."

"You never had any goals, Hadley, except to marry a man who could afford to keep you." He set his water goblet on the table. "Unfortunately, I was the third husband who tried and invariably failed to keep you from screwing around."

"Oh, do I detect a hint of remorse in your voice, Tyler?" She leered at him. "Who's to say you couldn't keep me happy in the future? We'll never know unless we try again."

He shifted his focus to the dining room. "I don't want to try again, Hadley. We've beaten this dead horse about as far as it will go."

As he explored the entrance to the restaurant, Monique walked in on the arm of Chris Donovan. He thought Donovan's hold on her tiny waist was too familiar and the way she gazed into the arrogant man's face made Tyler want to set out across the restaurant and beat the living shit out of him.

"Tyler?" Hadley called across the table. "Are you listening to me?"

But Tyler never turned away from Monique. He reveled in the slight curl of her hair, the way the dim light in the restaurant glistened in her gray eyes. How the fit of her black slacks hugged her narrow hips, and how her cream-colored shirt clung to her small breasts. Monique's appeal for Tyler had never been about her looks. He was mesmerized as she tilted her head back and laughed at something Donovan had said. Tyler could not hear her, but he remembered the tinkling sound of her mirth in his head. He had dreamed of her adorable giggle for years and how every time she laughed, her eyes would disappear behind her smile.

When Monique and her overbearing manager began walking toward their table, Tyler was overcome by a compulsion to leave the crowded restaurant. He immediately stood from his chair.

"What are you doing?" Hadley pestered.

"Getting out of here." He threw his napkin on his plate. "I'm suddenly not very hungry."

As Hadley curiously looked him over, Tyler knew he had to give her some excuse; otherwise she would hound him about his behavior. Despite her aversion to grasp anything intellectual, his soon-to-be ex-wife was capable of remembering every detail about people, places, and events.

Though she invariably chose to use that ability selectively when it proved to be beneficial to her, she was also capable of inflicting a great deal of harm with it; harm that could still be detrimental to his business affairs.

He took in Hadley's voluptuous figure and something stirred within him. He wanted—no, needed—to forget about Monique. As far as Tyler was concerned, there was only one way to forget about anything.

"Let's go back to my suite."

Hadley's face brightened. "What did you have in mind?"

He did not give her an answer, but marched toward the restaurant entrance. When he reached the teak and gold elevators in the hotel lobby, he punched the call button and kept his eyes on the doors. He never acknowledged Hadley when she rubbed up against him and placed her arm through his.

As they stood waiting for the elevator, Tyler kept thinking about Monique. How her hair had shimmered, the light in her eyes, and all the things that had haunted him about her through the years. His hands curled into fists as his longing for her consumed him. Hadley tugged on his arm and for an instant he wished it was Monique he was taking back to his room. But that would never happen, and at that moment anyone would suffice. He just needed to forget, and the woman he wrapped his arms about did not matter; all that mattered was that for a few blissful minutes his mind would stop hurtling back to the past, and Monique's charming face would be as blurry as all the rest.

After the elevator came to a stop on the twelfth floor, Tyler darted from the car, leaving Hadley to hurry behind on her pointy high heels. He stopped before his suite door and pulled the white key-card from his jacket pocket. Without looking over at his wife, he swiped the card through the lock, and when the small light on the door handle blinked green, he turned the doorknob.

The stale smell of re-circulated air hit him as Tyler moved through the compact entranceway. His eyes swept over the gold carpet, textured gold wallpaper, and plush gold sofa and chairs in the living room. In the bedroom, he spied his black suitcase and overnight bag waiting by the king-sized bed. Seeking a distraction, he went to the wide windows of his Ritz-Carlton suite to view the Dallas skyline.

"This is very nice." Hadley dumped her Louis Vuitton handbag onto a mahogany coffee table. "I can see why you prefer to stay here all the time."

Tyler tuned out Hadley's words as he marveled at the evening sky with its hues of gold, red, and orange. He closed his eyes and an image of Monique standing next to him in the downstairs bar flickered across his mind.

"Maybe I should get a suite here," Hadley proposed, easing away from the window.

As if just remembering she was there, Tyler followed her figure as she progressed deeper into the suite. "Take off that dress."

Surprised by his command, Hadley raised her eyebrows questioningly. "What, no famous Tyler Moore seduction? No champagne, strawberries, luxurious massage? When we were dating you used to pull out all the stops."

"Now that we're getting divorced, I figured I could do away with the pretense." He removed his jacket and headed toward the wide master bedroom off to the side of the living area. "You want romance, Hadley, go screw one of your boyfriends," he added over his shoulder.

She slowly made her way into the bedroom and as she kicked off her high heels, Hadley turned to the open private bath and in-mirror bathroom television. "I should have one of those installed in my bathroom."

Taylor came up to her as he pulled the gray tie from about his neck. He hastily lowered the zipper on the back of her green dress. "Don't talk, Hadley," he instructed as he slid the dress from her body.

25

When the flimsy fabric hit the warm gold carpet, her hands went to the fly of his pants. "Do you want me to be meek and mild? You always liked me that way in bed."

He unclasped her bra and let it drop from his hands. His mouth covered hers more out of a need to keep her quiet than a desire to taste her lips. When his tongue tempted her, Hadley hungrily opened her mouth wider.

A ripple of disappointment curdled in his gut. There was no excitement, no temptation, and no desire here. It was just mindless sex. The same kind he felt like he had been having for years with a bunch of different woman. Why had he never noticed before how empty their kisses had been?

Hadley's hands went to work undoing the buttons on his shirt as he backed her onto the king-sized bed. When he moved his lips down her neck to her right breast, she squirmed with excitement.

"Let me get on top," she mumbled, running her hands through his thick, black hair.

But the thought of looking up at her empty eyes was enough to turn Tyler off. Instead of giving her a reply, he simply flipped her over on the bed. After shoving her underwear down to her knees, he lifted her hips into the air. With his other hand he pushed his pants down over his crotch. Before his pants had even hit the floor, he forced his way deep inside her.

"Give a girl some warning," Hadley balked as she grasped the bedspread.

Tyler pushed into her flesh again, harder than before.

"That's it, baby." Hadley backed her hips firmly into his. "You know I like it when you go deep."

Tyler blocked out her voice, and instead of trying to please her, he went after what he wanted. He drove into her as fast and as deep as he could go, grunting as his hips pounded her, thrusting with all of his might, hoping to lose himself in the sensation. He was relieved when the wonderful tingle that started in the depths of his groin began to climb, burning his flesh along the way. Grimacing, he slammed his hips harder into her.

"Oh yeah," Hadley moaned beneath him.

Clasping her waist with both hands, he arched back and brutally rammed into her. The movement sent Hadley over the edge and she threw her head back with delight.

"Yes," she screamed into the bedroom.

Feeling his climax barreling upward, Tyler dove into her until his muscles tightened and the overwhelming cascade of release burst within him. When his body finally calmed, he pulled out and collapsed on the bed next to Hadley.

She tried to nuzzle against him, but Tyler rolled over on his side. Her hands slipped under his shirt and caressed his back, but he ignored her.

"You haven't been like that since…I can't remember when. Maybe if you'd screwed me like that before, I wouldn't have needed all those boyfriends."

He sat up in the bed. "Jesus, Hadley. You think for once we could have a conversation without bringing up the other men you have slept with."

She popped up next to him. "Sometimes I think that was the only way I could get you to pay attention to me. Your mind was always somewhere else during our marriage, Tyler. No matter what I did, how I dressed, you were never thinking of me. What did you expect me do to?"

His brief respite from Monique was over, and once again her endearing features and kissable lips drifted back to the forefront of his thoughts. He ran his hand over his face.

"Shit."

"What?" Hadley stretched out her arms to him.

He pushed her away, and then he stopped when her slender arm rested against him. He needed to forget again. Tyler rose quickly from the bed, ripped his shirt from his shoulders, and snatched up his tie from the floor. When he came back to the bed, Hadley was grinning.

"You want to tie me up this time?"

He never uttered a word as he bound her hands together above her wrists.

"I always loved it when you tied me up." She rose to her knees on the bed. "What do you want me to do?"

He placed his hand against her shoulder and shoved her back on the bed. Hadley fell backwards onto the gold bedspread. Before she could right herself, he hoisted her legs over his shoulders.

"You've never been like this," she exclaimed as he hiked her hips higher in the air, jamming her head into the bedspread.

He was not even all the way hard when he entered her again, but he did not care. Taking his ex to bed had never been about pleasure, but forgetting, and he planned on thrusting into her as many times as it took to force the image of Monique out of his head for good.

***

The veil of night was covering the twelfth floor windows of his suite when Tyler awoke from his brief nap. He heard the water in the shower running and remembered Hadley. In the afterglow of sex with his ex, he realized that it had been a mistake. In the restaurant, he had not considered the consequences of his actions. All he had wanted was to forget about Monique, and Chris Donovan's possessive grip on her body. But the hours he had spent with Hadley had not helped. Throwing the sheets aside, he sat up on the edge of the bed.

"You want to tell me what that was all about?" Hadley badgered from the wide bathroom entrance.

He ran his hands through his wavy hair. "What was about?"

She wrapped the oversized, white bath towel closer to her body. "Acting like a jackrabbit on Viagra." She came up to the bed. "I know we've had our fun in the past, but honestly, Tyler, it's never been like that."

He stood from the bed and walked to the bathroom. "I thought that was what you wanted."

She followed him to the doorway. "I wanted passion, tenderness, a bit of cuddling. You gave me raw, unfeeling sex, and will probably leave me sore as hell tomorrow."

He went to the shower and flipped the faucet to cold. "I didn't hear you complaining."

"And I didn't hear you say anything at all. I mean a girl likes a good pounding every now and then, but four times? Even when we were dating you were only good for two times in one night, tops."

He stepped into the jet stream of icy-cold water, hoping the painful blast would awaken him from the lethargy quickly taking over his body.

"Are you listening to me, Tyler?"

"No, Hadley. I'm not listening, so grab your shit and get out of my room."

She came to the open shower entrance. "What do you mean, get out? After what we did, you could send me away just like that?"

He leaned his strong arms against the shower wall. "Yeah, just like that. We're still getting divorced. One afternoon in the sack isn't going to change anything."

"You're a real bastard, Tyler Moore."

He wiped his hand over his wet face. "That's why you're divorcing me, isn't it?"

"For a while you had me thinking that Monique Delome was some long lost love, but now I know you've never loved anyone. How could a sadistic asshole like you even have a heart?"

"I love you, too, Hadley," he hurled back with a contemptuous sneer. "Now get the hell out of my room, and the next time Fred Bishop sends you divorce papers, sign them, or I will cut you off without a penny."

"You would, wouldn't you? You would cut me and Tessa off without any means of support."

He shook his head, teeming with annoyance. "Now Tessa finally comes into play, eh? Well, you got by before I came along, and you'll get by long after I am gone. Your kind always does."

She went to slap him, but Tyler simply deflected the blow with his hand. "Get out, Hadley."

Growling like a rabid dog, she backed away and then bolted from the bathroom.

He waited for the slam of the suite door, and when it finally came, he reclined against the shower wall.

"She's right, I am a grade 'A' bastard."

Closing his eyes as the cold water slowly revived him, he let his thoughts stray once more to Monique. He figured if an afternoon of vigorous sex with Hadley had not dispelled the woman from his mind, perhaps nothing would.

He recalled the first time he had met her. Dragged to a party by some long forgotten friend, Tyler had quickly grown bored with the college crowd gathered in the upper end, Highland Park home. He was about to leave when he observed her standing by a stone fireplace, gazing up at a Jackson Pollack painting. He remembered how out of place she had appeared. In her faded blue jeans and pale yellow sweater, he had thought her refreshingly innocent, but when he spoke to her, Tyler had been surprised to find a sharp mind behind that lovely face. At first, Monique had refused his suggestion to get away from the noisy party, but after a little cajoling, she had relented and followed him in her beat up blue Pinto to a coffee shop. They had talked until dawn, and when he finally escorted her back to her dorm, Tyler knew he had found someone special.

On their first date, he had been afraid to kiss her, but by the second, he could not get enough of kissing her. On their third date, he knew he was falling for her, but during their few months together, had never told her of his feelings. Tyler had thought himself weak for harboring such emotions, now he realized he had been a fool to let her go.

Monique could not have reappeared at a worse time in his life. Fighting with Hadley, struggling to keep his business successful, as well as fending off the insidious advance of middle age, Tyler figured this was some kind of punishment for years of emotionless affairs and assorted one-night stands. Somewhere down the line he must have pissed off the gods of sex.

Satisfied that his shower had done all that it could to lift him from his doldrums, he flipped off the tap and retrieved an extra wide bath towel from a glass shelf next to the shower stall. After hastily drying off, he wrapped the towel about his waist and went to the phone by the bed. Lifting the receiver, he hit "0" and waited. After two rings, a lilting female voice thanked him for choosing the Ritz-Carlton Hotel.

"This is Mr. Moore in suite 1201. I need to speak with Missy at the front desk."

Missy's perky voice quickly came on the line. "Mr. Moore, how can I help you?"

"Missy, can you get me tickets to this romance convention that everyone in the hotel seems to be going to?"

"Ah....yes, I can call the booking department for you."

"Charge the tickets to my room and I'll pick them up at the front desk in the morning." He paused as a thought struck him. "Where is this thing, by the way?"

"The Dallas Convention Center," Missy stated. "Would you like me to arrange for transportation to the facility?"

"Yes, have a car and driver waiting for me at ten in the morning." He envisioned Monique's seductive eyes. "I need to arrive in style."

Alexandrea Weis

Chapter 3

When the black Town Car from the hotel pulled up outside of the gleaming modern steel entrance of the Kay Bailey Hutchison Convention Center, Tyler surveyed the throngs of women heading to the row of glass doors. Many were dressed casually in shorts or light summer frocks to beat the torrid temperatures, and most were carrying a variety of colored canvas bags.

"Are you a writer?" the young driver asked Tyler, after parking the car.

Tyler contained a smug grin. "No, I came to see one."

The driver nodded to the steady flow of women passing in front of the car. "Looks like you're not alone."

The driver climbed out and came around to the rear passenger side door. As soon as Tyler stepped from the car, the sweltering morning heat made his gray tailored suit feel absolutely stifling.

"When should I return to pick you up, Mr. Moore?"

Tyler slipped his gray suit jacket from around his shoulders. "I'm not sure."

The driver removed a white business card from the embroidered pocket of his short-sleeved shirt. "This is the number for the car service at the hotel; you can call them when you're ready."

Tyler took the card and placed it in his trouser pocket. "You ever been to one of these things?" He motioned to the convention center doors.

"No, sir. My mom goes all the time, though. She's a romance fanatic." He shut the rear door. "Watch your back in there. My mom's told me these ladies can get pretty feisty when they're trying to get to their favorite author."

Tyler flung his jacket over his shoulder. "I'll keep that in mind."

The young man jogged around to the front driver's side door as the endless line of woman continued winding their way toward the convention center. Tyler fell in step behind a trio of middle-aged women in flowery summer dresses and flip-flops. When they reached the entrance, he opened one of the glass doors for them and waited as each of the women gave him a polite nod before stepping inside.

"Excuse me," he said to the last woman coming through the door. "Where do I get one of those?" He pointed to the red badge hanging about her neck.

The heavyset lady with a heart-shaped face gestured to a row of booths at the far end of a long lobby. "You need to check in at registration to get an ID badge before you can enter the exhibit hall."

Tyler thanked her and when he entered the air-conditioned lobby with its patterned gray and taupe floor, he made his way to the booths with a bright red banner reading, "Registration" hanging from the ceiling above. An attractive older attendant with curly gray hair was sitting behind one of the booths and he strolled right up to her.

"I was told I needed to check in to get an ID badge," he declared, flashing his well-rehearsed, engaging grin.

The woman's sallow complexion brightened as he stood before her. "Of course," she mustered with a feeble smile. "Do you have your ticket?"

Tyler pulled the ticket that Missy had gotten for him from his jacket pocket. "I am particularly interested in seeing Monique Delome. Do you know where she will be?" He handed the woman his ticket.

She rolled her tired-looking brown eyes. "Every person here wants to see her. Ms. Delome is the biggest draw at these conventions."

"I knew she was well-known, but I never imagined...."

The attendant cautiously inspected him. "Are you a fan?"

"A friend," Tyler admitted with a slight nod of his head. "I knew her before she became famous."

The curiosity in the woman's delicate features peaked. "Then why did you buy a ticket and come to this convention to see her?"

"I wanted to surprise her."

The woman handed him a red badge with the convention's name printed on it and a sleeve with a necklace to place it in. "Wear this when you're on the exhibit floor." She handed him a program. "This lists all the exhibits and book signings by the authors. Ms. Delome is currently signing books in the main exhibit hall, and then she is going to attend an author panel in one of the meeting rooms further down the lobby." She pointed past the entrance. "Just follow the signs to the meeting rooms."

Tyler put the program and his jacket down by the booth while he placed the necklace with his red badge over his head. "Do you know where in the main exhibit hall I can find Ms. Delome?"

She motioned to the steady stream of women filtering in through the entrance. "Just follow the crowds...when you hit the longest line, you've found her."

Tyler collected his jacket and program. "Thank you." He gleaned over the program cover and was staring at a picture of a muscle-bound man with his thick arms about a scantily clad woman when the attendant spoke up.

"I hope you don't mind my asking, but have you ever read any of Ms. Delome's books?"

Tyler fought to keep a straight face. "No, I haven't had the pleasure."

"Really?" She appeared intrigued. "I'd swear you remind me of Darryl. Then again you look a lot like her Luke, Denver, Blane, and—"

"Are these men from her books?" Tyler interrupted, confused.

"Yes, just some of the leading male characters she writes about. They all look the same. Kind of like you." She waved a hand down his lean figure. "I think it's the eyes she always describes best. Dark, cool, detached, and yet mischievous, a lot like yours. It's as if you're listening, but at the same time, plotting your next move with a woman."

Her candid statement took Tyler off guard for a moment, and then he leaned in closer to her booth. "Considering we just met, I'm not sure—"

Her bird-like twittering cut him off. "And I'm sure I'm not telling you something you don't already know. I've got a twenty-four-year-old son a lot like you. He tends to look at women the same way."

Tyler cleared his throat. "Exactly how many of Ms. Delome's books have you read?"

"All of them." The woman gestured to another person who had taken up position behind Tyler. "I hope you enjoy the convention." She turned her attention to a young woman carting a black suitcase behind her.

A few yards down from the registration area, Tyler caught sight of the entrance to the main exhibit hall. At the doors, a burly security guard—reminiscent of the muscular gentleman on the program cover— checked his badge and then waved him into the hall.

The floor of the expansive hall was divided into long aisles cluttered with a variety of exhibitors. As Tyler started down the first aisle from the entrance, he could see each of the exhibitors represented booksellers, publishers, or business owners hocking items that were related to the romance book industry. A few authors had even taken out exhibits to sell their books. The publishers represented ranged from smaller, more modest independent ones to the bigger, more successful houses whose exhibits towered over the rest.

He searched each of the aisles, checking for the large crowds he had been told to look for. On the third aisle, he spied a long line of women. He quickly proceeded down the black carpet covering the hall floor, and when he finally came to the end of the line, he discovered Monique. She was sitting behind a simple brown table and speaking with a gray-haired woman who was clinging to her every word.

He was spellbound by the movement of her pink lips, and how her gray eyes appeared attentive, but when he noted her feet tapping on the floor, he remembered how she always fidgeted when she was getting impatient. As her eyes scanned the line of people still waiting for autographs, she spotted him.

Monique tucked her hair behind her ear as he came up to her. "I can't believe you just showed up here, Ty."

"I figured I should see what it is you really do." He rested his hip against her table, and a few angry glances from those still standing in line were directed his way.

"Come around here." Monique waved behind the table. "If they think you've cut in front of the line, they'll get testy."

Tyler breezed up to her side. While he placed his jacket and program on the table next to Monique, a young girl, no more than fifteen, shyly walked up, holding out a worn paperback book. Tyler was instantly reminded of his stepdaughter, Tessa.

"Could you make it out to Elise?" the young girl implored. "I just love all your books, Ms. Delome."

"Thank you." Monique took her pen and scribbled something on the inside cover of the paperback. "I hope you are going to read my new book, *Blind and Delirious*."

"Oh, yes, ma'am," the soft-spoken girl replied. "I want to get to New Orleans one day and see all the places you write about."

Monique pushed the signed paperback across the table to her. "I hope you do." Monique waited as the pretty teenager stepped away, clutching her newly signed book to her chest.

"You're a celebrity," Tyler commented behind her.

She reached for another book being offered by an enthusiastic fan. "What are you doing here, Ty?"

Tyler eyed the fans still waiting for their books to be signed. "I wanted to see you in action."

She passed the book back across the table to a woman wearing a pair of ill-fitting shorts with overly teased red hair. "You want something. I could always tell when you wanted something. You hovered."

He had forgotten how she could read him better than anyone. Easing closer to her chair, he inhaled the faint fragrance of her lilac perfume, and an unfamiliar feeling of calm flowed through him.

"I don't want anything from you, Moe. I just wanted to see you again."

She took the book from the next person waiting in line. "Please, Ty. I know better. You were always very persistent when it came to getting what you wanted. God knows, no matter how many times I told you no...." She glanced up at the fan before her. "You know what I'm talking about."

He leaned in closer to her. "You can't blame a man for trying, and I respected your wishes. That never happened between us."

"Because I wouldn't let it," she protested.

"That's not the way I remember it. There was that one time, when I cooked dinner for us at my place. You were very drunk and wanted—"

"Where's your wife?" she edged in. "Will she be stopping by?" She dutifully smiled at her waiting fan.

"Hadley and I are getting a divorce."

"Funny, it didn't appear to me like you two were getting divorced last night when you left the restaurant together." She scribbled her name on the inside cover of another paperback.

He lightly chuckled. "Is that a hint of jealousy in your voice, Moe?"

"Christ, Ty." She shook her head. "You really haven't changed, have you?"

Tyler tilted his head slightly to the side and perused the title of the book she was signing. *"The Night of the Hunter's Moon?"* He knitted his brow. "I thought you wrote romance books?"

"I do." She pushed the book back across the table. "Some are contemporary romance, and some are paranormal."

"What's the difference?" Tyler paused when Chris Donovan bellied up to the table, carrying two white paper cups.

"Ah, Mr. Moore." He placed a cup next to Monique. "Your black coffee, my dear."

"Thank you, Chris." Monique lifted the cup to her lips.

Chris motioned to the other side of the aisle. "Perhaps we should let her work."

Reluctant to walk away, Tyler figured it would look better with Monique if he obliged her manager. "Sure," Tyler agreed, and then he placed his lips next to Monique's ear and whispered, "We need to talk. I'm in suite 1201."

She gave him an angry side-glance and then went back to signing books.

After picking up his jacket and program, Tyler stepped away from the table.

"Monique tries to give her fans her undivided attention," Chris explained as the two men walked over to an empty table across the aisle from Monique. When Chris placed his cup of coffee down, he added, "It's best if she doesn't have any distractions."

Putting his jacket and program on the table, Tyler then leveled his gaze on the man next to him. "I didn't realize I was being a 'distraction.'"

"I think you have always been a distraction for her."

"I'm not sure what you mean by that, Chris."

39

Chris's condescending blue eyes dissected Tyler. "She talked about you after your meeting in the bar yesterday. I got the impression things didn't end well between you two."

"No, it didn't. That is one of my many regrets. Moe was…good to me."

Chris took in the long line zigzagging down the aisle from Monique's table. "She's always good to people; too good, sometimes."

Tyler closely studied the man's stern profile and stiff posture. "How long have you and Moe been together?"

"Five years." Chris gripped the white cup of coffee on the table. "I met her at one of these conventions. She was with a small publisher then, but I read her books and knew she had the talent to go far in this business."

"So you got her where she is today?"

Chris took a sip from his steaming cup of coffee. "No, she got herself here; I just cleared the path of obstacles. Bottom line in this business is you have to have talent to get anywhere. Readers are pretty picky and when they find a writer that touches them, they tend to stick with them." He motioned the cup in his hand toward Monique's table. "That lady touches a lot of people with her words."

Tyler looked on as Monique posed for a picture with a fan. "I never knew Moe was into writing. When we were together, she never mentioned anything about it. But then again," he dipped his eyes to the black carpet, "I wasn't really paying a whole lot of attention to anybody in those days."

Chris gave slight smirk. "She told me she always dabbled in writing as a kid, but did not get serious about it until after she was married."

"Yeah, she mentioned she was divorced. Did you know him?"

"It happened before I met her. The guy's name was Mathew Klein. He's a big-time neurosurgeon in New Orleans. From the way Monique described him, he sounded like a real asshole."

"Asshole? Really?" Tyler's eyes returned to her table. "I always hoped she would find a great guy."

"Mat was far from that," Chris went on. "They met when he was in his residency and got married when he finished. After he got a job with some big medical group in New Orleans, she was left alone a good bit of the time. And even when they were together, she said it was never quite what she envisioned married life to be. That's when she really got into writing. I guess she used it to create the kind of world she had always hoped to have." He paused and shrugged. "When she started making a name for herself as a writer, Dr. Klein wasn't too pleased. It seems he only wanted one celebrity in the family."

"Yeah, sounds like a real asshole," Tyler concurred.

"I've only met him once, when he came to one of her book signings in New Orleans." Chris snickered slightly. "Son of a bitch had the nerve to show up with his new wife and baby in tow." He nodded to Monique. "I thought she was really going to lose it that day, but she was a lady about the whole mess. Was very cordial to her ex and his wife…even held their little girl. But when I got her in the car to take her home after, she broke down." He eyes plummeted to the coffee in his hands. "It tore me up to see her like that."

Tyler contemplated the concerned glint in Chris Donovan's eyes. "You care for her, don't you?"

"Enough to not want to see her get hurt." Chris placed his coffee cup on the table next to him. "I don't know you, Tyler, but I know your kind. A lot of men have tried to worm their way into Monique's life, but she never paid attention to any of them, until you. When I saw her at the bar with you yesterday, I knew you were trouble. Don't come here and think you can win her over again. She's not the same woman you knew. She's been through a hell of a lot, and I plan on protecting her from people like you for as long as I can."

"What makes you think I'm out to hurt her? You know nothing about what we once were, what we had."

41

"I know a lot more than you think." He walked over to a pile of paperback books on the side of Monique's table and grabbed a copy.

"You should read this." Chris handed the book to Tyler. "It's Monique's new book."

Tyler gleaned the cover picture of a man in a suit with dark eyes and handsome features, standing behind a petite blonde in a skimpy red dress. Then, he read the title. "*Blind and Delirious.*" Tyler frowned at Chris. "What is reading this going to do?"

Chris glimpsed the line of waiting fans. "Do you know any writers, Tyler?"

"No. In my business, there aren't a lot of creative people."

"What business is that?"

"Oil," Tyler curtly responded. "I run an oil and gas development company."

Chris picked up his cup of coffee. "Well, writers are very much like sponges; they absorb everything from the world that they see and put it into their stories. All the people they have known, emotions they have experienced, and the places they have been all go into their books. Monique is no exception, except her books are more about those emotions she has kept bottled up. All the joy, pain...and heartache she has known makes its way on to those pages." He pointed to the book in Tyler's hand. "I think you might find that pretty enlightening."

Tyler decided to play along. "Sure, I'll take a look at it later."

Chris took a sip from his coffee. "In the meantime, I would appreciate it if you let my client do her job."

"Are you asking me to stay away?"

Chris lowered the cup from his lips. "Yes, I believe I am."

Tyler hid his growing annoyance from his face. "And what if I'm not willing to do that?"

Chris put his coffee down on the table and folded his arms. "Monique respects me, Tyler. She listens to me and always takes my advice. If I were to tell her to stay away from you, she would stay away."

Tyler took a step closer to Chris. "I'm beginning to get the impression you don't like me very much."

"I don't like anything or anyone that comes between me and a client."

Tyler considered his comment. "Shouldn't a manager be more interested in Moe's bottom line and not her heart?"

"In this business, it's the same thing. If you mess with one, you destroy the other."

Tyler was beginning to understand Chris Donovan's true reasons for wanting to protect Monique. "Thank you for the book." He held up the paperback in his hand. "I'm sure we will see each other again."

Collecting his jacket and program from the table, Tyler was about to walk away when Chris's voice stopped him.

"She's too good for you...you realize that, don't you?"

"She's too good for both of us," Tyler countered, and then purposefully strode down the black carpet to the end of the aisle.

After leaving the exhibit hall, he went to the nearest trashcan. Tyler pitched his program into the tall bin and was about to do the same with Monique's book when he hesitated. Looking over the cover, he thought, *What could it hurt?*

Flipping through the book, he began to read a few lines on the first page he came to. As he continued to read, he moved off to the side of the lobby, out of the flow of traffic into the exhibit hall. Leaning his shoulder against a gray-tiled wall, Tyler soon became entranced by the words on the page.

Alexandrea Weis

Chapter 4

The glare of the bright lights from downtown Dallas was coming in through the bedroom window of Tyler's suite when he finally closed the book in his hands. Scattered about the bed were four other Monique Delome novels, all with equally racy covers of scantily clad women in the arms of brooding, tall, dark men. His gray suit jacket was strewn over the corner of the king-sized bed, and a tray of partially eaten grilled steak sat on the floor next to him.

Ever since Tyler opened the first book, he had been glued to the pages. He had read the book while waiting for his car and driver to return to the convention center to pick him up, and continued to read it on the short drive back to the hotel. Once he had been dropped at the hotel entrance, Tyler had gone straight to the gift shop, curious to see if they had any more of her books. After purchasing the four most recent novels the hotel was selling in honor of the convention goers and writers staying there, he had returned to his room, sat down on his bed, and started reading again.

But it was not the story, or the intense burning desire of the main characters, that captured his attention, it was the leading men Monique had written about. From the confident swagger, good looks, and deep-set brown eyes, Tyler recognized himself. He had been astounded to see various elements of his personality incorporated into each of the characters…from gestures, to his love of steak, even his former affinity for bourbon. In every book he read, there was something very familiar about each of the alpha males Monique described, including their common ruthless disregard for women. In the end of each book, the hero had been changed by the love of a good woman. It was as if Monique had written the happy ending into her novels that they had never achieved in real life.

The entire experience left Tyler feeling confused and humbled. Never before had he been confronted with all of his imperfections and idiosyncrasies in such an eloquent way. As he stared down at the cover of the book he was holding in his hand, he became filled with regret. Seeing his personality through someone else's eyes had been a rude awakening.

"I have been such an idiot," he mumbled as he perused the collection of books.

He ran his hand over his chin, hiding his smirk, and then he remembered a few of the male characters in the books doing the exact same thing. The realization made him laugh out loud.

Slowly, he nodded his head, knowing that there was only one way to settle this. Turning for his master bathroom, he went to the sink and ran some water over his face. As the cool liquid hit his skin, he thought of Monique, and how she had written one character as an executive in the oil industry, replicating almost in detail Tyler's position with Propel Oil and Gas.

Suddenly remembering the responsibilities he had with his company, Tyler turned off the tap. Grabbing a towel from the rack next to the dark oak vanity, he raced out of the bathroom and went to his iPhone on the nightstand next to the bed. He blew out a long breath when he found the twenty-two voice mails and assorted text messages waiting for him. Wanting peace to read the books without the constant buzz of his cell phone, he had switched the device off and forgotten to turn it back on.

He cursed while scrolling through the four texts from the client he had come to the hotel to meet. Hastily typing away on the keyboard, he punched in a plausible excuse for his being unavailable, offered to reschedule at any time convenient for his client, and apologized for the confusion.

"That should placate the greedy son of a bitch."

Tyler sat down on the edge of the bed and went through the rest of his messages and texts, deciding that none were imperative, and a few he could return later in the evening. The three voice mails from Hadley he immediately deleted.

After putting the tray of half-eaten steak in the hallway, he returned to his bed, collected his jacket, and slipped it over his shoulders. Then, almost as a second thought, he retrieved the novel Chris Donovan had given him at the convention center and placed it under his arm. It was time to pay Monique a visit.

Down in the lobby, he exited the elevator and immediately went to the reception desk. When Missy smiled up at him, he knew he would have to do some fast-talking to get the young desk clerk to cooperate with his plans.

"Hello, Mr. Moore," Missy chirped.

"Ah, there she is, the lovely Missy." He rested his elbow on the desk, eyeing her snug blue blazer. "I hope you can help me."

She held up her head, continuing to smile for him. "What can I do for you, Mr. Moore?"

"Besides dinner?"

Missy played with a few wisps of blonde hair that had fallen from her ponytail.

He traced his long fingers over the smooth teak-stained desk. "I need some information. Can you look something up for me?"

"If I can," she answered with a speck of uncertainty in her blue eyes.

"Can you tell me what room Monique Delome is staying in?" He held up the book from under his arm. "I want to get this autographed for my daughter. She just loves her books."

"I can't give out that information, Mr. Moore," she firmly asserted.

"Please, Missy. Besides, I know Moe won't mind. We go way back."

She curiously raised her eyebrows. "You do?"

47

"Years ago we were friends, and I promised my daughter I would get her to sign this book."

Her blue eyes softened and she bit her lower lip, giving Tyler a glimmer of hope. Then, she ran her fingers through her blonde ponytail and inquired, "How old is your daughter?"

He sighed, wistfully. "Fifteen going on thirty. She's at that age where I am trying like hell just to keep up. It's hard letting them go."

"I never figured you to be a devoted father, Mr. Moore."

He placed the book against his heart. "I'm hopelessly devoted to my Tessa. She's my world."

Missy shook her head and the girlish smile she had given him the day before reappeared. "Just don't tell anyone where you got this information, or it's my ass."

He ogled her round curves. "And what a lovely ass it is."

Missy let out a short giggle, and he knew he had her.

She quickly typed in something on her computer. "Ms. Delome is in suite 833."

He tucked the book back under his arm. "Thank you, Missy." He angled closer to the desk. "I hope you like Japanese."

She nodded. "Love it."

He stepped away from the desk as an older couple approached. "Then I owe you one Japanese dinner."

Missy's flirty smile was displaced by her businesslike persona. "Of course, Mr. Moore. I will ring your room when I get that information." She greeted the couple. "Welcome to the Ritz-Carlton Hotel. Are you checking in?"

Tyler made a hasty retreat to the main elevators and excitedly pressed the call button several times, hoping his sense of urgency had some magical influence on the elevator car's return to the lobby.

After several long minutes of waiting, the teak and gold doors opened and he stepped inside. As the car began its slow rise upward, Tyler went over the words he had practiced for their meeting. Glancing down at the expensive Italian watch

Hadley had given him for their first Christmas together, he hoped that he would find Monique in for the night, perhaps preparing for bed. Even though eight o'clock was not late for many, he had remembered Monique to be an early riser. It was something that had always bothered him during their time together. He had been the night owl, anxious to party until dawn, but she had been his practical conscience, reminding him of his responsibilities and the need for a good night's sleep. Over the years, he had often recalled her advice about tempering his wild side with some discipline. It was as if Monique's voice still whispered in his ear day after day, advising him on the best course of action. He had not realized it until that moment, but hers had been the voice of reason in his head, the strength that had guided him through his sobriety and eventual rise up the corporate ladder.

When the elevator doors opened on the eighth floor, his usually resilient confidence faltered. Perhaps this was a mistake. Maybe the Monique he had built up in his head over the years would not live up to the woman she had become. She could have acquired vices or hidden secrets that would disappoint him and eventually make him regret their reunion.

Tyler was still vacillating between returning to his room and knocking on her door when he found himself standing before the white oak door with the number "833" painted in gold above the peephole.

"What am I doing?" he groaned into the empty hallway.

Pulling the book from under his arm, he was about to raise his hand to knock on the door when it flew open.

She was standing in the doorway wrapped in a white hotel robe with a white towel coiled about her head like a turban. Her dark gray eyes scrunched together as she inspected him.

"Funny, you don't look like room service," she jested in the intrepid Monique-style he remembered.

"I come bearing one of your books, not a plate of risotto." He held up the paperback to her.

She frowned, drawing her pink lips together. "I hate risotto."

He nodded, staring at her perfect mouth. "I remember." He took a step closer to the door. "I wanted to tell you that I read your book."

"Is that why you showed up at my book signing?"

He leaned against the doorframe. "No, I went to see what it was you did."

"When did you read my book?"

"This afternoon."

The expression on her face changed from lighthearted fun to dark worry. She pulled at the collar on her complimentary fluffy robe. "And what did you think?"

He went around her and determinedly entered her suite. "We need to talk."

She gawked at him, her eyes round with astonishment. "Ty, you can't just come in here without asking."

He examined the modest suite with a small sitting room done in pale tones of amber and gold, then turned to the adjoining bedroom and modest bath. Motioning to a half-packed black suitcase on her bed, he asked, "Are you leaving?"

"Tomorrow." She shut her room door. "I'm heading to another convention in South Carolina."

He waved his hand about the suite while turning back to her. "Not as nice as mine."

"Well, I'm not a rich oil executive."

He lifted the right corner of his mouth in a half-smile. "No, you're a rich and famous author."

"Well-off and not famous…not yet anyway." She walked past him to her bedroom.

"Ah, there's a side of Monique Delome I don't know. Since when have you craved fame and fortune?"

She unwrapped the thick white towel from about her head, letting her wet blonde locks fall to her shoulders. "I'm not into fame or fortune, but I am into being successful enough not to have to worry about how I am going to eat tomorrow."

He moved toward her king-sized bed. "What, being married to a wealthy doctor didn't get you a hefty divorce settlement?"

Flinging the wet towel on the bed, she demanded, "How did you know Mat was a doctor?"

He removed her suitcase from the bed and placed it on the floor, then had a seat. "Your pit bull of a manager told me about him. Apparently, he's not too fond of the guy. He said he was an asshole to you."

She shrugged and combed her fingers through her wet hair. "That's one way of putting it." She observed him sitting on her bed. "What are you doing here, Ty? I would have thought you had enough of me earlier today."

He tossed the book onto the bed next to her wet towel. "You want to explain what I am doing in all of your books?"

She ran her fingers over her forehead, looking a bit uncomfortable, and then her features hardened. "That's one book, Ty. You can't generalize what you read in one—"

"I read four other ones, Moe."

She stood before him, saying nothing as her eyes flitted about the small suite.

"I think that's the longest lapse of speaking I've ever heard from you," he commented, grinning like a Cheshire cat.

Her furious eyes fixed on him. "I'm thinking!"

He stood from the bed. "Thinking is not explaining, Moe. Why did you write about me? Every man you wrote about had my mannerisms, my expressions; hell, they even had my eyes."

"So what if I did write about you, Ty? You're a hell of an interesting character where women are concerned. I've never known a man who could wrap a woman around his finger like you. You always got everything you wanted from every woman you ever met."

"I didn't get what I wanted from you."

"Great, you're still not going to let that go." She made a beeline for the bathroom.

51

He followed her. "Hey, I didn't think I was asking too much."

She halted at the bathroom door and when she turned around, he was right in front of her. Monique pulled her robe over her chest. "I was twenty and a virgin, Ty. I wasn't just going to hop into bed with a twenty-nine-year-old lothario who wouldn't have remembered my name in the morning."

"I didn't ask you to sleep with me until after we had been together for six months, Moe. I think I was pretty damn patient."

"I think you were an ass. Packing me up in your stepfather's corporate jet and carting me off to Mexico, thinking you were finally gonna get lucky with me if you showed me a good time."

"That wasn't what I was doing and you know it. You said you always wanted to see Acapulco and I wanted to surprise you. It wasn't until you found out that we were sharing a hotel room that you accused me of trying to seduce you. Christ, Moe!" He threw his hand in the air. "So what if I was trying to seduce you? Didn't you know how much I wanted to be with you?"

"How was I supposed to know that? I'm surprised you could fit me into your schedule, since you were screwing half the female population of Dallas."

"It was only that one girl, just one, and even then I was too drunk...." He took a step back from her. "I am not going to do this again with you. I did not come here to rehash the past. I came...." He pointed to the book on her bed. "You're a very good writer. Good luck with that."

He was marching toward the door when she came running up behind him. "I never intended to write about you. It just happened."

Tyler pulled up in the sitting room and slowly pivoted around to her.

"When I went home to New Orleans, I hoped, maybe, that you would come to me, but you never did. I wrote about you as a kind of therapy, a way to get over you. Then, I married Mat. When my marriage fell apart, I escaped into my imagination, and there you were."

Tyler took in her small, oval face, wary gray eyes, and the pink blush on her cheeks, and knew he had made a mistake in coming to see her.

"Why couldn't you just have said that, Moe?"

"And given you the satisfaction of knowing there was another woman in the world pining away for you? Not a chance."

"Pining?" He chuckled at the thought. "I could never picture you pining away for any man, even me."

She walked back to her bed. "It was never the same after I left Dallas." She plopped down on the bed. "I was never the same."

"Then why didn't you come back to me?"

"Why didn't you follow me to New Orleans?" she angrily shot back.

"I thought about it. I really did." He stuffed his hands in the pockets of his gray slacks. "But then my stepfather gave me the job with the company and I tried to concentrate all of my energy on that. Not long after, I met my first wife, and put everything behind me." He sat down next to her on the bed. "Or so I thought."

"You could have at least called, Ty. Those first few months after I left, I thought...hoped...you would try to contact me."

"And said what, Moe? Come back to me?"

A knock on the door made Monique jump from the bed. "That's my dinner."

As she rushed to the door, the sway of her slim hips beneath the thick fabric of her robe enticed him. He waited on the bed while she took the tray of food from the waiter and carried it to the bedroom. Monique carefully slid the tray onto a modest wooden desk in the corner of the room. When she turned back to Tyler, he was still watching her from the bed.

She yanked the belt tighter on her robe. "I…ah, really should finish packing."

Tyler rose from the bed, suddenly invigorated. He went to the desk and removed the silver lid from the plate of food.

"What is that?" He grimaced with disapproval.

"Grilled salmon. Why? What's wrong with it?"

He replaced the lid. "You don't want that."

"I don't?"

"You're in the mood for a greasy hamburger and french fries."

"No, I'm not," she argued.

"Then how about pizza, with extra cheese?"

"That's not fair." She pouted her lips together. "You know I can't turn down pizza."

"It just so happens that one of the best pizza places I know is not far from here." His eyes hopefully explored her face. "What do you say to dinner with me?"

She tilted her head to the side, as if she were weighing her options "Fine. But I am only going because I want pizza more than that salmon." She spun away from him. "Just don't read anything more into this, all right?"

His deep, hearty laughter filled the bedroom. "What are you talking about?"

"You know what I'm talking about, Ty. I'm having pizza with you as a friend. Don't think this is going to go any further." She disappeared into the bathroom and shut the door.

Tyler did not want to admit it, but he knew exactly what she meant. He went to the hotel phone by her bed and hit the number for the front desk.

"Thanks you for choosing the Ritz-Carlton Hotel. This is the front desk, how may I help you?"

"Ah, this is Mr. Moore in 1201. I'll need a car in twenty minutes for the evening."

"Of course, Mr. Moore. Will you be needing the car for the entire evening?"

He recognized Missy's sweet voice. "Yes, Missy, I'll need the car for the entire evening."

"Very good, Mr. Moore. I will make the arrangements for you."

After hanging up the phone, Tyler reasoned that he was getting too old for young women like Missy. Maybe Monique was the kind of woman he needed in his life. No one had held up a mirror to his empty existence quite like she had. The characters she had based on him had opened his eyes to the possibility that all was not right with his world. He had made mistakes, a lot of them, but perhaps there was always room for redemption. As he listened to the blow-dryer whirring in the bathroom, he resolved to turn over a new leaf. He was going to start again with Monique, only this time he was determined not to let her slip away. He hoped that she would be just as willing to embrace a second chance with him.

Alexandrea Weis

Chapter 5

Twenty minutes later, Tyler was sitting on her comfortable gold sofa when Monique exited the bathroom wearing jeans and a casual top.

"I hope this is okay for pizza." She clutched her small black purse against her chest.

Tyler stood up. "You look fine."

While adjusting his jacket, his eyes wandered over her tiny figure. He had forgotten how much she reminded him of a little girl. There were moments when she seemed so vulnerable, and other times when she was a mountain of strength.

He opened the door to her suite and held it as she stepped into the hall.

"Can I ask you a question, Ty?"

He shut her hotel room door. "Is this something I'm not going to want to answer?"

"Perhaps."

Tyler wondered where this was going. "What is it?" he grilled in a dubious tone.

"Why are you doing this?"

"Doing what? Taking you to dinner?" He smirked at her. "I'm saving you from that salmon."

"I'm being serious. In twenty-one years I haven't heard a single word from you. But today you show up at my book signing, knock on my hotel room door, and now you want to take me to dinner. Why?"

He rolled his eyes. "Christ, you always used to do that."

"Do what?"

57

"Interrogate me, just like you are doing now; why I took so long to kiss you on our first date; why I never introduced you to any of my friends. It's all starting to come back to me."

She dropped her gaze to the gold and burgundy carpet. "You've got a good memory."

Taking her elbow, he guided her down the hallway. "You're probably the only woman I know who would say such a thing. I've been accused by both my former wives of never listening to them."

"You always did have an immense talent for shutting people out."

"Yeah, well...." He tipped his head casually to the side. "My first wife, Serena, said I was a walking tree...dumb and blind to the people around me."

"Ouch." Monique giggled as they made their way to the central elevators. "What was she like, Serena?"

"She was pretty; rather empty-headed, but sweet." They stepped before the fancy gold-trimmed elevator door. "I remember every now and then, when she turned her head a certain way...." His eyes returned to Monique. "She reminded me of you." He pressed the call button. "I met her about six months after you left. At the time, I was trying hard as hell to stay sober and working as a manger at Propel. A year later, we were married. Six months after the wedding I got...bored. A year after that, Serena filed for divorce."

"Did you cheat on her?"

He shrugged his wide shoulders as the elevator doors opened.

Monique clucked with disapproval. "What about your current wife, Hadley? Did you cheat on her, too?"

"Ex-wife. As soon as she signs the papers, she'll be my ex." He waved her into the car.

"You didn't answer my question, Ty?" She entered the gold and teak elevator.

He followed her in and pressed the button for the lobby. "Yes, I did, but only after I caught her in bed with another man." He came alongside her. "After that, our marriage was just a technicality."

She shook her head as the elevator doors closed. "You and Mat would have had a lot in common."

Tyler was taken aback. "He cheated on you?"

The car started its slow decent to the lobby. "About three years in. There was a medical assistant in his office named Lou Ann."

He rested his shoulder against the side of the elevator car. "What did you do?"

"I wrote books. I figured success was my best revenge. If he didn't want me as a housewife, then maybe he would want me as a successful writer."

"Your manager told me he remarried and has a kid."

A momentary jolt of tension pulled her shoulders back. "He has two kids now, and he's still married to his medical assistant."

"He was a fool, Moe."

She turned her eyes to him. "Was he?"

The elevator stopped on the third floor and a younger couple entered, holding hands. They did not seem to register Tyler and Monique standing next to them on the ride down to the lobby. When the elevator doors opened, Tyler took Monique's hand and pulled her toward the front entrance of the hotel.

"I've got a car coming to take us to the restaurant," he told her as they quickly crossed the onyx marble floor.

"Why can't we walk?"

He scowled at the suggestion. "It's a hundred degrees out there. And the car is more convenient."

While passing before the front desk, Tyler purposefully kept his eyes focused on the ornate glass entrance, wanting to avoid seeing Missy.

"Ty?" Monique spoke up as she tugged on his hand. "What's the rush?"

"I'm just hungry," he grumpily complained.

When they stepped outside of the glass doors that led to the street, the stifling hot air hit them.

"It's after sunset and it's still sweltering," Monique commented as he escorted her to a waiting black Town Car.

"Now, aren't you glad I got the car?" Tyler ribbed as the driver opened the rear passenger door.

"All right." Monique slid into the backseat. "I'll admit it. You were right about the car. Just don't let it go to your head."

***

Coal Vines was a casual neighborhood restaurant a few minutes by car from the hotel. Stepping through the exterior patio set with dark walnut chairs covered in bright red cushions, they entered a cozy dining room. Decorated with racks of wine bottles and a light amber-bricked wall rising up behind an oak bar, the rich aroma of garlic, thyme, and oregano tempted their noses. A pretty hostess in a clingy black dress showed them to a table in the corner.

"This isn't where you usually take your women, is it?" Monique probed as he held out a chair for her.

"Very funny. I like to come here for lunch when I'm alone. My offices are not too far from here, and the food is good." He unbuttoned his gray suit jacket and had a seat.

"Do you like to eat alone?"

He sat back in his chair. "Sometimes. I get real tired of the predictability of people, and when I need a break from that, I like to go somewhere alone."

"The predictability of all people, or are we talking about only women?" She folded her arms over the table. "By the way, I saw the blonde at the front desk."

"What blonde?"

"The one that was staring at you as you dragged me across the lobby. What did you promise her?"

He casually waved his hand in the air. "She was very friendly when I checked in, and she has helped me out here and there. Nothing else happened." He clapped his hands together and rested them on the smooth surface of the table.

"My God, you haven't changed a bit." She sat back in her chair with a look of complete dismay on her delicate features. "It must be so hard for you, being such an asshole all the time. No wonder you need to get away."

"I am not an asshole," he indignantly refuted.

"Oh, come on, Ty. Look at you." She waved her hand down his lean figure. "You're good-looking, CEO of an oil company, and probably sleep with every women you meet. Of course you're an asshole."

He put his hand over his mouth, hiding his smug grin. "You always did have a nasty habit of telling me exactly what you thought."

"I told you the truth."

He gave her a weak smile. "You were the only one who ever did."

"Even in that big company you run, there's no one to tell you the truth?"

"Employees never tell you the truth, Moe." He shook his head while fighting off a disgusted frown. "They are too worried about keeping their jobs."

"Well then, what about ex-wives? Surely, they told you the truth."

The insistent frown worked its way across his thin lips. "The women I married were more like employees than wives. They said whatever it took to keep me happy and paying their credit card bills."

"I don't buy that, Ty. What made Hadley and Serena so different from all the other women you went out with?"

"Nothing." He flashed back to his previous evening with Hadley. "They turned out to be exactly what I expected. I just hoped they would be different, that's all."

A young woman with small black eyes and dark hair pulled back in a ponytail came to the table. Dressed in black pants and a long-sleeved white shirt, she held a white pad of paper in her hand and had two black menus wedged under her right arm.

"Welcome to Coal Vines. What can I get you two to drink tonight?"

"Just soda water for me." Tyler motioned to Monique. "I believe the lady would like a glass of chardonnay."

Monique nodded for the waitress. "That sounds great, thank you."

The young woman placed the vinyl-covered, black menus on the table. "I'll get your drinks while you look over the menu. Our specials tonight are a grilled salmon with crabmeat dressing and a beef tips rigatoni."

"Thank you." Tyler handed her his menu. "But I think tonight we're going to have a large white special pizza with some of your extra marinara sauce on the side."

The waitress jotted their order on her pad and then took their menus. "I'll get right on that." She quickly made her way to a black door cut into the amber-bricked wall behind the bar.

Monique rested her arms on the table. "You remembered I liked chardonnay and pizza?"

"How many times did we eat at Rick's Pizza Place? You always had pizza and chardonnay."

Appearing intrigued, she shifted closer to the table. "What else do you remember?"

He cocked his head to the right. "That you hate pepperoni; have an aversion to anchovies—"

She made a face. "Who doesn't?"

"You hated the opera, too."

"I still don't know why you wanted to bring me to the opening night of the season. It was so boring, Ty."

"It was the biggest social event of the year, Moe. My mother insisted I go, and I said I would only go with you. I thought it would be a chance for you two to get to know each other."

She sat back stiffly in her chair at the mention of his mother. "How is Barbara? Is she still milking the social scene for every bit of attention?"

Tyler slid his jacket from around his shoulders. "She and Gary moved to Austin to be with Gary's daughter, Helen, after he retired from Propel. I speak to her every now and then, but I haven't been down to see her in a while."

"I remember your mother was always obsessed with your social standing. Inviting you to all those parties, making you attend numerous charity benefits, and then there was the time she even tried to get you on the board of some museum. You remember that?"

"Yes, the Dallas Museum of Art. But, thankfully, it never worked out."

"You and Barbara never saw eye-to-eye on anything...including me." Monique fiddled with the knife on her place setting. "I swear that woman always hated me."

"She didn't hate you." He fixed his jacket around the back of his chair. "She just didn't understand why I chose to be with you and not the socially prominent misfits she always pushed on me."

"She hated me, Ty. I knew it the first time you introduced us at that company picnic your stepfather hosted. She looked me up and down, and I knew she had already made her mind up about me. What did she always call me, 'That New Orleans girl'?"

Tyler directed his eyes to a crowded table at the side of the room. "She didn't understand you."

"She didn't want to understand me. I remember all the fights you two had about me. She kept asking you to dump me, and you kept telling her to mind her business."

He drew his finger along the smooth edge of their walnut table. "After you left, she told me that she regretted trying to push us apart."

Monique's eyes became shadowed by doubt. "What changed after I left?"

"She knew how unhappy I was."

Folding her arms across her chest, she pressed her lips together, appearing unconvinced. "But I bet she still blamed me for your drinking."

"After you left, I quit drinking. I think she knew then that she had been wrong about you."

Her skeptical demeanor evaporated. "You've been sober since I left?"

He nodded. "Twenty years."

"Wow, I'm impressed. I never thought…I'm glad to hear it. Your drinking was…a real problem. When you were sober, you were wonderful to be around, but when you drank you were—"

"An even bigger asshole than I am now?" he injected. Monique opened her mouth to speak, but he held up his hand. "I know I wasn't the best boyfriend at the time, but I want to thank you for sticking by me for as long as you did. Without you, I might have chosen a different path. You made me see that I needed to walk away from the booze in order to get my life together."

"I can't take credit for that. You made the decision to stop, not me."

"You gave me the strength to make that decision, Moe."

She stroked the edge of the white plate in front of her. "You know the drinking had a lot to do with why I went back to New Orleans."

Dropping back in his chair, Tyler digested what she had just told him. He had suspected that his excessive drinking had pushed her away, but until that moment he had never truly accepted that as a reason for why their relationship had ended.

"Why didn't you say anything?"

"It doesn't matter." She put on a happy smile. "Everything turned out for the best. You have your company, and I have my writing career."

He placed his elbows on the table. "But if you had stayed, things might have been different for us."

"If I hadn't left, you might never have stopped drinking. You would never have taken over your stepfather's company and become the successful man you are."

"I would have stopped for you, Moe."

"We both know that's not true," she responded with a dismissive shake of her head.

Their waitress reappeared, and after placing their beverages on the table, she darted away.

Monique reached for her wine glass. "Besides, if I had not gone back to New Orleans, I might never have met Mat and become a writer."

Tyler ran his fingers along the rim of his glass of soda water. "Was he…the first?"

Monique's gray eyes searched his, and then she took a quick sip of her pale yellow wine. "No. My brother, Jake, set me up with one of his friends. I think he got sick of listening to me talk about you. I can't even remember his name. Randy, Raymond…something like that."

"Obviously, you didn't care for him."

"No, I didn't." She tossed back another gulp of the liquor. "He was just someone who was there. It happened about three months after I came home. I was lonely and I figured what the hell."

Lifting his beverage, that nagging burn for a shot of alcohol rose from his gut. "You should have called me."

"Called you for what? Sex?" Monique fidgeted in her chair. "Sleeping with you wouldn't have changed anything between us."

"No, it would have changed everything between us." He took a needed swig of soda water.

"I would have just turned into a number then, Ty. And I didn't want to end up being just another notch on your bedpost."

He plopped his glass on the table. "Jesus, you would never have been that."

Raising her wine to her lips, she conceded, "I guess we'll never know."

She sat across from him, heartily chugging her drink, when he realized her need for alcohol was just as great as his.

"Moe, haven't you ever wondered what we would have been like together?"

Monique almost choked on her drink. She patted her hand against her chest and banged her glass down on the table. "No!"

"Liar." He signaled their waitress, who was standing at the oak bar across the room.

"Ty, what are you doing?"

"I'm getting you some more wine."

"I don't need it, really." She held up her half-empty glass.

The waitress looked over at him and he pointed down to Monique's drink. When the dark-haired woman nodded her head with understanding, he glanced back at Monique. She was desperately clutching her wine with both hands.

He contemplated her apprehensive eyes. "Why are you looking so terrified all of a sudden? Are you afraid of me?"

"No, not of you." She avoided his gaze. "I'm afraid of what you are thinking."

"And what am I thinking?"

"I'm not going to sleep with you, if that's what this dinner is about." Monique guzzled more wine.

A ribbon of desire snaked its way through Tyler's body. "This is just dinner between two old friends. I have no expectations."

She whacked the empty glass down on the table. "Now who's lying?"

He raised his drink to his lips, but said nothing. He could feel it in his bones when a woman wanted him, and suddenly his insides were humming with excitement. But as he ran through a flurry of detailed sexual images of Monique, Tyler questioned if the actual act would live up to all of his expectations. Never before had he waited so long for a woman, and instead of adding to his desire, the idea of finally attaining what he had hoped for worried him. Would the reality of their sleeping together live up to the twenty plus years they had spent dreaming of the moment? Tyler had a sneaking suspicion that he was about to find out.

Alexandrea Weis

Chapter 6

It was well after eleven when Tyler helped a tipsy Monique out of the back of the black Town Car and into the hotel lobby.

"You shouldn't have let me drink so much," she admonished.

He put his arm about her shoulders. "You were the one who kept drinking the wine."

"Only because you kept ordering it for me. Honestly, Ty, I'm not one of your bimbos."

"I don't go out with bimbos, Moe. Many of the women I end up with are smart, classy, polished, and—"

"Easy," she piped in.

He laughed as the teak and gold doors of the main elevators loomed before them. "After forty a woman is not easy, she's interested. You're only easy in high school."

"Forty?" She chuckled against him. "I thought you liked them a lot younger than that."

While pressing the elevator call button, he slipped his hand about her waist to help hold her up. "I gave up dating anyone under forty a few years back. The conversations were too painful. The younger one's just kept reminding me how old I was getting."

"You'll never be old. You're still that twenty-nine-year-old guy who was way too good-looking for me."

"Too good-looking? You're joking?"

"I always thought you were never interested in me because I wasn't a model, or cheerleader, or any one of those ultra-gorgeous girls."

"Why on earth did you think that?" He dipped his head to her ear and whispered, "You were the most beautiful woman I ever knew. Still are."

She let go a loud disapproving snort. "Yeah, right."

He removed his arm from about her waist and cupped her face in his hands. "I mean it, Moe. To me, you are a very beautiful woman."

"Well, there you are," a deep voice called.

When Tyler turned, a casually dressed Chris Donovan emerged from an open elevator. Tyler let go of Monique and stood back from her. The sudden loss of his support made her wobble slightly on her feet.

Chris rushed to Monique's side. "Where have you been?"

Tyler bristled as Chris placed his arm about Monique's waist to steady her.

"We just came from dinner." Monique straightened up and pushed Chris away.

"How many chardonnays did you have with dinner?" Chris put his arm back about her waist and ushered her toward the waiting elevator.

Monique pushed him away once more. "I'm fine." She swayed slightly on her feet.

"You're drunk," he chided.

Tyler edged to her side. "I was going to see her back to her room."

Chris Donovan's angry blue eyes burned into Tyler. "I'll see her to her room. I think you've done enough for one evening."

Monique inched toward the elevator. "Chris, you don't need to take me up to my room. I'm fine."

"Monique, you're not fine." He came closer to her. "I'll get you some coffee."

"No, Chris. No coffee." She shuffled into the elevator. "I'm just going to go to my room and sleep it off."

Chris was about to walk into the elevator with Monique when Tyler stepped in front of him, blocking his path. "She said she'll be fine," Tyler growled.

"Yeah," Monique chimed in from the elevator car.

Chris took a step back, nodding his head. When Tyler turned around, he was surprised to find Monique holding the elevator doors open for him.

"Aren't you coming?" she implored.

Tyler grinned and entered the car.

As Monique pressed the button for the eighth floor, Tyler could not help but gloat when Chris's lips tightly pursed together in an angry scowl.

After the elevator doors had closed, Monique let out a heavy sigh. "Christ, he is getting impossible."

"What is it with that guy? Why is he so possessive of you?" Tyler demanded.

She shrugged and rested against the side of the car. "I'm his biggest client and he's terrified of losing me to some other publisher that will cut him out as my manager."

"Are you thinking of leaving your publisher?"

She waved off his question. "Hell no. Donovan Books has been good to me."

"Donovan Books? It's his publishing house?"

"His family's business," she acknowledged. "He has a brother, Hunter, who manages the publishing company while he runs a separate promotions company for the authors."

"No wonder he's so worried about losing you." Tyler rested his hand on his hip. "I thought maybe he was in love with you."

"He isn't in love with me...or at least I don't think he is."

"I can't believe you haven't noticed how he acts toward you, Moe."

"I know any man that shows the least bit of interest in me, Chris runs off. Until you came along, I didn't care who he ran off, because I never wanted—" She abruptly stepped over to the doors.

71

He came alongside her. "You never wanted what?"

"Forget it." She kept her eyes on the doors as the elevator came to a stop on the eighth floor.

He held on to her arm. "What is it, Moe?"

When the doors opened, she shirked off his hand and bolted from the car.

"Wait," he pleaded, following her down the hallway.

Monique was almost sprinting when he caught up to her. Grabbing her arm, he spun her around to face him.

"Tell me what you were going to say."

She struggled against his grip. "No."

Wriggling free of him, Monique scampered the last few yards to her room. Tyler followed dutifully behind her, determined to make her talk. When she reached her door, she had already removed the white key-card from her purse and was swiping it through the lock. But the gods of fortune were smiling down on Tyler, because the lock failed to register the key after her swipe and the red light on the lock blinked, denying her access.

Tyler came up behind her as she hurriedly swiped the card through again, only to be denied once more. He took the white card from her hand.

"Let me try." He ran the card through the lock, and the light switched to green.

Monique stood beside him as he opened her door. "You were right," she whispered.

"Right about what?"

Her gray eyes were filled with the same fear he had seen back at the restaurant. "When you asked me if I ever wondered what we would be like together. I did lie to you. I used to think about it all the time."

"Are you thinking about it now?"

She slowly nodded.

He pushed the door all the way open. "Ask me to stay."

"What if you're disappointed, or what if I don't live up to—?"

He placed his finger over her lips. "Moe, you could never disappoint me. If nothing happened between us tonight, I still wouldn't be disappointed."

She took in a deep breath, clasped his hand, and led him into her room. When they came to the edge of the bedroom, Monique let go of his hand, and then set her black purse on the wooden desk to the side. For several seconds, she just stood there with her back to him.

Placing his hands on her shoulders, Tyler turned her around. The panic swarming in her eyes made him smile.

"It's not like you haven't done this before, Moe."

"I just haven't done it with you." She rested her hands on his wide chest. "With you, I still feel like I'm that twenty-year old virgin."

His mouth was poised inches from hers. "Don't think of how we used to be. Just think of how much I want you." Tyler gently kissed her sumptuous pink lips.

At first, he was almost afraid to kiss her any harder, she felt so fragile next to him. He gingerly placed his arms about her slender figure and eased her closer. It was then that she kissed him back...tentatively, pressing her mouth ever so slightly against his. When his arms tightened about her, she parted her lips and tempted him with her tongue. Tyler quickly became undone; the softness of her velvety skin, the heat from her body, and the curve of her breasts against his chest were intoxicating. He deepened his kiss, hungry for more. Soon, his hands were running up and down her back, holding her firm, round behind in his hands, and lifting her from the floor. Tyler carried her to the bed, and when he set her down on the neatly turned down gold bedspread—complete with that complimentary chocolate on the pillow—Monique peeled the suit jacket from his shoulders.

"I don't remember it feeling like this." She nipped at his earlobe.

No longer intimidated, Tyler was pulling at her top, desperate to get to her skin. "It's better." He kissed her again.

Her hands went to his pale blue shirt, and after fumbling with the first few buttons, she ripped the shirt from his chest, popping buttons in the process.

Tyler reciprocated by tugging at her top, almost tearing the collar as he fought to pull it over her head. He nimbly unclasped her bra, and then his mouth covered her right nipple. He kissed her tender pink flesh, and when his teeth sank into her, she trembled in his arms. The sensation drove him over the edge. He was grabbing at the zipper of her jeans, yanking the fabric free of her hips while her nails scratched down the length of his back.

He bit the nape of her neck, wanting to get back at her. When her hands went to the fly of his slacks, his anticipation reached the breaking point. Eager to have her supple body beneath him, he hastily pushed her back on the bed. Before he climbed on top of her, he shoved his trousers and briefs down around his ankles, and then kicked them away along with his shoes.

Finally naked with her, he gradually lowered the last impediment of clothing from around her hips. After he wrestled her beige silk underwear free of her ankles, he let his lips travel slowly up her creamy white thighs while his hand slipped between her knees, urging her legs apart. He pulled her hips closer to him and kissed her inner thigh, letting his mouth work its way to the valley between her legs. When he spread her folds, ready to taste her moist flesh, Monique moaned.

He teased her with his tongue, feeling her undulate against him as her pleasure rose and ebbed. When she arched against the bed and cried out, Tyler's lips begin their slow ascent over her flat stomach to her left breast. He clamped his mouth over her nipple, relishing the taste of her.

"That wasn't so bad, was it?" he playfully said into the base of her neck.

"I can't believe…Mat never made me…do that."

He sat up on his elbow. "Are you saying Mat never gave you an orgasm?"

"Not like that." She bashfully covered her eyes with her hand. "I know that sounds really horrible, but when I married Mat and we...it was never very good."

"Did you tell him that?"

She removed her hand from her face and frowned at him. "You never critique a man in bed. I've at least learned that much about sex."

"But he was your husband." He caressed her cheek. "You two should have talked about how you felt."

"Mat never liked talking about sex. He said it made him uncomfortable."

He kissed her shoulder. "I like talking about sex, and it never makes me uncomfortable. I want to please you in every way, Moe, so don't be afraid to tell me when you don't like something, or when I don't satisfy you, all right?"

"But you've already satisfied me, Ty."

"Just wait." He kneeled between her legs and lifted her hips to him. "There's more to come."

When his tip penetrated her, he groaned into her neck as her wet flesh closed around his shaft. Monique clasped her arms about him when he pulled out and drove into her again.

"God, yes," she gasped into his hair.

Monique raised her hips higher, and Tyler took the invitation to move deeper. He could feel his orgasm rushing forward, faster than he had experienced in the past. Tyler could usually control himself so well, but not with her. He wanted her, wanted to keep moving faster and harder into her, like an unrelenting conqueror, taking what he wanted without remorse.

She was writhing in his arms, panting into his chest, and when her hands clutched his butt, he thrust into her with wild abandon, not caring about her anymore, just needing to satiate his desire.

As his muscles tensed right before his release, Monique's breath caught in her throat and her body shuddered in his arms. Her reaction sent him hurtling over the precipice. He smacked his hips into her, grunting against her neck, until he felt the rush of his release.

Completely spent, he lay on top of her, catching his breath and taking a moment to luxuriate in the feeling of satisfaction flowing through his veins.

"So that's what everyone keeps raving about?" she giggled against his cheek.

Tyler lightly chuckled into her chest. "I guess that means you liked it."

"Very much." She combed her fingers through his thick, black hair. "Was it worth the wait?"

"Hell of a wait, but worth it."

"Yes, definitely worth it," she agreed.

He gauged the contentment shining in her eyes. "I take it that means I've lived up to your expectations."

She traced the outline of his square jaw with her fingertips. "Like you said, I could never be disappointed with you."

"Don't go to your convention in South Carolina tomorrow," he pleaded. "Stay in Dallas for a little while longer."

"And do what?"

He sat up next to her. "Be with me. I'll take you out and show you the town. Wine you, dine you, whatever you want."

"Tempting offer, but...."

"Stay, Moe. Let's see where this goes."

Her body stiffened against him. "I already know where this is going, Ty." She edged away from him. "Perhaps we should just enjoy tonight and not plan on any more than that."

He tossed his arms about her. "Don't push me away."

She relaxed and patted her hand against his chest. "You were always the one pushing me away. I'm just being realistic."

"To hell with being realistic." He tumbled back with her onto the bed. "Let's pretend we are in one of your books; perhaps *Blind and Delirious.* I could be Darryl finding you in his hotel room for the first time. Remember that scene?"

"You really did read my book, didn't you?"

"Yes, I did. And I have to admit your steamy love scenes really did something for me." His lips passed lightly over her neck.

"I was thinking of you when I wrote every one."

He nibbled at her shoulder. "In that case, I can't wait to act them out."

"I'm sure you won't remember all the details."

His mouth hovered temptingly over hers. "Oh, I remember every single detail."

She pressed against him. "Prove it."

"If you insist." Then his lips came down hard on hers.

Alexandrea Weis

Chapter 7

The sunshine was creeping in through the window of Monique's hotel suite when Tyler stirred from his deep slumber. He yawned happily, feeling more relaxed than he had been in a long time. As his eyes adjusted, he realized where he was, and soon the memories of his night with Monique began to roll across his mind. He stretched out his hand to the spot next to him in the king-sized bed, and his heart plunged when he found that she was not there.

Sitting up, he gazed anxiously about the room, but there was no sign of her. He leapt from the bed and ducked into the bathroom, but it was empty. Even the vanity had been cleared of her toiletries. Back in the bedroom, he found that the black suitcase he had moved from the bed to the floor was gone. He did a quick turn of the modest suite and discovered that all of her clothes had been removed from the closet, and her purse was no longer sitting on the wooden desk across from the bed.

"Son of a bitch," he shouted into the empty hotel room.

Barefoot, and still wrestling his shirt around his shoulders, he walked out of the room and scrambled toward the elevators. When the elevator stopped on the twelfth floor, his cell phone began ringing in his jacket pocket. Ignoring the call, he searched for his key-card. Once in his room, he went straight to the hotel phone and hit the number for the front desk. He was relieved when a man's voice answered, not wanting to have to deal with the perky Missy again.

"This is Tyler Moore in 1201; can you tell me if Ms. Delome in 833 has checked out?" he blurted into the phone before the man could finish his well-rehearsed salutation.

"Just a moment, Mr. Moore."

A few seconds passed and then the man returned to the phone. "Yes, sir, about an hour ago."

"Did she say if she was heading to the airport?"

"I'm sorry, sir. I don't know."

"Thank you." Tyler smashed the phone back on its cradle. "Shit!"

He sat on the edge of his bed, trying to figure out what to do. This was a new experience for him. For years he had let women come after him, slept with the ones he wanted, and then in the morning had slipped away just like Monique. It felt odd to be on the receiving end of what he had been dishing out for so long.

"What in the hell is wrong with me?" He wiped his hands over his face and then looked down at his wrinkled pants and half-open shirt. Lifting his shirt, Tyler inspected the broken buttons along the inner seam. He remembered Monique popping the buttons as she tried to rip the shirt from his body. His head filled with images of her from the night before: the softness of her skin, the aroma of her lilac perfume, the taste of her lips. He could feel himself growing hard as he thought of her, and he groaned out loud with frustration.

Standing from the bed, he angrily wrenched the shirt from his shoulders and then fumbled with the fly on his trousers. It had been a long time since he had taken a cold shower to calm his ardor, but he desperately needed one this morning. Making his way to the bathroom, Tyler had a sneaking suspicion that he had better get used to this. Until he could get Monique Delome out from under his skin, he was going to be requiring a lot more cold showers.

***

After donning a sharply pressed black pinstripe suit, Tyler decided to go downstairs to have some coffee in a café that sat across the street from the hotel entrance. In the elevator, he scrolled through the messages on his iPhone, checking to see if his morning appointment with the client he had originally come to the hotel to meet was still set for ten. He was stepping from the elevator and staring down at his cell phone when he happened to bump shoulders with someone. Raising his head, Tyler was greeted by the patronizing blue eyes of Chris Donovan.

"I think it is time you and I had a little chat," Chris advised between his clenched teeth.

Tyler suppressed the urge to sock the man in the jaw, and instead painted an irritated half-smirk on his face. "What do we have to talk about?"

"She left early this morning. We were supposed to go to the airport together and head to South Carolina for another convention, but when I awoke I got a text that she had taken the first flight back to New Orleans." Chris folded his arms over his chest. "I can only imagine what happened between the two of you last night, and if you hurt her, or upset her in anyway, then you and I are going to have a big problem."

"What happened between us last night is none of your damned business. As for why she flew back to New Orleans, I haven't got the slightest idea. I woke up and she was gone. No note, no explanation."

Chris's ramrod posture relaxed somewhat and he ran a hand over his deeply etched brow. "Perhaps we should go somewhere and talk about this. I think you and I need to come to some kind of understanding about Monique."

"Why?" Tyler snapped.

Chris sighed, sounding frustrated. "It's obvious we both care for her, but I also have to manage her career, and I can't have you interfering with that. You could threaten everything we have worked so hard to build."

"I think you overestimate my influence on her. If I was such a threat, she wouldn't have run back to New Orleans."

"But that is exactly why she left." Chris's eyes searched Tyler's face. "You really don't know her, do you? Monique may be tough as nails on the outside, but inside she is just a vulnerable little girl in desperate need of being protected."

"I think you and I see two different women. Moe is the same girl I knew over twenty years ago. She doesn't want to be protected, she wants to be understood and respected."

"If you thought she wanted to be respected, then why did you sleep with her?" Chris barked.

Tyler's stomach rolled with indignation, and he took a cautious step back. "I think this conversation has gone far enough."

"Stay away from her," Chris warned. "You will only hurt her in the end."

"Don't threaten me, Donovan. I never stay away from the things I want."

"She's not a thing, but you wouldn't know that, would you? Women have always been objects to you, and I'm sure Monique is no different. You know, she told me all about you. Your escapades when you two were together before, your drinking, your trip to Mexico, the other women, all of it. You hurt her then; what makes you so sure you're not going to hurt her now?"

Tyler took another step back, wrestling with his anger. "Things are different between us this time."

"But you're not any different." Chris moved closer, pursuing him. "You're the same selfish son of a bitch who broke her heart all those years ago. Men like you don't change."

Tyler glared at Chris, wanting to forever wipe away the smug look on his face. Instead of lashing out with his fists, Tyler turned and promptly walked away. As he charged to the lobby exit, he gripped the cell phone in his hand, squeezing it as tight as he could. He wanted to hit someone, but he knew that was not an option. The one lesson his father had taught him before dropping out of his life for good was that violence never solved anything. It was the only advice he had ever heeded from any man, and he was not about to blow years of self-control on a worthless cretin like Chris Donovan, at least not yet.

***

The rest of the morning, Tyler was not able to concentrate on anything. Throughout his lunch meeting with his loquacious client from the Nagle Petroleum Engineering Firm, Tyler found gentle reminders of his previous night with Monique. The floral arrangement in the restaurant entrance reeked of lilacs. The pot-bellied client he had lunch with went into a long tangent about his recent trip to New Orleans. Even the milk he added to his foul-tasting coffee reminded him of the color of her creamy white skin. It seemed no matter what he did, or how hard he tried to focus, Tyler was drowning in memories of Monique.

Needing to end the pricey hotel lunch with the overzealous client, Tyler finally consented to entertain proposals from his small engineering firm. After returning to his room, Tyler packed up his clothes and proceeded to the lobby, anxious to check out. When he dropped his bags before the teak-stained front desk, Missy welcomed him with a bright smile.

"Checking out, Mr. Moore?"

"Afraid so, Missy. I've got a full schedule at the office in the morning and I need to get home."

She placed the bill in front of him. "I'm sorry you won't be staying longer."

"So am I," he mumbled as his eyes perused the room charges.

"Seems we have had a lot of hasty check outs lately. You, Ms. Delome…."

"Yes, I heard Moe left."

"Did you two have a nice dinner?"

Tyler grabbed a pen on the side of the counter and hastily signed his bill. "We caught up on old times," was all he offered.

"So I gathered. You ever get to New Orleans, Mr. Moore?"

83

Tyler crinkled his brow at the young woman's question. "No. My company doesn't do business in New Orleans."

She took the bill and placed it to the side of the desk. "I've read on the Internet that Ms. Delome has one of those lovely old houses in the Garden District of the city."

Tyler shook his head, feeling a bit confused. "May I ask why you are telling me this?"

"When the two of you returned from dinner last night, I got the impression you were very good old friends. After Ms. Delome checked out so unexpectedly this morning, appearing rather upset, I might add, I wondered if perhaps your friendship had hit a snag during the night."

"A snag?" Tyler took a breath as her blue eyes stayed on him. "What do you mean?"

"It's a hotel, Mr. Moore. There are cameras on every floor. We see all kinds of comings and goings, if you know what I mean." She pushed a piece of paper across the desk. "I figured you might need this sooner or later."

Tyler picked up the paper. "What is this?"

"Ms. Delome's home address. In case you ever get to New Orleans."

He chuckled at the young woman in the blue blazer, feeling that he had finally met his match. The perceptive desk clerk was better at reading people than the best executives Tyler had ever tangled with.

"Missy, if you ever want a job in the oil and gas business, you come and see me. I think you have a gift for figuring out just what it is your clients need."

Missy nodded her head, appearing pleased. "I just call 'em as I see 'em, Mr. Moore."

He pocketed the slip of paper. "You've gone above and beyond for me. Thank you for such stellar service."

"I'll have the valet bring your car around front for you. Good luck, Mr. Moore," she winked at him, "with everything."

Carrying his bags, Tyler made his way to the lobby entrance. The slip of paper felt like a ten-pound weight in his jacket pocket. But now that he had Monique's address, he questioned what was stopping him from picking up the phone and arranging for his company jet to take him to New Orleans.

As he stood outside beneath the shaded portico and waited for his car, a multitude of excuses swirled in his head. But by the time his black Cl550 Mercedes pulled up, he knew he would head straight home and never go near Love Field Airport. Somewhere in the pit of his gut, he had to wonder if there was really anything to pursue between them, or if last night had just been the result of the accumulation of twenty-one years of pent-up frustration.

After tipping the valet, he eased behind the burl walnut and leather steering wheel of his car. Pulling away from the hotel, he edged on to the road and closer to I-45, heading out of the city. It was time to put Monique behind him. The road ahead may not have been as alluring as the past, but it was all he knew, and the best that he could hope for.

Alexandrea Weis

Chapter 8

Monday morning, Tyler arrived early at his downtown office in the Energy Center on Bryan Street. Designed by I.M. Pei, the glass and concrete high rise was created using three triangles to produce its unique shape, making it the ninth tallest building in the Dallas skyline.

When he entered in his wide corner office on the thirtieth floor, he paused and took in the scenic views of the Dallas Central Business District through his widows. Arching his back, he could still feel the nagging tightness in his shoulders from the night before.

He had spent a little extra time in his gym at home to get rid of his nervous energy, but pushing himself harder on the expensive weight machine Hadley's trainer had talked him into buying did nothing to relieve his tension. After his workout, he had settled down in front of his wide screen television with a tall glass of orange juice, but all the channel surfing in the world could not distract him from thinking about Monique. Thoroughly frustrated, it had been well past two in the morning when he finally stumbled into bed.

As he stood in his office, facing a long day of meetings and monotonous phone calls, he debated if this was what he had truly wanted for his life. Suddenly, the challenge of his business paled in comparison to holding her.

"Mr. Moore," his devoted secretary, Lynn Stallmaster, called from his office doorway. "Mr. Harper from accounting is on line one. He says he needs to speak with you right away, and don't forget you have a ten o'clock in the conference room with the engineers on that new development in the Gulf."

Lynn's lively green eyes stood out against her yellow and blue-checked pantsuit. Always the fastidious dresser, the attractive, sharp, and tireless middle-aged brunette had been part of the reason for Tyler's successful climb up the corporate ladder.

"Fine, Lynn." He walked over to his desk.

"Are you all right, Mr. Moore?"

"It was just a long weekend." He pulled out his leather desk chair.

Lynn took a step into his office. "Did the guy from Nagle Engineering wear you out?"

"Among other things," he slyly remarked, taking a seat at his desk.

"I'll get your coffee started. I've got some new stuff in with chicory in it. You know, how they drink it in New Orleans."

Tyler froze at the mention of the city. "New Orleans?"

"Yeah, when Ed and I travelled there last year for our anniversary, we went to Café Du Monde and had beignets and coffee with chicory." She waved her hand at him. "It'll perk you right up, trust me. Ed had a caffeine buzz for two days after a cup of that stuff."

Tyler traced his finger over the antique mahogany Napoleon desk his stepfather had left for him in the office. The intricate carvings of laurel wreaths and olive branches reminded Tyler of his stepfather's fascination with all things related to the emperor who had ruled France so long ago.

"Did you like New Orleans, Lynn?" he queried, never looking up from a swirled olive branch on his desk.

"Of course, but you already know that. I thought I never shut up about the place."

He scooted his chair closer to his desk. "Never been there; not on vacation anyway. Went for a few conferences, but never saw much of the city."

"You should go back and take it in as a real tourist. It's a hell of a place."

He lifted the receiver on his phone. "Just make my coffee black this morning, Lynn. I think I'll need all the boost I can get from it."

She reached for the brass handles on his black leather-covered doors. "Sure thing, Mr. Moore."

Tyler waited for her to shut the doors to his office before he took the waiting phone call. He went to put his finger on the blinking white button on his phone, and Monique's dark gray eyes floated across his mind.

A knot spurred to life in his chest. "Shit," he mumbled. He pressed the white button. "Hello, Harry. What's wrong now?"

**

He had been to four meetings with assorted staff and the legal department, trying to put out fires on future projects. It was a little after one and his stomach was rumbling after three cups of coffee and no food. He was sitting at his desk, reading through the same budget proposal for the fourth time, when Lynn beeped in on his intercom.

"Fred Bishop is on line two for you, Mr. Moore."

Tyler sat back in his chair, a little surprised to be hearing from his divorce attorney. "All right, Lynn."

After taking a second to gather his thoughts, Tyler answered the phone. "Fred, is this good news or bad news?"

A deep rolling chortle greeted him. "That depends on how you feel about being divorced, buddy. Hadley was in my office first thing this morning."

"Hadley came to see you?" Tyler leaned forward in his chair. If Hadley had visited his divorce lawyer, it could not be good.

"Yeah, she came in my office and threw the final divorce papers at me. Not handed, mind you, threw them across my desk."

Tyler let out a pensive breath. "Why?"

89

"She signed them, Tyler. She accepted all the terms and signed the papers. Congratulations, you are now divorced."

"She signed them? But last Friday night she was telling me how much she liked being Mrs. Tyler Moore, and had no interest in ever settling the divorce."

"Well, this morning she marched in here, madder than a donkey in pig shit, and hurled the papers at me. She apparently wants nothing else to do with you." Fred paused and Tyler could hear another phone ringing in the background. "Whatever happened last weekend must have convinced her to sign the papers."

Tyler smirked and picked up a pen on his desk. "I doubt that."

"Well, now you're free of her. I'll file all the paperwork at the courthouse and send you copies for your records."

Tyler tapped the pen against his green blotter. "Thanks, Fred."

"No problem, Tyler. Just call me before you marry the next one so we can work out a prenup."

He slapped the pen down on the blotter. "I don't know if there will be another Mrs. Moore. I think two times is my limit."

"Nonsense," Fred balked in his baritone voice. "You just found the wrong women, that's all. Find yourself a good woman who gives a damn about you and not your money for a change."

Tyler thought of Monique sneaking out of her room while he was sleeping. "Already found one of those, Fred. But I don't think she wants me."

"I find that hard to believe. Every woman you meet wants to be the next Mrs. Moore. Maybe she needs further convincing?" Fred's mellow laughter came pouring through the phone speaker. "Don't ever give up on good woman, Tyler. Took two years for my Rita to agree to go out with me on a date. A year later, we got married, and we've been that way for twenty-five years. The good ones always take a lot of convincing."

Tyler mulled over his words. "How did you convince Rita you were the right one?"

"I hounded her morning, noon, and night until she went out with me. I never let up. When she finally did go out with me, she realized I was a pretty great guy. Yours will figure it out, too. Just keep on her. Good luck, my friend."

"Thanks, Fred. I'll let you know what happens."

"Just call me when you're ready for that prenup."

After Tyler hung up with his divorce attorney, Lynn stepped through his black leather-covered doors, carrying a pile of manila folders in her hands.

"I need these back this afternoon before you go. They're for the Jennings Refinery contracts, and beneath those are the new specs on the projected outputs on our gas wells in the panhandle. Elliot Winters needs those back from you by tomorrow."

Tyler sorted through the folders she placed in the middle of his desk. "Does it ever end?" He selected one of the folders and opened it.

"Only time things slow down around here is when you go on vacation, and you haven't done that in three years, Mr. Moore."

He flipped through the paperwork in the folder. "Sounds like I am overdue."

"I'll say." Lynn placed her hands on her ample hips. "I could use a break myself."

"You just got back from vacation two months ago, Lynn. You were gone over a week and everything was a mess without you."

"Yeah, but a girl can always use another vacation. I could head back to the Big Easy and hit a few of the restaurants I missed." She patted her hips. "I still need to lose the five pounds I gained last time I was there," she muttered as she walked away.

Tyler put the folder down on his desk. "That sounds like a hell of a good time, dining your way across New Orleans."

Lynn stopped at the office doors and turned back to him. "You should try it. Great place to just get away. I loved that town."

Tyler recalled Monique saying something very similar. He sat back in his black leather chair and eyed his secretary as an idea simmered in his head. "I guess I could leave after I finish this paperwork."

Lynn furrowed her creamy brow as her green eyes became like two small marbles. "Leave? You mean go home?"

"No, I mean leave Dallas. You did say I needed a vacation."

Lynn slowly approached his desk. "You do, but a vacation for you usually revolves around something related to the company, like a conference or going to check out a new drilling site. You never just spontaneously take off without a set itinerary of things to do."

"You make me sound like a control freak."

"You are," she maintained.

He gave her a disparaging glance. "Maybe I need to change things up a bit." He focused on the folders on his desk. "Call Love Field and tell them to get the jet ready to fly tonight."

"To where?" Lynn probed.

He never looked up at her. "New Orleans."

She put her hands on his desk and stared him down. "All right. What's up with you?"

"Up? Nothing is up."

"You're not the impulsive type, Mr. Moore. If you don't mind my asking, is there a woman involved?"

He scowled at her. "Okay, I do mind your asking."

She shrugged, then cut across the fine, beige European rug to his office doors. "Do you want me to call the Ritz-Carlton in New Orleans to get you a suite?" she queried over her shoulder.

"No, I have somewhere else I can stay."

She stopped at the office doors and spun around. "Somewhere else? But you always stay at the Ritz-Carlton."

"Don't worry about it, Lynn. I'll be fine. Just arrange for a car to pick me up at the airport and take me into the city."

"Are you sure about this, Mr. Moore? You're not really into roughing it on the road."

Tyler raised his eyes to her. "First, I'm a control freak, and now you're implying that I'm spoiled?"

Lynn snickered, sounding thoroughly amused. "You are spoiled." She turned for the doors. "You like order, and for everything to run smoothly. I'm not sure how you're going to adapt to just being spontaneous."

"I might surprise you, Lynn."

"I look forward to it, Mr. Moore. I've never met anyone who could use a swift change of pace more than you." She quietly shut the doors to his office.

Alone at his desk, Tyler speculated about how Monique would react when he showed up on her doorstep. "She'll probably hate it." He slowly grinned. "But I'm sure I can find a way to win her over, eventually."

Alexandrea Weis

Chapter 9

The sticky, hot air clung to Tyler's exposed skin as he walked through the open door of his Embraer Phenom 100 business jet at Lakefront Airport in New Orleans. He wiped the humidity from his bare arms, ran his hands over his blue jeans, and then adjusted his overnight bag on his shoulder before he climbed down the steps to the tarmac.

"You sure you don't want us to wait around in New Orleans for you, Mr. Moore?" a handsome young man with thick, curly brown hair spoke out from the top of the ladder.

Tyler waved his hand down his pilot's casual polo shirt and khaki pants. "I know you would love a few days in the city with me on the company tab, but not this time, Marty. You can head back to Dallas tonight. I'll make arrangements to fly commercial when I'm ready to return."

"You never said how long you were staying?" Marty carried Tyler's black suitcase down the steps.

Tyler pulled at the strap of his overnight bag. "Not sure how long I'll be here. It depends on a few things."

A dismayed grin broached Marty's rugged features. "You, not sure? Wow, that's a first."

Tyler frowned up at his very tall pilot. "Am I that much of a stickler? First, my secretary and now you; does everyone think I am controlling?"

Marty shrugged his wide shoulders. "Not controlling, you just always seem to be on a tight schedule. I never see you relax." He handed the black suitcase to Tyler. "I hope you try and enjoy yourself, Mr. Moore. It's a great town."

95

"You've spent time in New Orleans?"

Marty nodded. "When I flew for Southwest Airlines, we had quite a few layovers here. It's where I met my wife."

Tyler pulled out the metal handle on his suitcase. "Never understood why you didn't want to stay with Southwest, Marty. It's a good company, and I'm sure you were making more than you do with Propel."

"Yeah, but I was never home. With your company, I get to spend more time with my wife and little girl. There are some things more important than money, Mr. Moore."

"So I've been told." Tyler became distracted by a black Town Car pulling up to the side of the hangar a short distance from the plane. "I'll see you back in Dallas, Marty."

"Have a good time, Mr. Moore." Marty turned to the sleek white jet beside him and walked under the belly of the plane.

Tyler strolled to his waiting car parked next to the white hangar with "New Orleans Aviation" printed in red on the side.

"Mr. Moore?" A gangly young man wearing a black suit jumped to Tyler's side and took the suitcase from his hand. "I was sent to bring you into the city. I'm Clark, sir." He raced to the rear of the car and popped the trunk.

"Good to meet you, Clark." Tyler went around to the open rear passenger side door and pushed his overnight bag along the black leather seat.

"Where are you staying, Mr. Moore?" Clark asked, slamming the trunk closed.

Tyler removed the slip of paper Missy had given him from the pocket of his blue jeans. "2918 Prytania Street," he read from the paper.

Clark scratched his thick, bushy head of blond hair. "2918 Prytania? I don't recall a bed and breakfast bein' there, Mr. Moore. You sure you got the address right?"

"I'm staying at a friend's house," Tyler explained as he slid into the backseat.

"Sounds good to me," the young man drawled and then shut the passenger side door.

While Clark got comfortable behind the wheel, his small green eyes glimpsed Tyler through the rearview mirror. "I guess you plan on seein' some of the city while you're here, eh, Mr. Moore?"

Tyler nodded as his driver put the car into gear. "I hope to."

"You'll be stayin' at a real central location. You got Lafayette Cemetery right down the street from you, along with Commander's Palace, and then there's all them nice old houses in the Garden District you could visit. When you want to go to the Quarter, you could hop on a streetcar goin' down St. Charles Avenue. Great way to see N'awlins."

"You sound like a real proponent for city tourism, Clark."

"Just trying to get you psyched up 'bout stayin' here, sir. And, yeah, I'm always pluggin' my hometown."

"Tell me, Clark, are all New Orleanians like you? Everyone I've met from here loves it."

"Hell yeah! N'awlins is like no other place on earth, Mr. Moore. I should know. I did two tours in Iraq before I came back."

"You were in Iraq?" Tyler angled forward in his seat. "Well, I am impressed, Clark. Thank you for your service."

Clark drove the car up to a security gate located at the edge of the airfield. "Hey, the Army did me a favor." He waved to the guard in the security booth as he drove by. "I was a real screwed up kid in high school. Bad grades, bad attitude, bad reputation...you name it. After I barely graduated, I got into some trouble with the law and an uncle suggested the military. So, I joined up. Best thing I ever did. They got me in shape, cleaned me up, and gave me direction. I would have stayed in but my Humvee got hit with a roadside bomb in Tikrit. Lost the hearin' in my right ear, but I was lucky. A lot of guys I knew never came back."

"How did you end up doing this?" Tyler asked, intrigued by the exuberant young man.

"My uncle—the one who talked me into the military—he owns a car service and gave me a job as soon as I got home. It's good, you know? In a few years, he's gonna let me take over some of the management stuff for him, and who knows, in a while I could be runnin' the whole thing." The car careened off the airport road and merged into the street traffic. "One thing Iraq taught me was that life's good, no matter where it takes you. If you're breathin', then everthin's gonna be just fine."

"That's a great philosophy, Clark," Tyler pronounced.

"Not a philosophy, Mr. Moore. Just the truth; nothin' is as bad as it seems."

Tyler sat back in his seat as the streetlights zoomed by. He took in the dark shadows covering the shoreline of Lake Pontchartrain to his right as a sliver of the new moon reflected on the still, black water. His thoughts eventually turned to Monique and a flurry of anticipation stirred in his belly. As he tried to plan exactly what he was going to say when he stood on her doorstep, the cell phone in his overnight bag began ringing.

"Yes, Lynn," he said into the phone after recognizing his office number.

"You got in all right?"

Tyler chuckled at his secretary's propensity to always check to see if he had arrived in one piece. "Fine. Why do you always call and ask me that whenever I travel?"

"Just making sure you're still alive, so I know I have a job in the morning."

"That's very comforting, Lynn, thank you."

"Curtis Norman called from the gas line project in Oklahoma," she related, getting straight to business. "He says they have run into a problem with the zoning commission controlled by the state legislature there. They want to rescind the permits on construction."

Tyler ran his hand over his forehead, remembering that this was the reason he could never take vacations. "Did you call Mitch Douglass with this? The Oklahoma project is his baby."

"I did. He told me you would know some people in the legislature up there that might be able to smooth things over for us."

Tyler's gut tightened. "I don't know anyone, but...." He let a long sigh escape his lips. "There is someone I can call."

"I'll let Mr. Douglass know you're on it."

Tyler had another thought before he hung up. "Lynn, do me a favor."

"Yes, Mr. Moore?"

"Any other emergencies, funnel them to Mitch. He's the COO and should be handling things while I'm out of town."

Lynn took a moment. "So I am to tell everyone I can't get in touch with you from now on, is that it?"

Tyler relaxed against his seat, grateful for his secretary's ability to read between the lines. "You got it, Lynn. I'll check in with you in the morning after I get settled."

"I'm impressed. She must be something really special."

Tyler knitted his brow. "What are you talking about?"

"I've been juggling your messages, ordering flowers, and shopping for your wives and girlfriends for over ten years, Mr. Moore. But I've never known you to chase anyone."

He pictured her sitting at her desk with a whimsical smirk on her pretty face. "Lynn, I'm simply taking a break and getting away from the office for a while."

"If you say so." A reserved snicker came over the speaker. "Happy hunting, Mr. Moore." Lynn rang off.

Scrolling through his contact numbers, he found the one he was looking for. With a great deal of reservation, he hit the number and waited as the line rang on the other end.

"Hello, darling," a woman's velvety voice purred from the speaker.

Tyler slumped into his soft leather seat. "Hello, Mother, how are you?"

"Fine, just fine. Gary and I just got back from dinner at the club. Helen was there with the grandkids. They are getting so big. You should come down to Austin soon and see everyone."

"I can't right now, Mother."

"Are you still at work?" Her always carefully measured voice only rose slightly higher with feigned concern. "It's after eight, Tyler, you should go home. You can't keep pulling these late nights at the office."

"I'm not at the office, I'm in New Orleans."

Tyler counted off the seconds until her constantly composed voice returned on the line. "New Orleans? Are you at a conference?"

"No, I'm here to see an old friend. You remember Monique Delome." He grinned, knowing that should upend his mother's continuously controlled demeanor.

"Ah, when did this happen?"

The lights of the city's skyscrapers were growing brighter in the distance as the Town Car motored along I-10. "We ran into each other over the weekend when I was staying at the Ritz-Carlton for business. Monique was there for a convention."

"Yes, she's become a very good author."

"I'm surprised you knew about that."

"I've read two of her books. All my friends at the club have read her books. That's how I found out she was a writer." She paused and he could almost see her perfectly smooth white brow straining against the Botox holding it into place. "Is it serious?" she pressed, trying to sound indifferent.

"It's beginning, that's all."

"It will be serious between you two, soon enough, just like it was before." Her voice became uncharacteristically tense, making Tyler's grin grow even wider. "You were absolutely besotted with that New Orleans girl," she added.

"Her name's Monique, Mother."

"I know that! Is that why you called me, to gloat about getting back together with her?"

"No." He tapped his fingers on the thigh of his jeans, gratified that he had rattled her practiced patience. "I need to speak with Gary. Business."

100

"Be careful, Tyler. She broke your heart last time when she left for New Orleans, and she will do it again."

"Maybe this time it will be different. We've both grown up."

"Your body grows up, darling, but your mind is just as stupid as it was when you were young. That's the little irony of life. You may appear wiser because of gray hair and wrinkles, but it is only an illusion. Wisdom only comes to us when we're dead."

"Always the optimist, aren't you, Mother?"

"I'll get your father."

"Stepfather," Tyler quickly corrected.

"He's been more of a father to you than...don't start, Tyler. You'll give me another migraine if we go around in circles again about your father."

"I thought the migraines only came when we talked about Peter."

The silence on the line this time was completely expected. He knew mentioning that name would always elicit his mother's ire.

"You know I don't like talking about him, Tyler. I've told you that before. And please, don't get that nasty attitude like you always do whenever you bring up your brother."

"At least I talk about him. You act like he's dead." His hand tightened on the phone.

"He is dead to me. It's been thirty-six years since he left us. Not a word in all that time means he has to be dead. I said my good-byes long ago, Tyler. I suggest you do the same."

"Not until I have proof. I won't give up hope."

"You'd better, or it will destroy you just like it—here's your father." He heard the phone being passed away.

"Tyler?" a man's gravelly voice echoed over the line. "What's up?"

"Hey, Gary. I hope you don't mind but I need to ask you a favor."

"I take it this is about the company?"

101

That uncomfortable knot in Tyler's chest tightened. It was his usual reaction whenever he discussed business with his stepfather. "Yeah, I have a situation developing with that pipeline we are trying to run down from our gas wells in Oklahoma. It seems the state legislature is blocking our building permits."

"Sounds like the usual political bullshit. You pay off the right guys?"

Tyler withheld the insolent retort he wanted to let loose, not wanting to upset his stepfather. "Yeah, we locked in the locals a while ago, but I need someone at the state level. You still know people there?"

"You know you have to pay off at all levels in this game, Tyler. 'Men are more easily governed through their vices, than their virtues.' Napoleon said that." An episode of light wheezing could be heard over the phone. "Hal Askew is an old poker playing buddy of mine," Gary went on, sounding a little out of breath. "He's a majority leader of the Oklahoma State Legislature. I'll give him a call in the morning and set him straight. He can be swayed, but you'll probably have to wash his hands in return."

"What does he ask for?" Tyler questioned, familiar with the art of gift giving to political cronies.

"Trips abroad mostly, usually for him and his wife. I sent him to Italy twice when he got some of my projects pushed through committee. First class all the way, cost me a boatload, but he has a lot of clout in Oklahoma. You need him."

"Fine, just let me know what he wants. I've got to get this pipeline deal closed in the next six months."

"I'll pass that on." Gary took a ragged breath and then coughed. "Anything else? You taking care of my baby? I didn't build Propel from nothing to have you run it into the ground."

Tyler bit his tongue, not wanting to remind the man that he had been successfully running the company for ten years. When Gary had been forced into retirement, Tyler had hoped his stepfather would let loose the reins of control over Propel, but

Tyler had been wrong. He figured no matter what he did, Gary Leesburg would never see him as anything other than a second-rate replacement. "I'm taking care of the business, Gary. You got the last P&L report. We're doing very well."

"Could always be doing better, Tyler," Gary said in his usual patronizing way. "Your mother complains that you're working too hard."

"No harder than you did, Gary."

"If I hadn't had that damned heart attack, I'd still be running Propel. The only reason I left you in charge was because you're Barbara's son, and I thought you could handle it."

"I am handling it, Gary," Tyler replied, tempering the irritation in his voice.

"I heard something about New Orleans. You there on business for the company?"

The bright lights of the Mercedes-Benz Superdome came into view as the car reached the top of a high rise on the I-10. "No, I'm just taking a break for a few days, and catching up with an old friend."

"Well, don't stay away too long. Things fall apart when no one is at the helm." Gary coughed again. "I envy you. I feel like I am getting absolutely senile puttering around this house all day."

"You need to take it easy, Gary."

"So the doctors keep telling me. I'll get back to you about Hal Askew tomorrow, so check your messages."

"Will do, and thanks."

"Your mother wants to talk to you again."

"Forget it," Tyler returned. "We've already said enough."

Tyler hung up, feeling more anxious than relieved by the phone call. Dealing with his mother always brought out the worst in him. After all the years of battling with her to be the successful son Gary needed, he was not surprised that their every conversation ended badly. Tyler never blamed his stepfather for his mother's frenzied ambitions for her son. Gary had always given him the opportunity to make his career choices without any added pressure. But his mother always pushed Tyler to go above and beyond, especially when it came to making Gary happy. It was if she were making up for the loss of one son by forcing the other to be perfect. That had always been the underlying reason for the tension between them. Peter. Thirty-six years later, and it still hurt to think of him.

"We should be there in about ten more minutes," Clark reported from the front seat.

Tyler shook off the past and focused on the businesses spread out along the lower portion of the famous St. Charles Avenue. To his left, a green trolley hummed along the center of the avenue, reminding him of the uniqueness of New Orleans.

"That's quite a sight." Tyler pointed out the window to the trolley.

"Yeah," Clark agreed. "Until you try and cross the neutral ground and end up dodgin' them things. Always gotta look out for streetcars 'round here."

"What's a neutral ground?" Tyler inquired.

Clark lightly chuckled. "Sorry. Ya'll call them medians. In N'awlins, there ain't no medians, only neutral grounds. Anythin' that divides a street in two in this town is called a neutral ground."

"That's an odd name for it," Tyler commented.

"The term goes back to the days when the French Creoles were livin' in the French Quarter and the Americans occupied the other side of Canal Street, now called the CBD. The two groups always had tensions because of their different lifestyles, manners, and languages, but Canal Street was literally the one place they could go and not have any fights. So, it became the neutral ground and the term stuck in the city. That's how you always know somebody's from here. When they say neutral ground and not median, you've got a real New Orleanian."

"Interesting bit of history, Clark."

"It ain't history to us. It's just the way of things. There's so much tradition in this town, that's what I love about it. Nothin' changes. Oh, I'm sure we have our detractors out there, 'specially since Katrina, but people here are pretty devoted. I think that's what's hard for outsiders to understand. But you gotta be from here to get it."

"Actually, it would explain a great deal," Tyler remarked.

The commercial buildings on St. Charles Avenue gave way to stately mansions and architectural landmarks. Tyler watched in fascination as the streetlights cast an eerie glow on the homes, making them appear more horrific than historic, and awakening images of vampires, ghosts, and any other number of supernatural creatures that he had read about in books set against the backdrop of the Big Easy.

The Town Car took a left across the "neutral ground" and his gut twitched with misgivings. While the car maneuvered down narrow, bumpy streets with smaller, but still charming homes, Tyler debated if he had been a bit hasty in his decision to drop in on Monique. He figured he had been doing what she wanted, but as his journey came to an end, he began to consider if she would actually be as welcoming to him now as she might have been twenty-one years ago.

When Clark pulled the car in front of a raised gray and white, three-story home, Tyler was reminded of Monique. The house was like her in a way, not as ornate as others he had passed on the way down St. Charles Avenue, but reserved, classic, and distinctly unique.

Modest white Doric columns decorated a short porch and also supported an equally short second floor balcony. Rising from the second floor was a steep, slopping roof with dormer windows set on either side. A black iron fence ran about the edge of the property with manicured gardens of green shrubs in front. The porch lights were out, and none of the long windows facing the street had any light shining through them, making Tyler question if anyone was home.

He remembered what Chris Donovan had told him about Monique returning to New Orleans instead of attending her next convention, and speculated if perhaps she had gone on to fulfill her commitments.

"You sure someone is waitin' for you?" Clark asked, reading Tyler's mind. "Looks like no one's home."

A sudden flash of light from a second floor window made Tyler smile. "She's there."

Clark put the car into park and Tyler grabbed his overnight bag on the seat next to him. But when he put his hand on his door, Clark was already opening it for him.

"I hope you have a nice stay in N'awlins, Mr. Moore." Clark moved away from the passenger door and to the back of the car.

Tyler stood from the car. "I hope so, too."

He waited for the young man to lift his suitcase from the trunk as he slung his overnight bag on his shoulder.

"You want me to take this to the door for you?" Clark held up the suitcase.

"No, thanks." Tyler took his suitcase. "I'm good."

"Just call again if you need a lift back to the airport, Mr. Moore." Clark stood before him. "It's been nice meetin' you, sir."

Tyler extended his hand to the young driver. "Clark, it's been a privilege. I wish you all the best."

Clark shook his hand. "Thank you, Mr. Moore. Have a good time."

Tyler waited as the young man went around to the driver's side and climbed back behind the wheel.

After the black car had pulled away from the curb, Tyler turned to the imposing recessed oak door with a decorative glass fanlight above, and squared his shoulders.

"Here we go."

Chapter 10

Tyler entered the small black gate and progressed down a slender, red-bricked pathway to the front porch steps. He climbed the steps and listened as his footfalls echoed across the porch. Dropping his suitcase before the front door, he pressed the brass doorbell on his left.

The distant sound of chimes could be heard coming through the thick oak door. Seconds ticked by, and he could feel his heartbeat speed up as he listened for movement within. Lights suddenly shone through the fanlight overhead.

"Who is it?" a woman's voice called.

"Moe, it's Tyler."

At first, nothing happened. There was no rattling of security chains or creaking as the old door gave way. Tyler listened and after a few tense moments was relieved to hear the clap of a deadbolt and see the porch light above the door come to life.

When she opened the door, he detected the hint of lilac in the air. Then, he saw her bare feet on the dark hardwood floor. His eyes traveled up her faded blue jeans to her rumpled T-shirt, and he noted how her dirty-blonde hair draped around her shoulders. When he gazed into her face, her simple beauty enthralled him.

The faint pink blush on her cheeks stood out against her porcelain high cheekbones. Her deep gray eyes were resplendent beneath the porch light, accentuating her dark eyelashes. The dim light highlighted the curve of her jaw, and her pink lips appeared paler, but still as full and round as he remembered. He wanted to reach out and sweep away the wisp of bangs hanging in her eyes, but then the light changed and her eyes drew together.

"What in the hell are you doing here?"

"Lovely to see you again, Moe." He lifted his suitcase. "Aren't you going to invite me in?"

She pointed at his black suitcase. "What is that for?"

"I thought I would come for a visit."

She pushed the door all the way open and glowered at him. "What, are you stalking me?"

"I'm visiting, not stalking. If I was stalking, I wouldn't have used the doorbell."

"You can't stay here, Ty," she declared, standing in the doorway.

"Why not?"

"Because...because I don't...I don't want you here," she stammered.

"Well, it's too late for me to get a hotel."

"It's New Orleans. It's never too late to get a hotel."

"Come on, Moe." He moved closer to the door. "It's late, and I just got in. Don't make me have to call a cab and fight getting a hotel room at this hour."

She kept her body in front of the door, blocking his way. "Why are you here? I think we said about all there was to say back in Dallas."

He leaned his shoulder against the doorframe. "You left before we finished talking."

She folded her arms, appearing uncomfortable. "I figured I should leave you before you snuck out on me."

"I wasn't going to sneak out, Moe."

"Isn't that what you usually do with women, sneak out before they wake up?"

"Perhaps, but that wasn't what I wanted to do with you." He kept his eyes pinned on her. "I came to New Orleans because I didn't want to repeat the same mistake I made over twenty years ago. I'm making an effort here. Can you meet me halfway and allow me to come inside?" He hiked up the suitcase in his hand. "This isn't exactly light, you know?"

She nodded her head and moved aside.

Tyler shuffled in the door and put his suitcase and overnight bag down on the dull, hardwood floor. The small entryway around him led to a straight walnut staircase on the left, while a hallway ran along the side of the stairway to the right. Tall cypress doors with fanlights matching the one above the front entrance opened off the main hallway. The walls were done in cream-colored textured plaster with wainscoting of darkly stained beadboard beneath. Stately paintings of lush landscapes and green forests adorned the entranceway. Above, a lavish twenty-four light brass chandelier added a touch of opulence to the impressive décor.

"And here I thought you were living modestly." He lowered his eyes to her. "Rather a grand place for someone trying to make a living as a writer."

"It was part of my divorce settlement. It's all I got out of the six years we were together."

"You want to show me the rest of the place?"

Her eyes went wide. "No. You'll be leaving in the morning when you can get a hotel room."

He raised his eyebrows playfully. "Will I?"

She slammed the front door closed. "Don't do this, Ty. Don't come here and think you will make everything like you want it to be. I have a life now. I have a deadline for my next book, and I don't need you—"

"Sunday morning I ran into your manager. He was pretty pissed and told me you had skipped out on attending another convention when you came back to New Orleans. You want to tell me why?"

She ran her hands up and down her bare arms. "No."

"Moe, I came here to try and figure things out between us. I know I have a lousy track record with women, but I'm here and I'm trying to have something better with you. The least you can do is tell me why you left Dallas the way you did."

109

She went to the stairs and had a seat on the bottom step. "I woke up in the middle of the night with you next to me and I knew...I knew it would never work between us. Just like it would never have worked before. It doesn't matter what you do or try to be, Ty, we were never meant to be together." She motioned to him. "You are you, and I am...not want you want."

He came closer to the stairs. "How do you know what I want?"

"I know the kind of woman you want, and I'm not it. I figured it was better to go before...we had our night together, let's just leave it at that."

He had a seat next to her on the step. "Moe, in all my life, I have never known anyone like you. You've never been something you're not in order to please me. Do you know how refreshing that is? I guess that's why I never forgot about you."

She snorted at his disclosure. "You never forgot about me because I was the only woman you never slept with."

"But I did sleep with you, and here I am." He shimmied closer to her on the step. "If you would let me, I would like to spend some time with you, get to know you again."

Tyler angled slightly forward, desperately wanting to taste her lips, but Moe brusquely stood from the steps.

"You can stay in the guest bedroom upstairs, but in the morning you have to get a hotel room."

"Whatever you want," he told her, knowing he had no intention of leaving.

Tyler gathered up his bags as Moe waited in the middle of the staircase. Just as he was about to climb the steps, a small ball of white fur appeared on the second floor landing and started yapping at him.

"Bart, stop it," Monique called to the dog.

The small Chihuahua mix descended the steps. He had patches of white matted fur, a short snout, bulging black eyes, and a red tongue that hung out of the side of his mouth, waving like a flag.

"What's that?" Tyler demanded, staring at the mongrel.

"Bart," Monique answered. "I found him at an animal rescue benefit I attended a few years ago. He was up for adoption but no one wanted him because he was so...different."

"You mean ugly, don't you?" Tyler ribbed.

Monique held the small dog to her chest. "He's not ugly, and I don't like to use that word around him, because he's very sensitive."

Tyler nodded to the dog in her arms as he climbed the stairs. "I'm not going to kiss you if you keep holding that thing against you like that. You may catch something."

"I don't want you to kiss me."

Bart growled as Tyler drew closer.

"I never figured you to be into animals, Moe."

She ran her hand along Bart's patchy coat. "There's a lot you don't know about me."

"That's why I'm here." He came up to her and Bart gnashed his teeth. "Maybe you should have named him Chris."

"Not funny." Monique turned to the stairs. "Bart is just being protective."

"And what is Chris Donovan being?" Tyler followed her up the steps, relishing the view of her firm butt in front of him.

She stopped on the second floor landing. "He's being my manager."

Tyler climbed the last step to the second floor. "Manager or lover?"

"Chris is not my lover," she loudly clarified.

"He's not your type, Moe."

"Like you would know my type." Carrying Bart in her arms, she set out from the landing to a connecting wide hallway.

He eyed the pale yellow wallpaper, beige hall carpet, and tapering sconces on the walls shaped to look like candles and decided he liked this simpler style. It felt more like Monique to him. She had always been unimpressed with extravagance, and he was glad to see that this part of the home reflected that endearing quality.

Stopping before a tall cypress door, she placed her hand on the polished brass doorknob as Tyler stared at the still snarling dog.

"Please tell me you don't sleep with it, too?"

She turned the knob and pushed the door open. "Yes, I do. As a matter of fact, he's the only man I want to sleep with."

"You're standards must be slipping, Moe."

She smirked at him. "Well, I slept with you, didn't I?"

"Touché," Tyler replied, and then entered the room.

Monique flipped a switch, and the tastefully decorated, cream-colored bedroom glowed beneath the pale light coming from an antique ceiling fan. A mahogany trundle, queen-sized bed occupied the center of the room with matching night tables on either side. The walls were covered with framed black and white photographs. On closer inspection, Tyler discovered they were pictures of New Orleans from the turn of the century.

"Nice pieces." He pointed to a still of the Mississippi River front.

"I like to collect old photographs of the city," Monique admitted.

"I remember when you dragged me to that photography exhibit on the SMU campus. We spent hours wandering about. You checked out every photo."

She frowned at him. "I can't believe you remember that."

"I especially remember how much you enjoyed it. It was a side of you I had never seen before that night."

Scratching Bart's back, she turned to an open door next to a mahogany dresser. "There's a small guest bath so you don't have to use the one across the hall." Monique motioned to a slender door in the corner. "That's the closet, but you won't need it, since you'll be leaving in the morning."

Tyler went to the bed and tossed his suitcase on top of the tan and white comforter. "But I have all night to change your mind about that."

She headed for the entrance. "You're still impossible."

He plunked down the overnight bag on the bed next to his suitcase. "And still just as determined as I ever was."

Monique halted at the doorway. "Why bother being determined? You got what you wanted out of me. We slept together and can put all those years of wondering what it would be like behind us. You don't need anything else from me."

"Don't be so quick to judge me, Moe." He crept closer to her. "If all I wanted was to sleep with you, I wouldn't be here." He reached for a tendril of her silky hair and then Bart attempted to snap at him.

Tyler jerked his hand back. "Shouldn't you lock that up in a cage?"

She patted the dog's head. "You're the one who should be locked up." Monique stepped into the hallway. "If you're hungry, there's only fruit and cold cuts in the fridge. You're welcome to whatever you can find in the pantry. Just don't leave a mess behind in my kitchen. I've got to get back to work."

She was about to start down the hall when Tyler came bounding through the door. "Where's your room?"

Her eyes warily studied him and then she nodded to a door further down hall. "That's the master. It has a study connected to it, where I write. But don't think of sneaking in my room at night and pulling anything, Ty." She shoved the small dog toward him. "He may not bite hard, but he knows all your vulnerable spots."

Tyler gestured to the dog. "I hope that's not all you have for protection around here?"

"No. I also sleep with a .357 next to my bed."

"Now that sounds like the Moe I know and love."

The sullen expression she gave him was just what he intended. He needed to make her second-guess her first impressions of him, and put the question in her head if he was really being sincere. *But love?* If he had ever loved any woman, it had been Monique. She had gotten closer to him than anyone, and despite the passage of time, he had never been able to forget her. Maybe that was what love was all about. Not the passion, but the ability to never be able to erase the memory of another from the furthest reaches of your heart.

"I'll see you in the morning," she mumbled, and then departed down the hall to her bedroom.

Tyler grinned as she slinked through her door and quietly shut it behind her.

"Round one to me," he whispered.

Back in his room, he went straight to his suitcase. Opening the skinny closet door, he placed some slacks, an additional pair of jeans, a casual jacket, and a few dress shirts inside. After putting his suitcase in the closet, he carted the overnight bag to the bathroom.

He frowned as he stood in the narrow bathroom. "It's not the Ritz."

But somehow it felt more comfortable to Tyler than many of the numerous hotels he had stayed in through the years.

Once his unpacking was done, he returned to the bedroom and realized that there was no television.

"This could be a problem." Tyler hated to admit it, but the television had become something of a diversion for him. He always kept one on at home, wanting to stay abreast of current events. Deciding he would have to resort to other means to satiate his information fix, he went to his overnight bag and removed his iPad. Plopping down on his bed, he turned on the iPad, and hit the twenty-four-hour news app. While he flipped through different headlines, catching up on the weather and stock quotes, his mind worked its way back to Monique.

Half the battle was over. He was here, and had made his intentions known. Tyler just hoped this story turned out to have the happily ever after he was aiming for, and did not end up being just another disappointing tale filled with regrets and resentments.

"It will work out," he avowed, bolstering his confidence. Then, he remembered Clark and the young man's optimistic attitude toward life. "As long as I keep breathing, everything will be just fine."

Alexandrea Weis

Chapter 11

The travel clock on his night table read well after one in the morning when Tyler bolted upright in the queen-sized bed. He rubbed his eyes and glanced down at the iPad next to him. He remembered going through some e-mails and had decided to close his eyes for a few minutes. That had been over three hours ago.

Swinging his legs around to the side of the trundle bed, he sat up and stretched out the kink in his neck. Standing up, he gazed about the room, and then the rumbling of his stomach reminded him that he had not eaten anything since grabbing a bagel at Love Field before boarding the jet for New Orleans.

As he walked across the bedroom, the floorboards moaned. Would he be able to sneak down the stairs to the kitchen without having the creaking floors alert Monique and her sidekick, the ugly Bart, to his presence? Another insistent gurgle from his stomach made him decide he would risk it in order to be able to get back to sleep.

In the almost pitch-black hallway, Tyler had to practically feel his way toward the stairs. Checking beneath Monique's bedroom door, he was relieved to see that there was no light peeking through. He quickened his pace and eventually got down the steps with only a few resistant groans coming from the old walnut staircase.

On the first floor, the streetlights outside the front windows afforded him a better view of the hallway heading toward the back of the house. At the end of the hallway, he found a pair of open double white doors that led to a wide kitchen. After flipping on the lights, he was pleasantly surprised by a spacious kitchen with a built-in refrigerator, island cooktop, double-oven, and a black granite countertop set beneath light oak cabinets that went all the way up to the eighteen-foot ceiling. Recessed lighting behind the top of the cabinets gave the room a warm glow, while spotlights beneath the cabinets made the stainless appliances shine.

Nodding his head with approval, Tyler worked his way across the kitchen to the refrigerator. He hunted through the shelves filled with cold cuts, fresh fruits, and an assortment of cheeses. Settling on sliced turkey, some grapes, melon chunks, and crackers he found on the countertop, Tyler took his plate to a square kitchen table set against the wall, ready to enjoy his midnight snack.

He was piling a portion of turkey onto a cracker when he heard a gentle tip, tip, tip coming toward the kitchen from down the hall. Seconds later, Bart came trotting in through the open kitchen doors.

"Hey, Ugly."

Bart ignored him and went to a spot where a bright blue bowl of water and a matching blue bowl of dry food had been placed on the floor.

Tyler pointed his finger at the dog. "I think you and I need to have a serious man-to-man talk."

Bart lapped noisily at his water, only stopping every now and then to cough.

"Won't be much of a man-to-man talk," Monique voiced from the kitchen doorway, "considering he was neutered a few years back."

Resting her shoulder against the door frame, her arms were folded across her short red nightshirt. Tyler's eyes roamed over her toned legs and his hunger for food abated as a more pressing need arose within him.

"I thought you didn't like animals, Ty."

He sat back in his chair as she ambled to the refrigerator. "I like them fine, but they don't like me."

118

"You never had pets growing up?" She opened the refrigerator door and peeked inside, making her nightshirt cling to her round butt.

"We couldn't afford them. My mother was a single parent and worked in a department store. It was all she could do to keep food on the table for my brother and me. So pets were not an option."

"I forgot about Peter." She stood back from the refrigerator. "Have you ever heard from him?"

"No." Tyler picked up the paper napkin beside his plate. "My mother has given up completely on ever finding him. After I took over Propel, I hired a private investigator to track him down, but with no luck."

"I'm sorry to hear that. I know how much you admired him."

He wiped his hands on the napkin. "Admired may be the wrong word."

"No, it's not. I remember the way you spoke of him. You admired him a great deal."

"It doesn't matter now." He threw the napkin back on the table.

"Must be hard not knowing what happened to him," she continued.

"I'm over it. I was fourteen when Peter packed up all the clothes he could carry on his motorcycle and left." Tyler could still picture his brother's bike heading down the street outside the crappy little house they had lived in before his mother had met the fabulously wealthy Gary Leesburg. "When my mother remarried, she seemed to push Peter out of her mind and focus all of her efforts on me. In some ways, I hate Peter for leaving me at Barbara's mercy."

She came closer to the table. "I know if I had lost my brother, Jake, around the age you lost Peter, I might have turned out different. Perhaps I would have been just as mistrusting, and just as doubting about the intentions of others as you. I would also have felt guilty as hell, and stuck by my mother's side to spare her the agony of losing yet another child."

"Don't analyze me, Moe. I hated when you did that." He loaded a slice of turkey on a cracker. "If I am mistrusting and doubtful it is more a result of the nature of others, and not because of my past mishaps."

She took a seat in the chair next to his. "Yeah, I guess being a big oil executive makes you the target of a lot of plots and conspiracies."

"Would you stop saying it like that?"

She stole the turkey from his plate. "Saying what?"

"The way you say 'oil executive,' you make it sound something akin to executioner."

She munched on the turkey. "I guess to some environmentalists it could sound like one in the same."

He pulled his plate to him. "Go get your own turkey, Greenpeace."

She giggled and Tyler's heart damn near lifted out of his chest. "Yours tastes better." She snuck another slice of turkey from his plate. "What about your business? Don't you have to get back to your oil wells?"

He popped a grape into his mouth. "It's taken care of."

"For how long?" she challenged.

"For a while," he evasively responded.

She tilted forward in her chair. "It won't work, you know."

Wantonly, his eyes lingered over her red nightshirt. "What won't work?"

"Coming here and trying to win me over, or whatever it is you're doing. It won't help, Ty. What we had is behind us. One night in a hotel room—"

"One very hot night in a hotel room," he interjected.

She blushed and sat back in her chair. "Yeah, well, we were just living out our youthful passions...we're different people now."

"You might like to think that, Moe, but we both know that's not true. Look at us. This is just how we were twenty-one years ago. We could stay up all night and talk about silly things, important things, but we could talk to each other. I don't know about you, but it's been a really long time since I've felt this comfortable with anyone."

She snuck his last slice of turkey from his plate. "You're good. I could almost hear the violins playing in the background, but I won't budge on this. You're outta here in the morning, Mr. Moore." She stuffed the turkey in her mouth and stood from the chair. "Enjoy your snack."

Monique padded out of the kitchen, and just after she rounded the double doors, the white fluff ball that was Bart ran after her.

Tyler listened to Bart's feet ticking down the hallway. Reaching for a piece of melon, he plotted what to do next. He had time on his side; sooner or later, he would get her to lower her defenses, and then he would make sure he never let her walk away again.

Alexandrea Weis

Chapter 12

The smell of coffee roused Tyler out of a sound sleep, and then the sound of Bart's yapping compelled him from his bed. The sun was climbing in through a blue stained glass window as he walked into the bathroom and heard the traffic on Prytania Street outside.

After running some cold water over his face, checking his five o'clock shadow in the mirror, and making a mental note to shave later, he wrestled a fresh, long-sleeved shirt from its hanger. He put on his jeans from the night before and scrambled for the bedroom door, desperate for coffee. When he opened his door, Bart was sitting outside of his room with his tongue hanging from the side of his mouth.

"Son of a...." Tyler grabbed at his chest. "You scared the hell out of me, you little shit."

Seemingly satisfied that he had done exactly what he set out to do, Bart turned and trotted for the stairs.

"We're going to have a serious talk about privacy, Bart," Tyler called after him.

Closing his bedroom door, he unsuccessfully tried to suppress a loud yawn and then slowly walked toward the stairs. When he hit the first floor landing, the smell of bacon made him quicken his step. But at the kitchen doors, he came to a grinding halt the instant he saw Monique at the island cooktop.

She was flipping slices of french toast with a spatula in one hand and drinking from her mug with another. Wearing baggy jeans and a loose fitting T-shirt, she appeared more like a little girl than a grown woman. Her dirty-blonde hair was pulled back in a messy ponytail and she had not a touch of makeup on her face. At that moment, Tyler had never seen her look more beautiful. He found it odd that he had been with so many women who had primped and painted into what he had thought was the epitome of beauty, only to discover that they could not hold a candle to Monique.

"Hey, you're up," she said when she cast her eyes the doorway. "I made us some breakfast, and then I figured you could call a few hotels and find a room."

"You're still eager to get rid of me?"

"Absolutely. I need to work, and I can't have you hanging around here…disturbing me."

He folded his arms over his chest as he came up to the cooktop. "Disturbing you? I thought it was the other way around."

Growling erupted from the corner of the kitchen and Tyler turned to see Bart glaring at him from his food bowl.

"Your rabid mongrel scared the hell out of me when I walked out of my bedroom."

Monique nodded to Bart. "He parked outside of your door from the moment he left my room this morning. He's not used to strangers staying in the house."

Tyler motioned to the dog. "Perhaps you should tell him I'm not a stranger."

"Wouldn't help." She scooped the slices of battered toast onto two plates. "If it makes you feel any better, he hates it when Chris stays here, too. He follows him all over the house, growling."

The thought of Chris sharing Monique's home infuriated Tyler. "When does Chris stay here?"

She shrugged, ignoring his unpleasant tone. "When he is in town," she informed him, and picked up the plates.

Tyler followed her as she took the plates to the kitchen table. "How often does he come in town?"

Putting the plates down, Monique took a seat at the table and then reached for a tray of bacon across from her. "He comes in when he needs to see me, or whenever we have an event here." After placing two slices of bacon on her plate, she passed the tray to Tyler.

Tyler took the tray of bacon and whacked it down on the table. "I'll repeat the question, Moe. How often does he come in town and stay with you?" Waiting for an answer, he leaned over the table, and glared at her.

She sat back in her chair. "You want coffee?"

"Moe!"

"All right. He comes in town once a month."

"Are you sleeping with him?"

"Jesus! What is your problem?" She sprang from her chair and headed across the kitchen to the coffeemaker.

"You are sleeping with him, aren't you?" he hollered. "That's why he wanted to rip my head off back in Dallas."

"I told you last night, I'm not sleeping with him. He wants a relationship with me...he told me so, but I said no."

"When was this?"

Monique came back to the table with the coffeepot. "It was a little while after he started as my manager. I had been lonely since my divorce and I never dated anyone because I was too busy writing. Chris was there for me. He became my friend, manager, confidant...."

"Do you care for him?" Tyler pulled out his chair and had a seat.

She filled his blue coffee mug. "We're close, but I don't think it would be a good idea to get any closer. He has never given up hoping I'll change my mind." She put the mug down in front of him. "You want sugar?"

"No." He shook his head. "I mean, yes to the sugar. If you don't want more, then why do you let him stay here?"

Shrugging, she poured the coffee into her white mug. "Why not? It's convenient when we have things to do in town." She carried the coffeepot back to the coffeemaker on the counter.

"I don't think it's wise for the guy to stay with you. What if he wears you down one day and you two begin a relationship?"

Monique picked up a bowl of sugar by the coffeemaker. "Wear me down? Like you're trying to wear me down?" She brought the sugar to the table.

"This is different." He waited as she placed the sugar in front of him. "You don't care for him, you care for me."

"Cared for you, Ty. Past tense." She returned to her chair. "What we had was a long time ago."

"It was last weekend, Moe."

She lifted a small white jug next to her plate filled with maple syrup. "That was just sex," she admitted, covering her french toast with syrup.

He shook his spoon at her. "It was more than sex, and you know it."

"No, I'm pretty sure it was just about the sex."

He stabbed his spoon into the sugar bowl. "Why are you being so stubborn?"

She thumped the jug down on the table. "Why are you being so persistent?"

"I thought that was obvious." He dumped a spoonful of sugar into his coffee.

"Nothing with you is obvious, Ty. I learned a long time ago that nothing is as it appears with you."

He stirred his coffee. "Meaning what, exactly?"

"You always said one thing and meant another. I could never tell where I really stood with you half the time."

"Oh, come on, Moe." Tyler banged his spoon down on the table. "You knew exactly how I felt about you."

"Did I?" She looked over her plate of french toast and bacon. "Funny, I don't remember you ever saying how you felt about me."

"Yes, I did. Plenty of times. You just don't—" The chimes from the front doorbell interrupted him. "Let me guess," Tyler grumbled. "It's Chris."

126

Monique pushed her chair back from the table. "It's not Chris. I spoke to him yesterday. He's at the convention in South Carolina, covering for me." She stood and went to the kitchen doorway. Before she exited the kitchen, Monique turned to him. "Stay here. I don't need you starting shit, in case it is Chris."

Tyler stood from the table. "To hell with that."

Monique rolled her eyes. "Great."

She hustled to the entrance and Tyler followed close behind her. She waited with her hand on the front door when he came up to her side.

"Just behave," she whispered to him.

"I make no promises."

Monique uttered a frustrated sigh, shook her head, and turned the deadbolt.

A thick, muscular man of medium height with wild, light blond curly hair and piercing blue eyes was standing on the porch, holding up a newspaper wrapped in a blue plastic bag. His fitted, dark gray suit and yellow tie stood out against the white front doorframe. When his playful eyes found Monique, a wide grin brightened his round face.

"Hey, girl," the stranger called in a chipper voice. He then stepped inside the door and kissed Monique on the cheek. When he raised his eyes to Tyler, his cheerful countenance disappeared. "Sorry, did I, ah, interrupt something?"

"Jake, this is Tyler." Monique gestured to Tyler. "Tyler Moore; my friend from Dallas."

Jake's bright blue eyes clouded with concern. "Not *the* Tyler Moore?"

Monique nodded. "Yeah. Tyler this is my brother, Jake Delome."

Tyler stepped forward, extending his hand, but Jake refused it and took a step back, scowling at Tyler.

"Jake, stop it," Monique cautioned.

"This is the son of a bitch who made you a basket case when you came home from SMU!" Jake shouted.

127

Monique went to Tyler's side. "That was over twenty years ago, Jake."

Jake pointed at his sister. "Do you know what you did to her?"

"I can understand why you are angry, but I think your sister and I have worked things out," Tyler told him.

Bart trotted into the hallway, anxious to see what all the commotion was about. He had a seat on the floor and casually took in the show.

Monique spun around to her brother. "Jacob Martin Delome, you apologize right now!"

"For what?" Jake appeared indignant.

She went to the open front door and pointed outside. "If you can't be civil to my guest, then get out."

"Now I'm a guest. Last night I was a stalker," Tyler remarked behind her.

Jake then pointed his finger at Tyler. "Hey, I wasn't the asshole who dumped you all those years ago, Mojo."

"Mojo?" Tyler asked.

"He's always called me Mojo, since we were kids," Monique explained, glancing back at him.

"You want to tell me why he is here?" Jake implored, raising his voice.

Tyler turned to Jake. "I'm here because your sister and I ran into each other last weekend and I wanted to catch up."

Jake wrinkled his brow at Monique. "I thought you were in Dallas last weekend for a convention?"

Tyler came up to Monique's side and she waved her hand to him. "I was. We ran into each other at my hotel."

"And now he's here? Give me a break," Jake scoffed. "Sounds like you two are still hot for each other."

Monique blushed, and then dropped her eyes. "We're not 'hot' for each other."

"Could have fooled me." Jake knelt down and patted Bart on the head.

"I know I'm still hot for you," Tyler whispered to her.

128

Monique playfully slapped his arm. Tyler sensed the change in her, and knew he was making headway.

Jake rose from the floor and then begrudgingly motioned to Tyler. "Hey man, I'm sorry I jumped all over you." His eyes then swerved to his sister. "There, happy?"

She shut the front door with a loud bang. "You're such an idiot." She went back to Tyler. "Come on, let's finish our breakfast."

"Hey, Mojo, can I get a cup of coffee?"

"It's in the kitchen," she called over her shoulder to her brother as she escorted Tyler down the hall.

When they entered the kitchen, with Bart bringing up the rear, Jake went to the table and inspected the plates of french toast and bacon. "I want some," he whined, sounding more like a little boy than a grown man.

Monique went to the refrigerator. "You get coffee, and that's it."

Jake pitched the newspaper still in his hand onto the black granite countertop. "I got your paper for you. Isn't that worth a slice of bacon?"

"Fine. You can have mine." She waved to her place at the table.

"Cool." Jake went to the table, flung his tie over his shoulder, and straddled her chair. The man-child nabbed the fork next to the plate and happily dived into the soggy, syrup-coated french toast.

"You'll have to forgive my brother, Tyler. He got hit in the head a lot when he played baseball for LSU."

"Very funny. So why is he staying here?" Jake jammed a forkful of food into his mouth.

As Tyler stood next to the table, Monique came alongside him, carrying a butter dish. Placing her hand on his back, she deposited the dish next to her brother's spot at the table. When she stepped back, she smiled into Tyler's eyes and for a moment it was as if all the years apart had never happened. The same sense of awe he felt for her when they first met in front of that Jackson Pollack painting was still there.

"You finally slept with him, didn't you?" Jake's voice intruded.

"Jake!" Monique croaked.

Tyler tried to hide his grin.

"What?" Jake pointed his fork at her. "It's written all over your face. Why else would the guy be staying here?"

"Jake, I am here catching up with an old friend." Tyler pulled out his chair and had a seat. "Monique was kind enough to invite me to stop by whenever I was in New Orleans. I got a lucky break from work and decided to take her up on her offer." He reached for his blue coffee mug. "That's all there is to it," he declared.

"Yes, that's all there is," Monique confirmed. "He got in late last night, but he's getting a hotel room today. Right, Ty?"

Tyler purposefully did not respond and took a sip from his coffee.

Jake scowled at Tyler. "You do know you broke her heart before, don't you?"

Tyler nodded. "And she broke mine."

"I did?" Monique spoke up, a bit mystified.

Jake's blue eyes honed in on Monique's reaction. "What about Chris? Does he know Tyler is staying here?"

Tyler swiveled his dark eyes to Monique.

"It's none of his business," she groused and spun away from the table.

Jake let out a hoarse chuckle. "Yeah, right. If he even gets wind that you have another guy under this roof, he'll be here with a bazooka to blow him away."

"I'll make sure to keep an eye out for that bazooka," Tyler mumbled.

Huddled over his plate, Jake appraised the man across from him. "So what is it you do, Tyler? Mojo told me you came from money?"

"I'm the CEO of Propel Oil and Gas."

"I've heard of them. Well-established company." Jake shoved another slice of french toast into his mouth.

"What do you do, Jake?" Tyler sipped his coffee.

"I'm an attorney with Barton and Lubell. We handle mostly insurance cases, defending the insurance companies, not litigating against them."

Tyler raised his eyebrows. "Impressive."

Jake held out his white mug of coffee to Monique, who was standing by the kitchen counter. "Can you refill this for me…please?"

Monique sighed and retrieved the coffeepot from the warming plate.

"How long have you been with Propel?" Jake inquired.

"Over twenty years. I started with them after Monique returned to New Orleans."

Monique came to the table, carrying the coffeepot. "What are you doing here so early, Jake?"

"I've got a deposition at an attorney's office close by. So, I thought I would come and get a cup of coffee." He nodded to Tyler. "Didn't think I would see you with him here, though. I thought you had put this guy behind you, except of course in those trashy novels you write."

Tyler put his mug down on the table with a thud. "Am I the only one who didn't know I am in her books?"

"Her trashy novels, you mean," Jake infused. "Yeah, she told me about putting you in them after I read her first one. I thought it was weird."

"Would you stop calling my books 'trashy novels'?" She finished filling his white coffee mug. "Just call before you come next time, okay?"

"Why? I've never called before."

She walked back to the counter. "Yeah, and it used to drive Mat crazy when you would just show up at any hour."

"Mat was an asshole," Jake snorted.

"I keep hearing that," Tyler quipped.

"Mojo ever tell you about the time I beat the shit out of her husband?"

Monique thumped the coffeepot down on the counter. "Damn it, Jake."

"Oh, I'd love to hear this," Tyler imparted with a wicked grin.

"Yeah, I came over one morning and found Mojo crying her eyes out. Seems her dickhead husband let it slip about his affair with one of the girls from his office. I confronted him and he thought he could push me out the door." Jake's blue eyes danced with mischief. "Asshole Mat may have been an inch or two taller than me, but I had twenty pounds on his skinny ass. So when I pushed back, he raised his fist to me. Big mistake."

"You broke his nose," Monique scolded as she came back to the table.

"Yeah, and knocked out two of his teeth, too." Jake grinned. "Poor bastard had to get implants."

Tyler laughed and could not help but notice as Monique laughed, too.

"It was pretty cool," she admitted.

"Very cool," her brother added. "Anyway, a few days later, Mat the asshole moved out." He heaved another thick wedge of french toast into his mouth.

"Well, I'm glad Moe has always had you around to watch out for her."

"Me and Chris." Jake chewed his food. "That dude's got a twisted obsession with my sister."

Monique slapped her brother on the back of the head. "Don't say that about Chris. He has been good to me."

"He's a sick shit, Mojo." Jake checked his watch, greedily swallowed another bite, and then quickly slurped back a few gulps of coffee. After wiping his mouth with the paper napkin, he stood from his chair. "I gotta go." He peered over at Tyler. "How long are you staying?"

Tyler's eyes drifted to Monique. "That's depends."

She folded her arms over her chest and frowned at him.

Jake kissed his sister on the cheek. "Maybe we should get together this weekend and all go out for dinner?"

"He won't be here this weekend," Monique stated in a matter-of-fact tone.

"I won't?" Tyler came back, raising his dark eyebrows to her.

Jake pointed across the room to Bart, who was standing dutifully beside his food bowl. "Bart, my man!"

Bart stood up and wagged his tail.

Jake hurried to the door. "I'll see myself out. Tyler, don't screw up again with her, or I'm afraid I'll have to kill you next time." He pointed his finger to his sister. "She's always been in love with you; she's just too damn stubborn to admit it."

"Jake!" Monique yelped.

"Love ya, Mojo, gotta run." He darted out the double kitchen doors and his heavy footfalls could be heard heading toward the front of the house.

After the front door slammed, Tyler turned to Monique.

She nodded to his plate. "You better finish up so you can find that hotel." After clearing the half-eaten plate her brother had left behind, she went to the sink.

"Was he right?" he softly asked.

Monique did not respond and turned on the faucet at the sink. The kitchen filled with the sound of water rushing over dirty dishes.

Tyler stood from his chair, walked over to the sink, and came up behind her. Her hands glided over the dirty dishes, washing the food from the plates and pans, and after a few seconds, he noticed that she was shaking.

Tyler put a supportive hand on her shoulder. "Moe, was he right?"

She never stopped washing the dishes. "My brother exaggerates about a lot of things."

"Not about this." He turned off the tap.

Monique's shoulders slumped forward when the water stopped. "Don't, Ty."

133

Swerving her around, he forced her to look him in the eye. "I need to hear it from you."

She brushed her bangs aside with a soapy hand. "I don't know; maybe I was in love with you and that is why it hurt so much when I came home, but it was a long time ago."

"For me, we were just a few days ago."

"What good would it do for us to rehash it, Ty? We're done."

"I'm not done, Moe." He moved his lips closer to her mouth. "I have never been done with you. You were the one woman I could never forget."

Her eyes softened. "Is that the truth, Ty?"

"Moe." His mouth lingered hungrily over hers. "Stop doubting me."

When their lips met, Tyler swore it was better than the last time. He could taste the hint of coffee on her, and as her body crushed against him, his desire for her surged out of control. Throwing his arms about her, he held her tight, never wanting to let go.

When he lifted her onto the countertop next to the sink, she giggled. "You need to shave before you give me beard burn." Her fingers ran along his stubbled cheek.

"I'll shave after." He kissed her neck and then sank his teeth into her flesh.

She tilted her head back and let her fingers play in the touch of gray hair about his right temple. "Why can't I say no to you?"

"Because you're still in love with me; admit it, Moe."

She shoved him away.

"Don't do this." He rested his head against her chest. "Don't pull away right when we are opening up to each other."

She tried to shimmy off the counter but he held her in his arms. "You're not opening up to me, Ty. You're just screwing me. You don't open up to anyone."

"Me?" He let her go. "You're the one who never opens up. I'm here. I came to show you how I feel."

"Showing me isn't telling me how you feel, Ty. It was always this way before. You would claim to show me how you felt, but never once did you ever say how you felt." She pushed him away and hopped from the counter.

"Yes, I did. That time in Mexico, at the hotel, I told you I loved you."

"You told me you loved me after you hit on the waitress at the bar and had five shots of tequila. That's not what I would call a sincere statement."

"Well...I meant it."

"You meant it?" she roared. "Don't you see? You only meant it when you were drunk. When you were drunk you loved me, when you were sober you always said we were good friends. Do you know how hard that was for me?"

"But you never told me how you felt, Moe."

"How could I when I wasn't sure how you felt?"

He ran his hands over his face. "Why is everything like pulling teeth with you?" he griped in a menacing tone.

"This isn't about me." She folded her arms defiantly over her chest. "You didn't come here to show me how you felt. So why did you come?"

The cold rejection in her eyes caused something to snap in him. He didn't want her be like Hadley or Serena, or even his mother. Tyler had seen enough women look at him with disgust and disappointment, but he could not stomach it from Monique.

"I'm not going to do this with you." He pulled her close.

"Ty, stop it." She struggled against him.

"Just give in to me, Moe Let's not fight each other and ruin things. Let me in," he whispered against her mouth. "Just once, let me take what I want without having to ask."

Allowing all the need and passion he had been holding back to come shooting to the surface, he crushed her body to his and kissed her. Tyler expected Monique to push him away, but instead she yielded to his strength and allowed him to take her completely.

135

Lifting her tiny body back onto the counter, Tyler pressed his lips harder against hers. When he tugged at the zipper of her jeans, Monique did not resist, and helped him ease the baggy pants from her hips. After dropping her jeans and underwear to the floor, he unzipped his fly. Her hands impatiently pushed the heavy denim fabric over his round backside and then fondled his erection. Tyler kicked his jeans aside and pulled her hips to the edge of the counter. When he entered her in one slow motion, Monique moaned. Giving in to him, she shifted back on the counter, allowing him to go deeper.

Tyler did not hold back and thrust into her again and again, wanting to satiate his intense desire. With her head resting against his shoulder, he could feel her body arching with tension as he drove into her. On the verge of letting go, Tyler heard Monique gasp into his chest and then shudder against him. Before she could relax, he gripped her hips, made one final push, and then loudly groaned as his orgasm exploded.

When he glimpsed her face, beads of sweat were gathering above her upper lip. "I'm sorry. I shouldn't have—"

"No. Don't apologize, Ty. I liked you that way."

He angled back from her. "You did?"

"Yeah. I don't want you to hold back."

Tyler pulled her closer. "What did you like about it?"

She nibbled on his earlobe. "The way you took control. How you took what you wanted."

"Do you trust me, Moe?"

She tucked her head into his neck. "Yes."

"Then let me show you what I really like to do."

He carried her out of the kitchen and to the stairs. As she giggled into his chest, he could hear the tip, tip, tip of Bart following behind them.

"I forgot about Ugly," he said, taking the steps two at a time. "I hope he wasn't too traumatized by what we just did in the kitchen.

"I'm afraid his eyesight is pretty bad, so he may not have gotten a good look at everything."

"Thank God. It was bad enough having to explain myself to your brother, but Bart…."

When he placed his hand on the doorknob to his bedroom, Bart trotted right up next to him. Shaking his head, he pushed the door open, and before he could carry Monique inside, Bart strolled into the room.

Monique snickered at Bart's audacity. But her laughter was soon silenced when Tyler lowered her onto his bed, kissing the nape of her neck and reaching for her T-shirt. After throwing her shirt to the floor, his hands caressed her naked body as she reclined on the pale cream sheets.

"Lie back," he directed as he undid the buttons on his long-sleeved shirt.

"What do you want me to do?"

Binding her hands together with his shirt, he kept an eye out for any sign of fear, but her gray orbs only seemed to burn brighter with excitement. With her hands secured, he grasped her hips and flipped her over onto her stomach.

He caressed her smooth, white butt. "Now, I'm going to show you why I like being the one in charge." Having her helpless beneath him made Tyler grow hard. He traced his fingers up and down her back. "I can do whatever I want with you, and you will submit to me, right Moe?"

"Yes," she breathlessly sighed into the bed.

Lifting her hips, he forced her knees underneath her. His hand slid between her legs, and she sucked in a ragged breath when he his fingers lightly traced her delicate folds. Monique backed her hips into his hand, making him pull away.

He put his lips to her ear. "The game is you can't move or say anything. You're mine to control. I tell you when to move and how to move. The more you submit to me, the greater your pleasure." Putting his hand back between her legs, he murmured, "Let's try this again."

This time, she did not move or make a sound. Tyler was gentle at first and then his hand became more demanding, pressing harder into her wet flesh. When he dipped his fingers into her, she trembled.

"Spread your legs," he commanded.

Monique did as she was told, and he spread her folds open. Then, he thrust into her, pushing her apart until he fully penetrated her. Wrapping his arms about her waist, Tyler held on to her as he pulled out and pounded into her once more. She grunted beneath him, but did not move. He withdrew again, but this time he teased her with fingers. Tyler could feel her pleasure rising, and when she was getting close to orgasm he stopped, waited until she relaxed, and then drove deep into her once more. He repeated the process over and over, and soon Monique was damp with sweat. Every time she came close to release, Tyler would pause and watch her reaction.

"You want to let go, don't you, Moe?" He kissed the back of her neck. "When I allow you to come, I promise it will be worth it, but until then, you are mine to control."

He pushed into her, but this time, he had no intention of stopping. Moving slowly at first, he soon increased his speed and before long he was hurtling toward his climax. When she bucked beneath him, he stimulated her with his fingers. As Monique was rocking her hips, he lost all sense of control and came inside her.

Enjoying the swell of relaxation pervading his muscles, Tyler rested against the small of her back and closed his eyes. When he raised his head, he pulled her to him and untied her hands.

"Did you enjoy that?" He pitched his shirt to the floor.

"Where did you learn to do that?"

He plopped back on the bed. "My first wife, Serena, was into all kinds of kinky stuff. She taught me a few things."

She nestled against his chest. "Is that why you married her?"

"Perhaps. She was different from all the other women I knew. Every one I met was some social debutante or wealthy businessman's daughter. They were all spoiled, selfish, and looking for a husband who would make them look good, but not necessarily feel good. Serena didn't care about any of that."

"What happened to her?"

His fingers played in her silky hair. "She remarried a politician and moved to Washington DC. I haven't seen her in years."

"When my marriage began falling apart, I bought some things to help us out…you know, toys." She sat up. "Mat was horrified when I showed him what I had bought. He called me a deviant, and that was the last time I ever tried anything different."

Tyler leered suggestively at her. "Still got the toys?"

"I threw them out when he left. I never thought I'd want to be with a man again."

He sat up in the bed next to her. "Why would you think that?"

"When Mat ended everything, I figured there was something wrong with me. I had decided that my life was going to be writing my books, and any sex I did have was going to happen on my computer screen, and not in my bed." She flopped back on the bed and let out a long sigh. "So I lived vicariously through my novels."

He scooted down in the bed and curled against her. "I'm sorry I let you get away the first time. I should have come after you and then, perhaps, you might never have ended up with Mat."

"But you're here now."

Tyler enveloped her in his arms. "Yes, I am, and I want to stay, if you'll have me."

"What about your company, your life in Dallas?'

"It will keep for a little while. Right now, I want to concentrate all of my efforts on you."

Monique took a moment, and then slowly nodded. "All right, Ty. You can stay, for now."

"That's all I am asking for. All I want is a chance, Moe."

"And what if we fail again?"

He held her close and closed his eyes. "I would rather fail a thousand times with you than never take the chance."

"That's some line, Mr. Moore," she whispered beside him. "I might have to steal it and put it in one of my books."

"It's no line, Ms. Delome. It's the truth, even if it does sound like fiction."

Chapter 13

Tyler was dreaming of being breathed on by a fiery dragon when he awoke with a start to find Bart sitting in the bed next to him. The dog's long tongue was hanging out of his mouth and dripping saliva on Tyler's bare chest.

"You've got to be kidding me," Tyler cried out.

Looking about the room, he set the dog on the floor. There was no sign of Monique, and the bright morning sun was still streaming in through his wide bedroom window. He climbed from the trundle bed, retrieved his wrinkled long-sleeved shirt from the floor, and shrugged it on.

Bart casually trotted out the open bedroom door and Tyler followed him, entertained at the way the dog waddled down the hall. When Bart disappeared into Monique's open bedroom door, Tyler went back to his closet and grabbed for a pair of casual blue pants.

Zipping up his fly, he stepped inside Monique's room. He was surprised to see how feminine the room appeared, with pastel floral wallpaper and a matching floral bedspread of pale yellow and blue on the king-sized pine bed. The furniture was rustic and some of the pieces were unfinished. A round, pale blue rug covered most of the hardwood floor, while colorful paintings of countryside meadows decorated the walls.

As he crept further into the room, he heard the sound of someone avidly typing away on a keyboard. A small sitting area to the left of the bedroom had walls covered with bookshelves that were crammed with an assortment of books and papers. In the corner, beside a picture window, was a small desk with a laptop computer, printer, and piles of blue sticky notes scattered about. Wearing only the T-shirt he had stripped from her earlier, Monique was riveted to the computer screen before her.

Impressed by the speed of her typing, Tyler moved closer to the desk. He waited for her to turn to him, but she was so engrossed in her book that she did not even hear the floorboards moan as he walked into the cozy sitting room. However, when Bart stomped up to her desk and gave an insistent whine, she stopped typing.

Turning from her keyboard, she petted the dog, and then beheld Tyler. "You fell asleep so I decided to get some work done."

"You could have woken me." He kissed her lips.

She gazed up into his face. "You looked so peaceful, I didn't have the heart."

"But you had the heart to leave Bart with me? I woke up and found him in the bed next to me."

"He usually sleeps in that bed during the day when I'm writing. I guess he figured he would share it with you."

"What are you working on?" He tried to read some of the page on the computer screen.

"Something my publisher has been waiting for, but I haven't quite finished it. After our morning together, I got some ideas for things to add to the book."

Tyler chuckled and leaned in closer to her computer screen. "I can only imagine what you are putting in there." He pivoted his eyes to her. "About this morning…I meant what I said, about wanting a chance with you."

"I know." She rested her hands on the keyboard. "If I didn't believe you, I would have packed you up and shipped you off to a hotel." She began typing again.

"I'm going to take a shower and make some calls while you work."

"Just give me another hour, all right?"

He kissed her cheek. "Whatever you want, my Moe."

Leaving her to her book, he went back down the hallway to his bedroom. Peeling the clothes from his body, he disappeared into his bathroom and turned on the hot water in the shower. While he was waiting for the water to warm, he reflected on their morning of lovemaking. Never would he have guessed that Monique would have been so receptive to his interests. Stepping into the shower, he thought ahead to the nights to come, and all the things he would do to her.

***

After a dozen phone calls, Tyler felt confident that all possible problems had been handled at Propel. Having fulfilled his duties with the company, he was free for a few hours to relax with Monique. When he walked into her bedroom, he found her still at her desk. Her eyes were scanning the computer screen in front of her.

"Hey, you about ready for some lunch?" he asked, resting his hands on her shoulders.

She tilted her head back, gazing up at him. "Yes, I'm starved, especially since I didn't get to eat my breakfast."

He kissed the top of her head. "You've been writing the whole time."

"Just about. It's almost done." She stood from the chair and stretched.

Tyler delighted in the way her T-shirt rode up her thighs as she lifted her arms. "What's this one called?"

She waved at the computer screen. "I'm thinking of calling it *A Chance with You*."

"I like it," he admitted with a nod of his head. "What's it about?"

"A couple that tried once to make a go at a relationship and failed. They meet up years later and fall for each other again."

"Do they make it?"

She tossed her head to the side, avoiding his eyes. "I haven't decided. Might be a more poignant love story if they fail, but it could have a happily ever after if they succeed."

"Which do you prefer?"

"I don't know." She wrapped her arms about her body. "I think all love might grow stale with time; perhaps the best love is the one that never gets realized. Maybe our minds can create a better ending for us than reality eventually gives us."

"Do you feel that way about us? That things would have been better if we had spent the rest of our lives wondering 'what if' instead of where we are?"

"No, I prefer where we are but...I have to confess I'm nervous. We have over twenty years of expectations to either fulfill or not live up to. It's a bit daunting."

He put his arms about her waist. "Moe, I don't have any expectations, and neither should you. Let's just enjoy what we have without bringing the past into it. Who we were is not who we are now."

"But who we were has made us who we are. So how do you separate the two?"

He arched an eyebrow at her. "Are you sure you're not a psychologist instead of a writer?"

"Sometimes I think they are one in the same. All writers, no matter romance, horror, or comedy, analyze human nature in some form or another. After all, writers are observers. We just put what we see on paper, and leave it for others to interpret."

"You were always way too philosophical for me." He shook his head, smiling. "I remember it used to take me at least two bourbons before I could even begin to keep up with you."

"I seem to remember that after two bourbons you tended to be a lot less philosophical rather than more." Her eyes rolled with annoyance. "You also tended to get a lot more obnoxious."

He inwardly cringed at the notion of how he used to be when he drank. Tyler had heard enough stories through the years from friends and his mother about how bad his drinking had been, but somehow when Monique described it, she made him sound so much more pathetic.

"Allow me to begin to make amends by taking you to an extremely fancy restaurant for lunch and spending an exorbitant amount of money on you."

She pulled away and walked back into her bedroom. "How 'bout you buy me a root beer and a po-boy at this great little sandwich place I know, and we go to The Butterfly and eat them on the levee?"

"What's The Butterfly?"

***

Standing on a large embankment where Audubon Park met the bend of the Mississippi River, Tyler surveyed the park-like setting of "The Butterfly." A levee located along the border rose fifty feet in the air, blocking the view of the Mississippi River beyond. After climbing to the top of the levee with their brown paper bags filled with shrimp stuffed po-boys, french fries, and two cans of Barq's Root Beer, Tyler and Monique had a seat on the grass as a mammoth oil tanker maneuvered the tight curves of the muddy river.

"This sure beats the hell out of sitting in a restaurant." Tyler unfurled his well-wrapped sandwich and then popped the top on his can of root beer.

"I used to love hanging out here when I was a teenager," Monique confessed. "I'd skip out of class and come here with friends. We'd smoke and drink beer, thinking we were pretty cool for sixteen."

He turned his dark eyes to her. "You, a juvenile delinquent? I don't see it."

She shrugged and freed her shrimp po-boy from its white paper wrapping. "I was bored throughout high school, except for my English classes. I always went to those."

As Tyler hoisted his jumbo sandwich to his lips, the aroma of freshly fried shrimp, ketchup, and mayonnaise hit his nose, making his mouth water. He attempted to open his mouth wide enough to take in a whole bite of the french bread and fried shrimp.

After several minutes of chewing, Tyler put his sandwich on the white paper spread out before of him. "This should be illegal. It's really good."

Monique eyed her sandwich. "This is the real New Orleans. Not the fancy restaurants you read about in magazines, or the tourist-driven sights of the French Quarter. Po-boy lunches on the levee, snowballs on a street corner after school, beignets after a night of drinking, Camellia Grill breakfasts at 2 A.M., and pancakes at Rick's on Canal Street when you are waiting for the sun to come up. That's what I remember best about growing up here; places and, of course, the people."

"I read in one of your books about a character who attended a local college in the city. She was working on her degree in English but got sidelined by a doctor." He stole a french fry from the paper carton next to him. "Is that what happened when you came back?"

She put her po-boy down and reached for her can of Barq's Root Beer. "I was starting on my master's degree in English at Tulane when I met Mat. I was also teaching at a local high school."

"I don't remember you ever talking about teaching."

She rolled the can between her hands. "I think I must have switched majors about three times at SMU. I wasn't sure what I wanted to do. The only thing I liked was writing." She took a gulp of her soda.

"You never told me about the writing." He gripped his can of root beer. "Why is that?"

"You were never interested in hearing about what I did, Ty. All our conversations tended to migrate to you. When you were sober you wanted to know about me, but near the end you were drunk more than sober."

After taking a sip, he put his soda down. "Why on earth did you stay with me?"

She wrapped her hands around her sandwich. "I liked you. You were more fun sober than drunk, and I hoped I would get to see you when you were sober, but even when you were drunk you were okay. You weren't all hung up on image like most other guys I knew. I guess you were the most honest man I had met up until that point in my life."

"And who was the next honest man you met?"

She took another bite from her po-boy. "Mat," she mumbled, chewing on her food, and then swigged some root beer. "I thought he was charming and funny and...all the things you secretly hope for in a man."

His eyes outlined her exquisite profile. "When did everything go bad?"

"Right after we got married." She put her sandwich down. "Once the excitement of the wedding and buying our new house wore off, I think we realized there was nothing between us, or at least I realized it. I thought about going back to school or even going back to teaching, but then I started putting my feelings down on paper. After a while, it turned into a story. That was my first book, *The Taskmaster's Bride*."

Tyler negotiated his hands around his po-boy. "Still can't believe you're a writer."

"I was always a writer, Ty."

They sat on the grass, enjoying their food as the heat of the summer sun bared down on them. Occasionally, an ominous storm cloud would block out the rays of the sun, bringing a welcomed bit of relief from the heat.

Tyler was surprised to find that he had soon nearly finished the oversized sandwich and let the last remnants of french bread fall onto the white paper. Wiping his hands on a napkin, he turned to Monique, who was picking at some of the greasy fries.

"Why is it I feel like I am just getting to know the real you?"

She tapped a french fry against the side of the paper dish. "Perhaps you are just getting to know me. Those few months we were together you weren't exactly at your best." Monique popped the french fry into her mouth.

"I'm not at my best now, either, Moe."

Chewing on her fry, she lay back on the green grass. "I don't think that. You're more together now."

He spread out beside her. "Together or falling apart? It's a matter of perspective."

"I like you better this way."

He pulled her into his arms. "But you don't know me, Moe, at least not the real me."

She kissed his neck. "I know you, Ty. A lot better than you think." Her teeth teased the skin along his neck. "For instance, I know what you're thinking right now."

"You do?"

Her hands traveled to the crotch on his pants. "You ever done it out in the open?"

He laughed at her audacity. "Not like this."

"Then it will be a first for both of us."

Chapter 14

They arrived back at her house just as a thunderstorm released its fury over the city. Ducking in her front door, he held on to her wet body while she tugged at his soaked shirt.

"Again," she whispered to him as he kicked the front door closed.

A loud clap of thunder shook the house and the lights in the entranceway flickered.

"You're relentless." He pulled her wet T-shirt over her head.

"I can't get enough of you." She unzipped the front of his blue trousers.

He unclasped her bra. "But now I get to do what I want with you." He bit her earlobe as he secured her hands behind her back and then tied them above the wrists with the damp, beige bra.

She kissed his naked chest. "I'll do whatever you want."

Tyler's body surged with lust. He wrapped his wet shirt around his hands, and then positioned it over her eyes. Blindfolding her with the shirt, he tied it snuggly behind her head.

"Whatever I want?" He pinched her right nipple. "But you don't know what I want?"

She swayed slightly next to him. "I don't care."

He unzipped her jeans and pushed them to the floor. "That's what I like to hear." Looking over her semi-naked body, Tyler fingered the elastic waistband of her beige silk panties. "I think I'm going to see just how much you can take

149

from me." He placed his lips against her ear. "It will be fun to see how long you can last before you are begging me to stop. You would like that, wouldn't you?"

"Yes," she moaned.

"Get down on your knees."

Tyler waited as she did as he requested. Kneeling behind her, he peeled her underwear from her hips.

A giant clap of thunder hit right above the house and then the lights went out. Unperturbed by the darkness, Tyler continued.

"Bend over," he commanded in a firm voice.

With her hands tied behind her, Moe gingerly rested her head on the hardwood floor.

Raising her hips higher, he let his fingers pass lightly over her wet folds. "This excites you," he whispered.

Her body quivered as he lightly stimulated her. Slowly, he applied more pressure to her sensitive flesh, making her rock beneath him.

He withdrew his hand. "You cannot move, cannot make a sound, or I will stop."

Reaching down, he pressed even harder into her folds, making her flinch slightly, but then she stilled. As his fingers brought her to climax, she remained perfectly still. When the orgasm erupted through her, she only slightly bucked against his hand, but remained silent. He did not stop when her body relaxed and kept on with his firm stroking, and soon he could see her skin flushing as her next orgasm came even faster than the first.

Her fists clenched when he kept on. Her back arched as he applied even more pressure, and he could hear her rapid breaths. She was rocking against his hand when her third release seized her.

Tyler smiled as he continued stimulating her, determined to see how much she could take. Unable to hold back, her body shuddered as he fondled her. She grunted when he slipped three fingers from his left hand into her, while his other hand kept teasing her. When she threw her head back and let out a deep guttural moan, he still kept on with his sweet torture.

With every orgasm, he increased the speed of his fingers. Soon, his arms were burning against the exertion, and when she climaxed for the fifth time in a row, her body rolled over slightly to the side. She was covered in sweat and breathing hard. Feeling her body shaking with exhaustion, Tyler finally stopped.

"Good girl." He placed her on her right side. "But I'm not done."

She whimpered as he brought her knees to her chest and kneeled over her. Quickly dropping his pants and briefs, he then spread her folds apart and entered her.

Her body tightened as he pushed into her. Wrapping her in his arms, he pounded into her, holding nothing back. The image of bringing her to climax again and again had excited him like nothing he had ever known. He needed to drive hard and deep into her flesh. She lay still in his arms as he thrust into her. When he finally came, she never even moved.

He was on top of her, listening to the sound of his labored breathing and feeling her damp skin against him. Kissing her cheek, Tyler removed the blindfold from her eyes.

"Did the lights go out?"

He untied the bra from about her hands. "Right after I blindfolded you."

"I never knew you could come that many times in a row." She stretched out next to him. "After the third one, everything became one big blur."

"That's the idea, baby."

He stood, picked her up from the floor, and cradled her naked body against his wide chest. Carrying her up the stairs in the dark, he listened as the heavy rain hammered the house, sounding like a thousand fingers drumming along the roof.

After finding his way to her bedroom, he placed her on the bed. He went to the adjoining master bathroom and fumbled along in the half-light to an old, claw-footed bathtub in the corner. He turned on the hot and cold taps, and left the tub to fill.

"Come with me, my Moe." Lifting her from the bed, he carried her into the bathroom.

Tyler checked the temperature of the water before lowering Monique into the half-full bathtub. As he flipped off the taps, she eased against the tub and then motioned to the double vanity across from her.

"I have some candles on the counter there."

Tyler went to the vanity and found three round white candles next to a box of matches. As he lit the candles, the soft light reflected off the pale beige walls of the bathroom, adding to the relaxing ambience. Then, he heard a soft panting sound coming from the floor.

When Tyler looked down, he was startled by Bart's presence. "One day that dog is going to give me heart attack."

"He was probably hiding under my bed. He always goes there during a storm."

He climbed in and Monique cuddled against him. Holding her in his arms, he settled back against the tub and closed his eyes. Soon, Bart's continued panting chipped away at his patience.

"That's just what I needed to hear."

"At least he's not snoring. Snores like mad when he's sleeping next to me in the bed. Just give him a minute and he will settle down."

Within seconds the loud panting subsided and all Tyler could hear was the rain falling outside.

"That's better. We need some peace after our strenuous workout."

She giggled into his chest. "It sure beats the gym."

"But you liked it, didn't you, Moe?"

"I never thought submitting to someone else could feel so...liberating."

He ran his finger along her right shoulder. "Some women aren't brave enough to embrace it."

"Have you ever been with any that didn't like it?"

He nodded. "A few. It's easy to read the signals. You can tell when it's going to be just straight up sex or when you can push the boundaries."

"When could you tell that you could push the boundaries with me?"

"From the moment I saw you standing next to me in the bar. You took a chance and came to say hello. I knew then that you would be adventurous."

Her hand swirled about in the water. "Quite a talent you have there."

"It comes from years of dealing with people, in both business and in life."

"Do you like what you do, Ty? I mean do you like the oil business?"

"At times, but then there are times…forget it."

"No, tell me," she insisted with a nudge.

He hesitated. "I've wanted to do more with the company. Expand into different areas."

"Like what?"

He let out a long breath, uncomfortable with sharing his plans. "Well…I've always been interested in alternative fuel development. You know, solar, wind power, things like that. I've dreamed of bringing Propel into the twenty-first century, but there has never been a right time."

"You can't wait for the right time. You just have to do it. If I had waited for the right time to start writing, I would still be waiting."

"But I'm not like you, Moe." He twirled a lock of her hair about his little finger. "I don't have any talents or gifts that can make people happy. Changing up my business would create a lot of problems and make a lot of people, including my stepfather, very nervous. Things are fine where they are."

She sat up, facing him. "But if you could change it, would you?"

"Ever since my mother married Gary, it was pretty much written in stone that I was going to run his company. And running the company meant sticking to the status quo."

"But what if you did shake things up? Imagine the possibilities, Ty."

"I'm not in the business of imagining, that's your job." He pulled her back down to him. "Not everyone in the world is meant to change it. Some of us are here to help the others who are special. Maybe that's what I am here to do, make you happy."

She traced her fingers over his chest. "You've already done that."

"Ah, but I have a few more tricks up my sleeve."

"Like what?"

He kissed her forehead. "Patience, Moe. Just relax and let the warm water do it's magic, otherwise you're going to be sore later."

She snuggled against him. "Yes, Ty."

He rested his head against hers. "I promise there is more fun to come."

***

It was well after six that evening when the lights finally flickered back on. Anxious to return to her book, Monique retreated to her sitting room with Bart while Tyler went to the kitchen to prepare dinner. He carried his cell phone with him, figuring he could check e-mails and voice messages as he cooked.

He was rummaging through Monique's pantry as he listened to Lynn's updates on certain projects, potential problems, and a few small fires that she had redirected to different department heads. As her lovely voice filled the kitchen, Tyler made a mental note to give the woman a raise when he returned to Dallas. Lynn was one of the reasons Propel ran so smoothly. Reaching for a packet of spaghetti, a thought crossed his mind. What if he never returned to Dallas? What if he stayed with Monique in New Orleans? Settled down with her and retired to a life of taking care of her interests?

He stood in the corner walk-in pantry and was momentarily stunned. He had never considered changing his world for a woman, and a life after Propel had never occurred to him. Just like his stepfather, who had been forced into retirement by a two-pack a day cigarette-induced heart attack, Tyler had never contemplated not working. Up until that moment, work was the only thing that had given him satisfaction in life. But now he had Monique, and suddenly the idea of going back to Propel lacked the completeness of being with her. He had never before experienced such an emotion. Completeness was foreign to him; one of those adult life goals often strived for but never truly attained. He thought of a future with her, and soon his mind was overrun with concerns for his business.

Holding the pasta in his hands, he wrestled with which department head could take over for him at Propel. As he ran through the litany of names, the ringing of the black cordless phone on the wall next to the refrigerator interrupted his thoughts.

After four rings an answering machine on the counter picked up the call, and then a man's voice blared out from the speaker.

"Monique, where in the hell are you? I've tried your cell and this damned number all day. Where are the pages you promised me? We need to get this manuscript to editing by the end of the week to have it ready for a fall release. Send me what you have so we can get moving. Hunter is all over my ass on this one. He's already set up your release date with bookstores and is fuming that we have not gone into editing yet. Do you want me to come in? I can run errands and cook for you again, so you can just write. You know I'll do anything you need. Love you, baby. Call me."

Tyler tightened his hold on the fragile spaghetti, and the sound of the pasta breaking in his hand awoke him from the stupor Chris Donovan's message had invoked.

Glaring at the answering machine, he exited the pantry and put the spaghetti on the black granite countertop. After bolting from the kitchen, he was taking the stairs two at a time when the lights went out again. Thankfully, just enough daylight was coming in through the downstairs windows so he could finish getting up the steps. When he arrived at the landing, he heard footfalls on the floor just ahead of him.

"Moe?"

"I'm here. Damn power cut out again just when I was in the middle of working on a really good scene."

He could see the outline of her figure in the fading light from the window at the end of the hallway.

"Chris just left a message on your answering machine in the kitchen," he told her.

"He always calls."

She was about to walk past him when he seized her arm. "Does he usually sign off by saying 'love you, baby'?"

"You know there is nothing between Chris and me."

He let go of her arm. "He seemed real damned confident on that machine."

"Ty." She patted his chest. "I didn't write any books about Chris, did I?"

Her words soothed his anger. "No, you didn't. But still…the way he said it…."

"It doesn't mean anything," she assured him.

"If you say so." He put his arm around her. "Come on. While the lights are out you can show me where everything is in the kitchen so I can cook us dinner."

"We could order in."

He started down the staircase, keeping her at his side. "No, I want to prepare dinner for you, and when the lights come back on, I'll leave you to write. Chris sounded pretty adamant about you getting this book finished."

"He's always hot for the next book. He wants to read them all before they go to editing so he can give me his opinion."

156

"What will his opinion be of this one? Is it another bestseller?"

She chuckled beside him as they stepped onto the first floor landing. "I think he may be in for a shock."

"Why is that?"

"Never mind." She took his hand. "Come on, I'll show you where—"

The lights flickered and then came back on.

"That will make things easier," he remarked.

Monique urged him down the narrow hallway toward the kitchen. "Hurry up so I can get back to writing. If I pull an all-nighter, I can finish up the book and then we can have some fun tomorrow."

"What did you have in mind?" Tyler probed when they came to the double white doors to the kitchen.

"I thought we could go to the Quarter and see the sites. But only if I finish this book." Monique went to the kitchen cabinet beside the sink. She opened the cabinet to the left of the sink. "Pots and pans are there." She left the cabinet door open and walked over to a drawer located below the island cooktop. "Cooking utensils are here." She pulled out the drawer. "There is some ground meat in the freezer, and I think I have some frozen garlic bread up there, too. You can put that in the oven and warm it up." She came back to his side and patted his firm butt. "I expect everything to be hot and ready in one hour when I come back down. Got it, baby?"

He threw his arms about her. "Now who is the one issuing orders?"

"I kind of like this. Maybe I can tie you up next time." She pressed her hand into the crotch of his jeans. "Would you like that?"

"No." He removed her hand and spun her around. "Get back to work, you tease." He slapped her behind.

She looked seductively over her shoulder. "I like it when you spank me. Maybe you could do it again, later."

He tried to control his desire to take her right there in the kitchen. "Don't you think you've had enough for one day?"

She headed for the door, shaking her butt for him as she strutted away.

After she had exited the kitchen, Tyler tried to calm his rising libido. "Christ, she's going to be the death of me." He wiped his hand over his face and returned to the pantry.

Finding the jar of spaghetti sauce and a container of Parmesan cheese, Tyler was about to turn from the pantry shelves when a bottle of Jack Daniels sitting on the floor caught his attention. Before sobriety he would have found that bottle too tempting to ignore. Now, he felt not an inkling of desire for his former favorite vice. Returning to the countertop, he retrieved the broken spaghetti. As he prepared dinner, his eyes kept going back to the blinking red light on the answering machine and Chris Donovan's waiting message.

"I think it's time Moe found another manager," Tyler mumbled. "This one has definitely worn out his welcome."

Chapter 15

The next morning Tyler awoke in his trundle bed alone. He had gone to his room after checking on Monique before midnight, but she had been so engrossed in her book that he had given up. He had hoped when Monique was done she would join him, but he began to wonder if this was the price one paid for being with a writer.

Rolling over and taking in the early morning light coming through the picture window next to his bed, he briefly mulled over what it would be like to spend the rest of his days with Monique.

Alarmed by his imaginings, he sat up. "Don't go there, Tyler."

A knock on his door made him stand from the bed, eager to see Monique. But when the door opened, a familiar ugly face trotted inside.

"You're not the first person I want to see this morning, Bart."

The dog pranced past him and jumped on the bed.

"He's been waiting for you to get up." Monique came into the room, carrying a small blue tray with two white mugs of steaming coffee on it.

"Good morning." Tyler kissed her lips.

She nodded to his green pajama bottoms. "Very sexy."

He looked over her red nightshirt. "What time did you get to bed?"

"I crashed after four." She handed him one of the mugs from the tray. "This one is yours. I added some sugar."

"Did you finish your book?"

She took her mug and placed the tray on the dresser. "I got it done. I stayed up and went over a few things." She cupped her hands around the coffee mug. "But I e-mailed it to Chris this morning. Let's see what he thinks of it."

Tyler gulped his coffee, thankful for the added jolt. "I'm sure he'll love it. I have a feeling as long as you keep writing, he'll be happy with your books."

"He may not be too thrilled about this one." She took a sip from her mug. "It's a bit of a departure from my usual storyline, but it's timely."

"How is this one different?"

"It's got a few things my readers have not seen before."

He put his coffee on the night table beside his bed. "That's a good thing, right? Changing it up a bit keeps everyone from getting bored." Tyler walked into the bathroom.

"Sometimes, but then again you have readers that aren't too happy with changes from their favorite authors," she remarked from the bathroom doorway.

At the sink, he splashed some cold water on his face, and then glanced back at her. "What will you do if they don't like it? Go back to what you wrote before?"

"I can't go back." Monique leaned against the doorframe. "Things have changed." Monique waited as he dried his face with the towel. "Are we still on for a day in the French Quarter?"

He ran his hand over the dark stubble on his face. "You sure you're not too tired for a day out after staying up so late?"

"When I finish a book, I'm always keyed up. I'll probably crash later tonight, but right now I just want to get out in the world."

Resting his hip against the beige vanity countertop, he grinned at her. "You really like being a writer, don't you?"

She slowly nodded her head. "It's hard to describe. The only time I feel whole is when I write. It's like I am using all of my brain, and not just pieces of it."

"You have a passion, Moe. That's a blessing."

"You have a passion, too. You have Propel. I think you feel the same way about your company."

He folded his arms over his chest. "That's just my job. For years I thought it was everything, but lately I've discovered maybe I want other things in life."

She swept her bangs from her face. "Like what?"

"I'm getting older and I've realized life isn't all about work. Maybe I want a family and a life outside of Propel."

"A family?" She appeared taken aback. "I thought you never wanted children."

"I wanted them, even tried with Hadley in the beginning, but we found out she couldn't have any more." His eyes skimmed the curves beneath her red nightshirt. "I know we should have talked about this before now, but...." He paused and wiped his hand across his chin. "Are you on birth control? Because we haven't been using anything."

Her eyes plunged to her coffee. "No; I mean I haven't...but the chances of me getting pregnant are pretty slim."

"But there is a chance?"

"You don't have to worry, Ty. I'm not one of those women who would want child support or anything."

He took the mug from her hand and placed it on the bathroom vanity. "I wasn't hinting at that, Moe. I would embrace any chance of us having a baby together." He lifted her head to him and tenderly kissed her lips. "But I thought I should bring it up since I plan on spending a lot of time in your bed."

"I gave up on the whole kid option years ago. I figured once I hit forty, I was too old."

"Well, I just wanted you to know that if you want me to use condoms from now on, I will. I'm usually pretty adamant about using something, but with you I have been somewhat...forgetful."

"Forgetful?" She giggled. "I appreciate your...candor, but I'm pretty sure condoms won't be necessary. When Mat and I were thinking about kids, the doctor told me I would have problems conceiving. He said the chances were pretty good that I would never have children."

Tyler silently berated his callousness. Here he was trying to be responsible, and it blew up in his face. "I'm sorry. I shouldn't have brought it up."

"It's fine, Ty, really. I'm glad we talked about it." She stood back from him. "Why don't you get dressed and I'll take a quick shower, then we can head out."

"What about breakfast?"

"Breakfast?" Her dark blonde eyebrows went up in dismay. "We're going to the Quarter. Our tour will begin with breakfast at Brennan's."

***

After parking her white Toyota Forerunner in a lot next to Jax Brewery, Monique led Tyler across Decatur Street to the black iron fence surrounding Jackson Square.

"First place you have to see when you come to the French Quarter." She motioned to the majestic view of St. Louis Cathedral with the famous statue of Andrew Jackson sitting atop his horse in the foreground.

"I've been here for a few oil and gas conventions, but I'm afraid I never took the time to see the sites." Tyler ran his eyes along the balconies of the Pontalba Apartments. "I even considered trying to find you, but I wasn't sure you would want to see me," he sheepishly added.

"That wasn't the first convention I attended in Dallas. I even got the address to the Propel offices one time and was going to see if you were there, and then I thought maybe you had forgotten about me."

"We both know that never happened." He wrapped her arm about his. "Didn't you tell me once that you grew up around here?"

"I can't believe you remembered that." Monique shook her head as they walked down the gray cobblestoned street, heading toward St. Louis Cathedral. "My aunt had a gift shop here, and

I used to work with her every summer when I was a kid. I got to run around the French Quarter and grew up learning more than many about the city's past."

The clip clop of horse drawn carriages blended with the roar of passing tour buses on Decatur Street. Tyler breathed in the heavy air laden with the aroma of rich coffee and frying beignets from Café Du Monde across the street.

He viewed the line of artists who had set up shop along the black iron fence. "You never told me about your aunt."

"She died when I was sixteen. Aunt Mags was a real character."

"How did she die?" Tyler inquired, inspecting the arches of the Cabildo Museum up ahead.

"Mags had emphysema," Monique told him. "She smoked like a chimney."

He turned to her. "Didn't your mother have that, too?"

"Yes, along with frequent bouts of pneumonia. The last time Mom got really sick, she never recovered and that was when Dad asked me to come home from college. That last year with her was pretty tough."

He stopped beneath the shadows of the Cabildo Museum. "I don't know which is worse, seeing them go before your eyes, or always wondering if they are gone."

"I think the not knowing would be worse," she proposed as they turned down St. Peter Street to the left of the Cabildo. "You can put it behind you eventually when you see them go, but with your brother it will never end, will it? The not knowing where he is or if he is alive must be hell."

"It also makes you very angry. You keep asking why, but you never get answers, and that hurts worst of all." He took in the tourists around them on the street. "Everyone needs answers. We need closure to move on. When we can't move on, we fester, we tire, and we give up."

"Don't give up, Ty. One day you'll find the answers you need."

Encouraged by words, Tyler could not help but smile. "You're the first person to ever say that to me. Both of my wives told me to put it behind me, but I never could."

She shrugged as they walked on. "Maybe they never understood how much Peter meant to you."

"I think the women I married were too into themselves to notice what was important to me."

Monique held his hand. "Yes, Hadley did seem a tad bit self-centered."

"Just a tad," he returned as she urged him forward.

On Royal Street, Tyler admired the tightly compact Creole architecture and overhead balconies draped in elegant swirls of black wrought iron.

"This way. It's about three blocks up," Monique said, pulling him to the left.

When Tyler passed before a window showcasing decorative perfume bottles, a recollection stirred. "What book was it where you wrote about this place?"

"*Margot's Passion.* It was the one about a woman who had a perfume business in the French Quarter and fell in love with the shopkeeper next door. They longed for each other for years, but never got together until the woman became very ill."

Tyler was suddenly struck by an idea. "That was about your aunt, wasn't it? The one you just told me about, Mags?"

She gazed about at the quaint stucco-covered buildings painted in a variety of colors. "Mags was short for Margot. There was a shopkeeper she was in love with who was on the next block down on Royal Street. His name was Riley, like in the book, but he and my aunt never got together before he was killed in a motorcycle accident. My aunt cried for days after she found out. I guess I wanted to give her the happy ending she always wanted with Riley, so I wrote their story."

"But I seem to remember Riley looked an awful lot like me."

She gave him a flirtatious side-glance. "Yeah, well, I took a little poetic license, but the good intention was there."

"This book you just finished. How did it end, will you tell me?"

"I'll send you a copy when it comes out," she kidded.

He jerked on her hand, stopping her. "I would like to read it before then, Moe."

"What I wrote isn't some kind of glimpse into the future, Ty. It's just a story."

He stared into her eyes, purposefully keeping her waiting for his response. "It may not be how you mean for us to end, but it offers some insight into your thoughts, and your feelings. All your books do."

She pulled her hand away from him. "In that case, I'd better not let you look at it."

His deep, harmonious laughter made several people on the street look their way. "You're going to let me read it, even if I have to tie you to your bed while I do it."

She cocked one eyebrow at him. "Promise?"

He stretched his arm about her shoulders. "We'd better get to this restaurant soon, before I change my mind."

Brennan's Restaurant was located in the old Morphy Mansion that had once been the home to the celebrated chess player, Paul Morphy, who died there in 1884. The restaurant had been at that location since 1956, and was renowned for decadent breakfasts and the creation of the world famous Bananas Foster.

"I have never eaten here before," Tyler divulged as they entered the double doors under the black canopy at 417 Royal Street.

They walked into a narrow entranceway with potted ferns against white-painted walls, taupe floors, and a lavish twenty-four light, crystal-beaded chandelier hanging before a wide archway.

Tyler breathed with restraint as the smell of heady Cajun spices commingled with an acrid odor of something akin to burnt sugar lingered in the air. As they stood before a dark oak reception desk, he leaned closer to Monique.

"What is that funny smell?"

"Bananas Foster. Whenever you walk in here, the place reeks of it. It's the sugar, cinnamon, and banana liqueur they use to make it."

A tall hostess with short black hair led them to the main dining room where round tables were decorated with dark umber tablecloths placed atop white ones. Pale pink carnations set in glass vases adorned the center of the tables, while paintings of the French Quarter hung on the beige-colored walls.

"We are serving breakfast in our main dining room because there is a business breakfast meeting taking place on the patio this morning. I hope this will do?" the hostess asked as she motioned to a table by a wall of windows.

"This will be fine," Tyler stated as they were seated.

She placed their tall red menus over the white plates embossed with the Brennan's logo of a rainbow-colored rooster. "Your server is Sheldon, and he will be right with you." The dark-eyed beauty quickly walked away.

Tyler motioned to the empty dining room. "No one is here."

"It's early yet." Monique perused her menu.

Outside the wide picture windows was a lush green courtyard with an assortment of men in suits sitting about the black iron tables.

"Reminds me of me," he added, pointing to the windows.

She turned to the windows. "Do you have company meetings at restaurants?"

"Twice a year we hold the board of directors meetings at different restaurants in Dallas. Then every quarter, I meet with my department heads at a dinner meeting, held at some tastefully expensive, but equally boring restaurant. And then there are the assorted personal meetings I have to attend with clients. I think I spend half my time in restaurants, having meetings."

"What do you do when you're not working?"

166

Tyler opened his menu. "When I'm done at the office I go home, check e-mails, watch the news, return missed phone calls, and then go to bed. When I'm not working, I'm still working."

"But what do you do for fun? You must have something you enjoy doing other than running your company?"

"My time is so consumed by Propel that it's hard to have any kind of life. Coming to see you is the first real vacation I've had in years."

She closed her menu, skeptically eyeing him. "That doesn't sound good."

"I don't like that look. You're analyzing me again, aren't you?"

"No, I'm not. Merely wondering what happens to us when you go back to your company? Will I get lost in the shuffle?"

He closed his menu. "Of course not. We'll work something out."

"Work something out?" She let out a callous snicker.

He put his tall red menu to the side of his plate. "You could consider moving to Dallas."

"Moving to Dallas? Don't you think it's a bit soon to be discussing this?"

"Soon? We've known each other over twenty years, Moe. How slow do we need to go?"

She slapped her menu down on her plate. "I'm not talking about how fast we are moving, I'm talking about—"

"Monique, is that you?" someone called from the arched entrance to the dining room.

When Tyler turned, a man in a black, double-breasted suit was coming toward their table.

"Oh, shit," Monique quietly cursed beside him.

Somewhere around middle age, the stranger appeared to be very fit, like he worked out with weights, and had the self-assured swagger of someone who was very much into their body. As he halted before their table, Tyler analyzed the man's sloping nose, flat cheekbones, receding chin, and soft jaw, and was instantly reminded of a rat.

"I thought that was you," the visitor announced, pocketing his cell phone.

"Mat." Monique quickly stood from her chair. "What are you doing here?"

The distress in her voice surprised Tyler. His eyes returned to Mat as the realization hit him. *So this was the asshole ex-husband?*

Mat came up to Monique's side and gently pecked her cheek. "I am here for a breakfast meeting with my medical group."

She motioned to Tyler. "Mat, I...I want you to meet—"

"Tyler Moore." Tyler stood from the table and held out his hand.

"Dr. Mathew Klein." Mat's voice was higher than Tyler would have expected from someone who tried so hard to give off an air of masculine superiority. "Tyler Moore? Why does that name sound familiar?"

"Tyler is an old friend from Dallas," Monique quickly interjected.

Mat's beady brown eyes examined Tyler from head to toe. "You're not the same Tyler Moore who dated Monique when she was at SMU?"

Tyler nodded his head and diverted his gaze to Monique. "Afraid so."

Mat brushed a comma of light brown hair from his brow. "What brings you to New Orleans, Tyler?"

"Tyler is in town to visit," Monique explained. "We ran into each other last weekend at a convention I was attending in Dallas. We thought we would...catch up."

"Catch up?" Mat's rodent-like features reflected his disapproval. "I'm stunned he could pull you away from that computer of yours. God knows I never could." He raised his head to Tyler. "Do you know she put you in all of her books?"

168

"Really?" Tyler gave Monique a brilliant smile. "No, I didn't know that."

"Yes, Monique said you made an unforgettable character," Mat replied with an insolent smirk.

"Well, Moe left quite an impression on me, as well. We were once crazy about each other. I even wanted to marry her, but she knew I wasn't ready."

Mat turned to his ex-wife. "You never told me that, Monique."

Tyler placed his hands behind his back, beginning to enjoy himself.

"So, ah, Mat?" Monique's voice wavered slightly. "I'm surprised we ran into you."

Mat motioned to the patio beyond the picture window. "Yes, I was going to make a call when I saw you sitting in here with...him." He nodded to Tyler.

"Yes, we came in for breakfast," Tyler elaborated. "Moe told me this is something of a New Orleans tradition."

Mat's smirk slipped a little. "How long are you in town for, Tyler?"

Tyler grinned. "Until Moe kicks me out."

Mat's dark eyebrows went up. "You're staying with Monique?"

Tyler's grinned deepened. "It allows us even more time together to...catch up."

Monique's red face dropped to the floor.

"Well, that is...something." Mat's obvious discomfort hung in the air like the pungent aroma of Bananas Foster.

"Yes, it is." Tyler kept his eyes on the stocky man, making sure to accentuate his added height over the condescending doctor.

"I should be going." Mat patted Monique's shoulder. "I just wanted to say hello."

Monique took her chair. "Good to see you, Mat."

When Mat's brown eyes rose to Tyler, the dislike in them was palpable. "Tyler, it was nice to finally meet you."

169

Tyler held out his hand. "Mat, it was great to meet you."

The two men quickly shook hands and Mat stepped away from the table. Once he had exited the dining room, Monique whirled around to Tyler.

"What in the hell was that about? Why did you tell him those lies?"

Tyler resumed his chair. "Just making the asshole wonder about you, that's all. Now he'll question how close our relationship really was, and if all the years you were married to him, you were still in love with me."

"He read my books, Ty. He knows how I felt about you."

"Perhaps." Tyler reached for his napkin beside his plate. "But he doesn't know the feeling was mutual. He thought you were just obsessed with a man you couldn't have. Now he knows otherwise, and it will eat at him, trust me."

"And I'm telling you, Mat could care less about me or you."

Tyler leaned in closer to her. "Moe, men are very possessive creatures; even when they don't want you, if they think they can't have you, then they'll want you. Your ex was just given a new perspective about you. He will be second-guessing your marriage in his head for weeks to come."

"I don't get it. Why did you do that?"

He raised his menu. "Because he hurt you, and he deserved it."

Monique sat back in her chair and after a few seconds, she slowly smiled. "Yeah, he did deserve it."

She opened her menu just as a short man dressed in white entered the room, carrying a basket of bread and a plate of butter.

"I am so sorry for the delay." The man in white placed the basket and plate between Tyler and Monique. "I am Sheldon, your waiter. Welcome to Brennan's. What can I get you this morning?"

Cover to Covers

Chapter 16

After dining on eggs benedict, spicy fried shrimp covered with a Hollandaise sauce, and Banana's Foster, Tyler and Monique set out to tour the cracked sidewalks of the French Quarter. They wandered down Royal Street, peering into different shops until they came to a wide bay window exhibiting old photographs of the city.

Tyler was amused at the way Monique hungrily scoured the pictures. "Would you like to go inside?"

She shook her head. "No, I'd probably spend a small fortune in there."

He moved over to the door. "Lucky for you I have a small fortune to spend."

"I don't want you spending any money on me."

He opened the glass inlaid french door that served as the entrance to the establishment. "Moe, I flew here in a private jet that cost more to fuel up than you could possibly spend in this one store."

"But I didn't ask you to come," she pointed out.

"But I'm here, so allow me to buy you a gift."

She turned to the door. "No. If I find something, I'll buy it."

"You don't know how refreshing that is to hear," he muttered behind her.

The small store was crammed from wall to ceiling with hundreds of black and white photographs from the turn of the century to the late fifties. Some were of sites in New Orleans, while others were of historic landmarks or people captured from the past.

As if in a trance, Monique was drawn to a corner of the room where several large photos of the French Quarter were hanging on the wall. Beneath the photographs, a table was filled with matted, unframed pictures. She enthusiastically began thumbing through the pictures, shaking her head at some, and then smiling at others.

Gazing about the gallery, Tyler became intrigued by a row of skylines of different big cities in the United States. He walked across the jam-packed store to study the photographs further.

"You and your wife looking for something in particular?" a raspy-sounding older man asked as he came up to Tyler.

Tyler turned to the gray-haired gentleman with thick, black-rimmed glasses. "She might be," he admitted. "She likes to collect old photographs of New Orleans."

"Well, I got plenty. I can even ship them home for you."

Tyler took in the man's dark eyes. "Oh, she lives here. I'm just visiting from out of state."

"You two married?"

Tyler shook his head. "No."

"Gonna get married?" the insistent shopkeeper posed. "Cause if you ain't gonna marry her, I might give it a try." His lighthearted chuckle made Tyler smile.

Tyler glanced back at Monique. "I think we are still working on that."

"Well, as long as you're working on it. That's all that matters." He held out his hand. "My name's Joe, by the way. Joe Krieger."

"Tyler Moore." Tyler shook his hand and noted Joe's serene, wrinkled countenance.

When Tyler's eyes returned to Monique, she was holding two pictures in her hands, as if trying to decide which one she wanted.

173

"The pictures on that table." Tyler gestured to the table Monique was standing in front of. "How much for all the pictures you have there, Joe?"

"The entire New Orleans collection?" Joe crinkled his eyebrows together as he reflected on the question. "I don't know, I guess...." He scratched his head. "Fifteen hundred, maybe? How does that sound?"

Tyler faced him and lowered his voice. "I want to keep it as a surprise, so could you wrap up all the pictures and have them delivered to her house?"

"Sure, just give me an address and I can have them delivered day after tomorrow, if you like."

Monique came toward them, carrying a picture in her hand.

"Did you find one you wanted, Moe?"

"Yes." She noticed the older man next to Tyler. "Is this your store?"

"Sure is." Joe nodded. "You found something you like?"

"I did." She held out a very pretty, large black and white matted photograph of St. Louis Cathedral taken from the river at sunrise. "I'm getting this one."

Tyler pulled out his wallet. "I'll buy it for you."

"Ty, I told you I would get my own—"

"Let your man buy you the picture, darlin'," Joe interrupted with a wave of his gnarled hand. "It makes a man feel useful when he can buy a woman a gift."

"But it makes a woman feel empowered when she can buy what she wants with her money and doesn't need a man to do it for her," Monique debated.

Joe elbowed Tyler. "You got your hands full with this one."

Tyler raised his hand to his mouth and covered his cocky grin.

Monique glared at him. "I see you found an ally."

"Why don't you let him buy this for you?" Joe suggested, taking the picture from her. "Then, you can buy him something. That way you will both be appeased." He turned away, holding

174

the picture in his hands. "I can even have it delivered to your house, so you won't have to lug it around the Quarter with you." He carried the picture back to a wide counter set in the corner of the store that was hidden behind easels displaying huge framed photographs of famous jazz musicians.

"Oh, no, that won't be necessary," Monique declared, advancing toward the counter. "I can carry it. It's not that heavy."

Joe waved off her suggestion. "Nonsense. I can frame it for you and then it will be ready to hang when it arrives at your home."

"You don't have to frame it," she insisted.

Joe grinned at her. "Let me frame it for you, sweetheart. My treat. It's not every day I get such a handsome couple in here."

Monique's determination caved in to the shopkeeper's request. "All right," she finally agreed.

Joe handed her a pen and receipt pad. "Write down your address at the top, and I will have it delivered day after tomorrow via FedEx."

Tyler stepped closer to the counter and removed his black American Express card from his wallet as Monique wrote down her address.

He winked at the shop owner. "I appreciate all of your help, Joe."

"No problem." Joe took Tyler's credit card and started for the far end of the counter. "Let me just total everything up."

Monique finished filling out her information and scowled at Tyler. "But I still get to buy you something."

"If that makes you feel better, you can buy me an ice cream cone."

She pushed the receipt pad across the counter. "It has to be something you want."

"Well, I want an ice cream cone."

"If you don't tell me what you want, I will buy something I think you want, and then you might end up with something you

175

don't want and I will have wasted my money. Do you want that on your conscience, Ty?"

He gaped at her. "Is that really how your brain works? That makes no sense, Moe."

"It makes perfect sense, Ty. You just don't want to understand it."

"Can I offer a bit of advice?" Joe came back from the end of the counter and handed Tyler his credit card and receipt. "Never argue with a woman's logic. You can't win, son."

Monique motioned to the older man. "See, he gets it."

Tyler tucked the credit card and receipt into his wallet. "I'll keep that in mind, Joe."

After bidding farewell to Joe, Tyler closed the door of the picture shop as Monique surveyed Royal Street with her keen gray eyes.

"What can we buy you?"

"Moe, really, don't buy me anything," Tyler affirmed.

"No, I would feel better buying you something." She peered down the busy street as people milled about, peeking into shop windows and enjoying a quartet of street musicians that were playing a snappy melody on the corner next to them. "I've got it," she gleefully proclaimed. "There's a store on Chartres, not far from here. I think you might find something you would like there."

He took a step closer to her, studying her devious grin. "Somehow, I don't think I am going to like this."

She gripped his hand. "Trust me, you'll love it."

After a short walk down Bienville Street, passing before rows of trendy shops and boutique hotels, they came to a red Creole townhouse with stucco archways decorating the first floor. Above, a second-floor balcony with white cornices over the windows added to the postcard-like ambience. As Tyler read the colorful sign hanging over the front entrance, his mouth fell open.

"Mr. Binky's Boutique?" He gawked at the assortment of blow-up dolls and silhouettes of naked woman draped in pink

176

boas covering the entrance, and knew where she had taken him. "I'm not going in there, Moe," he loudly asserted.

"What did that old man at that shop say, 'don't argue with a woman'?" She tugged on his arm.

"He wasn't talking about this." He pointed to the adult store next to them.

"What? You're into different things in bed. I don't understand why going into a place like this bothers you."

Tyler nervously pulled at the collar on his blue knit polo shirt. "I don't like advertising what we do in the privacy of our bedroom."

Monique inched closer to the open french doors at the entrance. "Just think of it as research for my books."

"But you write romance...." He waved at the building. "Not this."

She chuckled at his obvious embarrassment. "Come on, Mr. Prude. Let's get you something to loosen you up."

He plodded forward. "That is not funny, Moe."

As Monique led him through a smaller pink door right behind the entrance, Tyler became immersed in a world of naughty lingerie, assorted lubricants, and an endless hodgepodge of sexual paraphernalia. When his eyes settled on the enhancement devices, he wanted to run for the front door.

"I think I know just the thing you need." Monique pulled him toward a corner of the store with a sign reading, "Bondage" hanging from the ceiling.

Tyler browsed the whips, chains, black leather hoods, and harnesses, wondering what exactly Monique had in mind. She selected a pair of pink, feather-lined handcuffs on the wall.

"What do you think? Or is pink not your color?" she asked, brandishing the handcuffs.

He chose a black riding crop with tassels on the end of it from a table beside him and waved it in front of her. "You're sure you don't want a riding crop to go with that?"

Monique took the crop from him and put it back on the table. "Nah, I prefer you use your hands."

Undone by her bravado, he ran his hand behind his neck. "Have you no shame, woman?"

She tilted her head to the side, puzzled by his reaction. "No, why be ashamed? It's just sex, Ty. If I have learned one thing from being a writer, it is that everyone has fantasies about how they want to be in bed, or how they want to be treated, but very few people act on them. We are so stifled by what is expected of us, that we rarely do what we actually want. Being a writer means being open to new experiences. That's all I'm doing."

He moved closer to her. "I like the pink," he whispered.

"All right. I'll get you these, but I don't think it is quite enough. That picture you got me cost five times what these handcuffs run, so I need to get you something else."

He placed his hands in the front pockets of his khaki pants. "I'm still in the mood for that ice cream."

Monique shook her head. "Ice cream and handcuffs. God, you are so easy."

***

At a stand in Woldenberg Park, Monique bought two vanilla ice cream cones. A peaceful oasis located next to the Mississippi River, the park was landscaped with green grassy knolls, shady trees, and ample benches surrounding a wide, bricked walkway that extended from Audubon's Aquarium of the Americas to the Moonwalk.

Tyler and Monique stood at the heavy iron railing next to the riverbank enjoying their cool treats as the muddy water swirled and coursed below. In the background, the calliope organ of the nearby steamboat *Natchez* played a familiar ragtime tune, while on the bricked walkway behind them, joggers, bikers, and ambling tourists passed by.

"This is a side of New Orleans I never saw when I came before," he admitted, staring down into the dark water.

She slipped the black bag with the handcuffs under her arm. "Why not?"

"Too busy, I guess, and being a tourist never appealed to me. I was just in a hurry to get my business done and head home."

She licked her ice cream cone. "All the places you have traveled to and you never once took any time to enjoy yourself? That's sad, Ty."

He pitched the remains of his ice cream cone in a nearby garbage can and rubbed his hands together, trying to remove the sticky mess from his fingers. "It's business, Moe."

As her hair stirred in the humid breeze coming off the river, Monique leaned against the thick iron railing and studied him. "When did you change? You used to be a lot of fun."

"I guess I grew up."

"You grew old," she teased.

"No, responsibility makes you realize that your needs must come behind those of your employees and company." He motioned to her. "Like you with your writing. You have to keep the needs of your readers in your thoughts when you write, don't you?"

She threw her cone in the trashcan. "I write for me, not for the readers. I have to write what I believe in and not just put something out there for commercial success." She pulled the black bag from under her arm.

"But you have commercial success, too."

"Only because what I write resonates with readers. You have to write with your heart, otherwise what you write won't feel…real."

When Tyler rested his back against the railing, he saw a small group of young women coming down the bricked walkway toward them. They were huddled together talking and giggling, as girls tend to do. Tyler was reminded of Tessa. He wondered what she was up to back in Dallas, and how she was taking the news of his divorce from her mother.

One of the girls spotted Monique and stared at her for several seconds. The dark-haired young woman came closer. "Excuse me? But are you…Monique Delome, the writer?"

Monique's posture stiffened and she put on a fake smile. "Yes, I'm Monique Delome."

Squealing began, and Tyler wanted to place his hands over his ears as the painful noise went on for what felt like an eternity.

"Oh, I'm your biggest fan," the dark-haired girl shrieked, clasping her hands to her chest.

"Can I have your autograph?" another from the group called.

"Oh, me too," yet another voice cried out.

Within seconds, a swarm of frenzied female fans surrounded Monique. As the girls searched purses and backpacks for any scrap of paper for her to sign, Monique handed the black bag from Mr. Binky's Boutique to Tyler.

"I just loved *Blossoms Become Her*. Your Beau Haskins was to die for," the dark-haired girl beamed.

Tyler slowly stepped back while Monique fielded the different pieces of paper being shoved at her. He waited off to the side as she diligently signed every autograph, making sure to get the name of the girl wanting it.

One of the young women approached Tyler. "Are you with her?"

He nodded. "I'm a friend."

"You look very familiar." The girl paused and closely examined his features.

"I'm not anyone." Tyler waved the girl back to Monique. "Better get your autograph."

Monique answered a few questions about her books, posed for a picture, and then received a round of hugs. When the posse of exuberant fans had moved on, Tyler glided to Monique's side.

"Does that happen often?"

She wiped her hand across her brow. "Don't ask me why, but for some reason teenage girls are my biggest fans. I don't know how they know it's me."

"Perhaps the photograph of you on the back of your book gives it away," he cracked, handing the black bag back to her.

"I never thought people would pay attention to that, but they do. I've been stopped at the grocery, the hardware store, and in the mall. The first time it happened I was shocked, now I'm a bit overwhelmed."

"Why? You're famous."

"I want my books to be famous. Me? I just want to live my life and write my stories." Monique sagged against the railing behind her. "You seemed to have shied away from the spotlight."

He rested his hip next to her. "I prefer to keep a low profile."

"How can you do that as CEO of your company?"

"In my business, it's rather a necessity not to attract a lot of recognition."

"Why is that?"

"When my stepfather, Gary, was CEO, he and my mother were pretty active in the Dallas social scene. You know how Barbara was. Well, a few years before he retired, Gary started getting death threats. He even hired security guards for my mother and his daughter, Helen. After that, I thought it best if I did not follow in my stepfather's footsteps in quite the same way. When I married Hadley, I became even more paranoid about protecting her daughter, Tessa."

"Tessa, you mentioned her before. Are you two close?"

"When she and Hadley moved in with me, I tried to get to know her." He shrugged. "But no matter what I did she remained…distant. After a while, I gave up."

Monique gazed out over the rushing water. "It must have been tough for her being bounced around like that. I can understand why she would be apprehensive about you. She didn't want to get close to you only to end up being hurt again."

"Somehow I get the impression we're not just talking about Tessa." He positioned his arm about her shoulders. "We never got to finish our talk at the restaurant…about us."

"I know." Monique settled against him. "How about we get out of this hot sun and head on home?"

Tyler removed his Porsche sunglasses from the front pocket of his polo shirt and slid them over his eyes. "Good idea."

Monique held up her black bag in front of him. "I want to try out these handcuffs."

Tyler softly chuckled. "I think I've created a monster."

Cover to Covers

Chapter 17

After they walked in the door of Monique's home, Tyler reveled in the brisk embrace of the air-conditioning. Despite the ride back from the French Quarter in Monique's cool Toyota Forerunner, his body was still moist with perspiration.

"The humidity here is awful." Tyler pulled his polo shirt over his head.

"Yeah, it takes a bit of getting used to." Monique shut the front door.

"Not sure if I will ever get used to it."

She paused as she flung her black bag from Mr. Binky's Boutique on the stairs. "Does that mean you would prefer living in Dallas as opposed to New Orleans?"

He gave her a questioning glance. "Where did that come from?"

"You just made it sound like living here would never be an option."

"That's not what I meant." He paused, looking her over. "Do you want me to consider living in New Orleans?"

"Perhaps commuting or something…." She tossed her hands up. "I don't know."

Monique quickly headed down the hallway next to the stairs. Tyler took a few long strides to catch up with her and then clasped his hand over her arm.

"Are you asking me to move here, Moe?"

She confidently raised her head to him; her face was completely bereft of any emotion. "I was just suggesting you might want to come back and…see more of the city."

"If I come back, it won't be to see the city."

Monique arched back from him. "If you come back? Am I supposed to beg?"

"No, want." He pulled her into his arms. "Want me to come back. Want to be with me."

"I want to be with you, Ty." She smiled obstinately. "How's that?"

"You...." He was about to kiss her when the ringing of the phone from the kitchen distracted him.

She twisted her head toward the kitchen doors just as a man's voice came out over the speaker of the answering machine.

"God damn it, Monique! What in the hell is this shit you sent me? We can't publish this. You'd better call me ASAP. And why aren't you picking up your cell phone? Call me back now!"

She crashed her head into Tyler's chest, groaning.

"What is it, Moe?"

"It would seem Chris read my new book." She leaned back. "I knew he would hate it."

"Why? What's wrong with it?"

She wiggled out of his arms. "I'd better call him back. I left my cell phone here this morning, hoping to avoid this."

"Moe, what's wrong with the book?"

She casually waved her hand at him. "It's about you. The real you this time, and there are parts that are...how should I put this...risqué."

"You mean the sex?"

She nodded. "Rough sex, bondage, and a few things that I got online doing some research."

Tyler ran his hand through his hair as he remembered the young girls crowding around Monique at the riverfront. "But you told me your fans were mostly teenage girls. You can't write things like...." He let his voice trail off as he began to comprehend why Chris Donovan was so furious. "Moe, you could hurt your career," he vehemently added.

185

"It's my career, Ty. I told you before, I only write what I want, and I won't have my stories dictated by the desires of my reader."

"But if your audience doesn't like the new stuff you write, you could lose them and in the process your publisher and your income could suffer."

"But it's what I want. It's what I'm feeling, and that is what goes into my books. Not the commercial benefits I hope to gain, the emotional release I need to write about." She set her eyes on the kitchen doors. "I'll call Chris and straighten it out."

After she slipped into the kitchen, Tyler was gripped by a sickening wave of guilt. Was he the cause of her sudden change in writing styles? What if he was threatening her successful career? He knew Monique was only the tip of the big business machine working behind the scenes. There were a lot of other people whose jobs were dependent on her book sales.

But instead of following her into the kitchen to talk her out of pursuing her latest novel, he went to the stairs and climbed the steps. Perhaps it was best if he did not interfere. It was her business, after all. The one thing he had learned from his marriages was to never tell a woman what you were thinking. That way you did not spend the rest of your life wishing you had never opened your mouth in the first place.

***

Later that evening, after a quick shower, Tyler checked the messages on his cell phone that he had let roll over to voice mail while touring the French Quarter. Spotting the three missed calls and assorted texts from his stepfather, he silently cursed.

"Gary, I'm sorry I missed you," he began when he returned his call. "But I was—"

"Where in the hell have you been, Tyler?" Gary shouted, interrupting him. "I've had to call Hal Askew back twice when I couldn't get you. He's been waiting to talk to you about the mess in Oklahoma."

"I've been tied up," Tyler asserted.

"Tied up with some woman, I'll bet. When are you going to get your head out of your dick, boy, and start devoting yourself to the business?"

"I have been devoting myself to the business for ten years now, Gary. I've even got the two failed marriages to prove it."

"You married a bimbo and a gold digger, what else did you expect?" Gary took in a labored breath. "Now, I've texted you Askew's contact information, and—"

"I got it," Tyler cut in.

"Then call him and set up a meeting for tomorrow. You need to settle this mess."

"Tomorrow is not good for me," Tyler insisted.

"Son, Napoleon once said, 'fortune is like a woman. If you miss her today, think not to find her tomorrow.' So get your ass to Oklahoma, before the business suffers for your...stupidity."

Gary hung up, and Tyler had to sit on the edge of his bed for several minutes, trying to quell his outrage. Deciding to leave the rest of his messages unanswered, he turned off the iPhone and rose from the bed. With his stepfather's words still burning in his ears, he left the bedroom in search of Monique.

When he walked into the kitchen, she was chopping carrots on a cutting board next to the sink. "What are you doing?"

"Making dinner." She carried a handful of carrots to a pan on the cooktop. "It's just some stir-fry chicken and vegetables. Nothing too fancy." She eyed his casual jeans and fresh T-shirt. "You took a shower?"

"Then I returned a bunch of messages from the office." He went to the cooktop and inspected the vegetables simmering in the frying pan.

She wiped her hands over the white apron she had covering her black slacks. "Everything all right?"

"Just playing political games with some state representatives in Oklahoma." Tyler leaned his hip against the island cooktop. "Gary has been trying to smooth things over with a project we have going into construction there, but it's been touch and go."

Monique lifted the pan and stirred the vegetables. "I thought he was retired."

"He still likes to butt in every now and then."

"Butt in?" She rolled her eyes. "That doesn't sound good."

"I don't have much choice in the matter. Gary still thinks of Propel as his."

"You have a choice, Ty. You run Propel, not Gary."

"Well, sometimes it doesn't feel that way." Wanting to change the subject, he quickly asked. "How did it go with Chris?"

She turned to the counter. "He yelled, I listened, and then I hung up on him."

Tyler moved toward her. "That bad?"

She wrenched a chicken breast from a sheet of wax paper and slapped it on the cutting board. "I don't want to talk about it."

"Moe, if he thinks it's a bad idea for you to publish this book, maybe you should listen to him. He is your manager and—"

She stared at Tyler. "I thought you hated him?"

"I do," he admitted. "But the man is also looking out for your interest. Would I prefer you hire someone else to be your manager? Of course, but in the meantime, I—"

"Are you dictating whom I can and cannot have as a manager?" She gripped the knife on the cutting board.

"No, I would simply prefer someone who isn't in love with you."

"You're getting awfully possessive for a man who isn't sure if he even wants to be in my life." She hacked into the chicken breast on the cutting board.

"I never said that," he contended.

She kept her eyes on the chicken. "You didn't have to."

He removed the knife from her hand. "Before you decide to slice into me with that thing, let's talk about what we are." He put the knife down on the black granite countertop. "What do you want to do? To work this out, or when this vacation of mine ends do you want me to leave and never come back?"

Monique rested her hands on the counter. "I don't want to scare you away. If I say I want more, I'm afraid you'll run."

He placed a lock of hair behind her ear that had fallen from her ponytail. "That is exactly what I have been thinking. I didn't want to get too serious in case you got scared."

"So what do we do?"

Her voice sounded so frail and childlike that Tyler almost did not recognize it. He had never perceived her as vulnerable, but in that instant she became that little girl in desperate need of protection that Chris Donovan had spoken of.

A loud crackling noise from the vegetables in the pan on the cooktop resonated throughout the kitchen.

Tyler motioned to the cooktop. "Don't burn dinner."

Monique cursed as she scooted to the gas cooktop and turned down the flame. "I hope you like your stir-fry crispy."

He came behind her and placed his hands on her shoulders, kneading them. "Maybe we're scared because we both want this to work this time."

She leaned her head back against his chest. "Or maybe we both know it can't."

"It can work, Moe."

"What if you get bored with me?"

Tyler gently spun her around to face him. "I could never get bored with you."

"The sex could get boring."

He rested his forehead against hers. "Then we'll have to go back to Mr. Binky's to find something new."

"All right, Ty. I'm willing if you are."

"That's my Moe." He kissed her cheek. "Now what about my dinner?"

She sarcastically saluted him. "Yes, sir." Monique went around him and back to the kitchen counter. "Why is it a man's emotions are directly linked to his stomach and not his heart?"

"But I am not your typical man," he argued.

189

Grasping the knife, Monique began slicing the chicken again. "No, you're not. You're more into control than most men."

"What are you talking about?"

"You know what I mean, Ty. You like being in control of your emotions and your women."

His dark brown eyes went wide with disbelief. "Lord, Moe, you make me sound like some kind of...Svengali."

She finished slicing up the chicken breast and reached for another on the wax paper next to the cutting bored. "You are in a way. I can see how you like to stay on top of every situation. Even during sex, you like telling a woman what to do."

He waved his hand in the air, feeling defensive. "I am open to letting a woman take control in bed, but in my experience women like it when a man acts like a man between the sheets."

Monique slid the sliced chicken breasts from the cutting board to a plate, and then carried the plate to the cooktop. "You really don't know women, do you?" She dropped the chicken into the skillet of sautéing vegetables. "A woman lets a man think he is in charge, but it is really the woman who is in charge. Don't you see?"

"There's that strange logic of yours again."

"Not logic, fact." She stirred the chicken with the vegetables with a wooden spoon. "What if I was to take control in bed? How would you feel about that?"

He shrugged as he stood next to her. "I might like it."

"You like being in control, Ty. Admit it...the thought of giving up control scares you."

He picked out a piece of broccoli from the pan. "No, I just don't like sneak attacks." Tyler popped the broccoli in his mouth.

"I think if you ever did let go and hand control to someone else you would discover a whole new side to yourself."

"Moe, stop sounding like a shrink; you're beginning to frighten me."

190

She pointed her wooden spoon at him. "You see, I was right."

"I can't win with you, can I?"

She grinned. "Now you're getting the idea."

Chapter 18

They had dined on the very crispy chicken stir-fry and after dinner had retreated to her television room on the second floor to watch a movie. Bart was settled between them on a bright green and white sofa next to a wide window that overlooked the garden in Monique's back yard. The walls were filled with more old black and white photographs of landmarks in the city. As Tyler sat on the sofa, he anticipated Monique's reaction to the coming cache being delivered.

"When did you get into collecting photographs of New Orleans?"

"After I married Mat, I wanted to decorate the house with a New Orleans theme. But instead of the gold fleur-de-lis, so common around here, I went with black and white photos from the city's past. I thought it was different." She snorted. "Mat called them cheesy."

Tyler diverted his eyes to Bart, who was avidly watching the wide screen television. "Yeah, he struck me as a bit of a snob at the restaurant."

"He was that. Thought he was God's gift to women." Monique's gray eyes whirled around to him. "Kind of like you," she added.

Tyler nodded, deciding to play along. "But I am God's gift to women."

Monique's mouth fell open and then she lunged across the sofa at him, making Bart growl with annoyance.

"I will be the judge of that." She sat on his lap.

Tyler wrapped his arms about her. "What will it take to convince you?"

She suggestively rocked her hips back and forth. "I have a few ideas."

Grabbing her slender hips, Tyler stood from the sofa. Lifting her body in his arms, he carried her to the door and out into the hallway.

"Let's do it in my room," she whispered.

By the time he entered her bedroom, Monique had already removed her shirt, and was working on her bra. Kissing her neck and cheeks, he hurried across the pale blue rug to her wide pine bed. After they fell on top of her blue and yellow floral bedspread, Tyler pulled his T-shirt over his head and threw it to the floor.

Her hands roamed the muscles in his back, and then her nails raked from his shoulders down to his backside. "Do you like that?"

Tyler grimaced. "Perhaps not quite so hard, baby."

Pushing his jeans and briefs over his round rear, Monique asked, "What do you like?"

"Breakfast in bed, long walks on the beach, romantic dinners," he joked in her ear.

She slapped his naked butt. "I'm serious. What do you want me to do to please you?"

He eased the black slacks from around her hips. "Moe, you already please me." He let her underwear and pants fall to the floor.

She rolled him onto his back and straddled his hips. "Tell me."

He winced when his back hit the sheets and then relaxed against the bed. "You know what I like."

Her fingers traced the muscles in his chest. "What else have you tried?"

"That works for me." His hands stroked up and down her slender thighs. "Why bother with anything else?"

She glimpsed the gold Italian watch on his wrist. Monique removed the watch and put it on the night table next to the bed.

"What are you doing?"

"It will get in the way," she told him. Lifting his arms over his head, she kissed his chest. When her teeth grazed his left nipple, Tyler sucked in an excited breath.

Still holding his arms over his head, she angled over him, her right breast hovering above his mouth. "Perhaps it's time we change things up a bit."

Tyler heard a click above his head as he felt something soft latch around his wrists. He fought to sit upright, and then realized his hands were secured to the round corner bedpost. When he peered up, the pink fur-lined handcuffs loomed above him.

"You're not serious?"

Her hands swept down his chest, and then settled over his erection. "It's time to let me have some fun."

"Moe, I'm really not—"

She kissed his lips, silencing his protests. "Leave it to me. Relax, I'll take care of you."

"But this is—"

"Do you trust me, Ty?"

He closed his eyes and tried to settle against the bed, fighting his urge to get out of the handcuffs.

"You didn't answer me." She dragged her nail down the center of his chest.

"Yes, all right." He flinched away from her. "Is this payback for yesterday?"

"No." She planted kisses down his chest. "This is something I think you need to experience."

Monique teasingly nuzzled his lower stomach, making him swell with desire. "You're killing me, Moe."

"This is just the beginning." Her lips slowly descended over his erection.

Tyler quickly forgot about the handcuffs and gave into the pleasure her mouth was creating. Blood surged to his groin as her lips moved slowly up and down his shaft. He wanted to reach down and grab her head, forcing her to move faster, but then the handcuffs stopped him. When the tension in his loins was about to pass the point of no return, she suddenly stopped.

"God, no, don't stop!"

Moe's lips traveled to his right nipple. She bit down hard into his flesh, and then her fingers delicately stroked him.

Tyler yanked against the handcuffs.

"Shh, baby." She kissed his neck. "All good things come to those who wait."

He groaned, knowing what she had in mind.

When her lips once again moved down his stomach to his rigid member, he closed his eyes and prepared for what was to come. She stimulated him with her mouth, bringing him almost to climax, and just before he could hurtle over the edge, she stopped.

"God, no," he howled. "Moe, you can't do this."

She giggled against this chest. "Yes, I can. You're my prisoner."

Monique would bring him close to orgasm, and then stop. With every touch of her lips, stroke of her fingers, and nip of her teeth, he was becoming more and more sensitive. Soon, Tyler found his strict self-control giving in to her. When she finally straddled his hips, he almost cried out loud with relief. He was so swollen, so in need of release that he could think of nothing else.

Very gently, she lowered her hips over him, taking him all the way into her. Closing his eyes as she slowly rode him, he pushed his hips higher, desperate to go deeper. Tyler was grunting wildly and pulling against the handcuffs above him. His arms were burning and his wrists throbbing, but he did not care. Monique's ragged breaths filled his ears. She was clasping at his neck and grimacing as her body grew taught with anticipation.

Tyler cried out her name, arching his back as the powerful orgasm roared through him. Seconds later, he heard Monique moan above him and then go limp. She was slumped over him, breathing hard into his cheek when he opened his eyes. He ached to put his arms about her, but then again he wanted to put her over his lap and spank her for what she had done to him.

"Did you enjoy that, Ty?"

"I can't feel my hands, Moe."

She hastily undid the handcuffs. Letting out a relieved, long breath, Tyler shook out his hands as Monique lay on top of him. Once the tingling had abated in his fingers, he clasped his arms about her and flipped her body beneath him.

"That was dirty," he grumbled. He bit her neck and sucked on her skin.

"Oow!" She squirmed beneath him. Lifting her arms over her head she whispered, "Do you want to get even with me?"

But he did not want to get even. If anything he felt closer to her than ever. No woman had ever flipped the tables on him, and for some reason he was relieved.

"No, not this time." He passionately kissed her lips.

Incredibly, he could feel himself growing hard again as he kissed her. Parting her lips with his tongue, he deepened his kiss, and as Monique slipped her arms about his shoulders, he felt something change in him. His hands caressed her breasts, hips, thighs, and when he settled his fingers between her legs, she sighed into his hair.

"Don't you want to tie me up?"

He kissed her lips again. "No."

Kneeling between her legs, he slowly slid into her. Hugging her petite body, Tyler indulged in the sensation of her warm, soft skin. He kissed her neck, pulled out, and then gently entered her once more.

"I like this even better," she whispered.

Tyler did not understand why it was better this time, but it was. He wanted her so much, and his yearning made him want to please her in every way. Fighting to control his need to dive deep into her flesh, he opted for short, steady thrusts, heightening her pleasure. When Monique moaned into his chest, Tyler held back, wanting to bring her to climax again. As the second orgasm hit her, Monique quivered and her scream filled the bedroom. Unable to stand it any longer, Tyler pushed all the way into her until that intense wave of satisfaction overtook him.

After, they lay holding each other in the darkness of her room. Tyler kissed her shoulder and was brushing the hair from her face when she opened her eyes.

"You were different that time. You felt...almost tender."

He rolled off her and placed his hand behind his head. "It wasn't different, Moe," he asserted, feeling a bit alarmed that she had felt it, too.

She cuddled into his side. "It was different, Ty. It was the real you."

He listened as her breathing slowed and her body relaxed beside him. In a short time, she had drifted off to sleep, but Tyler was still wide-awake, weighing her words.

Was that the real Tyler Moore? Sex had always been for release, and not so much about emotion with him, but this time he had felt the emotion. Most of his life, emotions had been something Tyler had kept buried beneath the surface. Even when he was married, he had never shared such intense feelings with his wives.

He wiggled out from under Monique, trying not to wake her. As she curled up in the bed, he tenderly covered her naked body with a corner of the blue and yellow bedspread.

What was happening to him? Tyler stood from the bed and rubbed his hands over his face. His body craved something to take the edge off. He needed to suppress the rising dread in his stomach. She was getting too close, and he needed something to give him the strength to block her out.

The patter of tiny feet on the hardwood floor by the door made him turn from the bed. Bart was standing in the doorway, staring up at Tyler as if to say, "What's your problem?"

Tyler looked past the dog to the hallway outside, and then he remembered the bottle of bourbon in the bottom of the kitchen pantry.

He was halfway down the stairs when he realized what he was doing. "Over twenty years of sobriety and I'm going to blow it now?"

But all the self-recriminations did not seem to stop his feet as they purposefully moved closer to the kitchen. Once inside the white double doors, he flipped on the lights and pondered the pantry door, fighting for any excuse to head back up the stairs to her bed. But the churning in his gut became even more insistent. He needed that fix of alcohol on his lips like nothing he had experienced in years.

Staggering across the kitchen, he flung the pantry door open and yanked the Jack Daniel's from the floor. The bottle glistened in the pale light from the streetlights outside the kitchen window. When he turned the cap, the crack of the seal echoed about the kitchen. He put the tip of the bottle to his lips, hoping the smell would satiate his need, but no such luck. The aroma of the alcohol only seemed to infuriate his thirst even more.

While a swirl of conflict squeezed his gut, Tyler touched the bottle to his lips. At first, the taste of alcohol was unpleasant in his mouth, almost nauseating. But soon the warmth of the liquid began to soothe his torment, prompting Tyler to take in a little more. As the bourbon burned its way to his stomach, he tossed his head back and he let out a long, defeated breath. In that instant, he had never felt so low. He had given in to the temptation he had fought so long to suppress.

Sitting down with a thud on a chair next to the kitchen table, he murmured, "What in the hell is wrong with me?"

After downing another long sip, his body trembled. Resting the bottle on the table, he sat back in his chair and struggled for control. It seemed that Monique had gotten to him, again. Tyler had stopped drinking when she had walked out of his life, and it took her return to make him reach for alcohol once more.

Standing from the table, he placed the cap back on the bottle. "I can't do this," he mouthed. Tyler then set the bottle back on the pantry floor.

As he bounded up the walnut staircase, he thought of what to do. When he came to her bedroom door, Tyler rested his shoulder against the doorframe, debating a course of action.

A light wheezing sound came from around his feet, and Tyler looked down to find Bart watching his every move. The accusatory glint Tyler swore he detected in the animal's round, black eyes only seemed to compound his guilt.

Unable to stand the din of questions circling his mind, Tyler returned to the bed. He wanted to have a little more time with Monique before he had to make any decisions about what to do. Lifting the bedspread, he slipped into the bed and wrapped their bodies beneath the covers. She woke briefly as he settled in next to her, nestled against his chest, and fell back asleep. He encircled her in his arms and tucked her head beneath his chin. Holding Monique was as close as Tyler figured he would ever get to heaven on earth. He had once heard it said that a lifetime could be summed up in a single moment. For Tyler Moore, that moment was now.

Chapter 19

Opening his eyes to strange pastel floral wallpaper made Tyler sit up, confused by his surroundings. The yellow and blue bedspread was twisted about his naked body and tufts of dirty-blonde hair were protruding from beneath the covers next to him. When he spied the pink, fur-lined handcuffs still hanging from a post on the pine bed, a montage of images from the night before came back to him. Gargled snoring from the floor next to the bed disrupted his reflection. Leaning over, Tyler saw Bart sleeping on his back on a pillow that had fallen from the bed. His pink tongue was flapping up and down outside of his mouth as he slept.

"God, that's hideous."

Monique stirred beside him, and then a single gray eye peeked out from under the bedspread. "Is it morning already?"

He kissed her forehead. "'Fraid so." He unraveled the bedspread from about his legs.

Monique stretched beside him, yawning. "I haven't slept that well in years."

He swung his legs over the side of the bed. "Must have been all of your…exertions last night."

"Oh, God. Did I do that?" She sat up and traced her fingers over his back.

Tyler flinched. "What is it?"

"You have red scratches all down your back."

Tyler lightly chuckled. "Unless Bart climbed in bed with us last night, I'm pretty sure that was you."

She scooted next to him and gently raised his wrist. "Does that hurt?"

He examined the black and blue line about his right wrist. "No, looks worse than it feels. Handcuffs always bruise. That's why I never use them. I only use soft ties." He kissed the side of her cheek.

"Why didn't you say anything last night?"

"Would you have listened to me when you had me handcuffed to the bed?"

With a straight face, she thought about it for a second or two. "Probably not," she concluded.

He patted her thigh. "I rest my case."

"I guess I got a little carried away with your back and all." She kissed his shoulder. "But the second time without the handcuffs was even better." Monique slid her arms about his waist.

A hint of uneasiness cut through him. "Yeah, it was great." He stood from the bed, massaging his right wrist. "I need a shower." He retrieved his gold watch from the table and slipped it on.

"Hey." Monique stood up next to him. "Is something wrong?"

Tyler silently chastised himself for being so abrupt. "No, nothing is wrong." He embraced her and smelled the remnants of her lilac perfume. Why did he feel like such an ass? "You just wore me out, my Moe," he added, hoping to reassure her.

She tilted back from his embrace. "I'll make it up to you with a nice breakfast. How does that sound?"

He gave her a genuine, warm smile. "Wonderful."

She stepped out of his arms and went to her bathroom door. Grabbing a fluffy blue robe from behind the door, she shrugged it over her shoulders and tied it at the waist.

"You take your shower while I'll make breakfast. Then you can think of something you want to do today. We could see plantation homes outside of the city, or take a trolley ride,

201

whatever you're in the mood for." She paused and grinned at him. "I promise, no more stores like Mr. Binky's."

He ran his hand over his face as she walked to the bedroom door. "I need to make a few calls this morning. I have to check on that business in Oklahoma."

"All right, I can do some work on the computer while you are making calls."

Monique was about to leave when he stopped her. "Last night really was wonderful, Moe."

Her eyes met his. "Yes, it was." She clapped her hands at Bart. "Come on, buddy. Let's go get some breakfast."

After she was gone, the guilt rose in Tyler like flood water behind a dam. Refusing to listen to the constant chatter in his head, he gathered his clothes from the floor and quickly escaped to his bedroom.

After tossing his clothes to his bed, he stepped beneath his shower and turned the tap all the way to cold. The icy water felt like pins shooting into his skin. Tyler closed his eyes and forced himself to stand there and take his punishment. For the first time in his life, he was beginning to truly comprehend the stinging pain of regret.

***

After breakfast with Monique and Bart, Tyler returned to his room and checked his cell phone. Seeing the thirty-four unanswered e-mails and twenty-six voice mails made him flop down on his bed with disgust.

"Something's happened," he whispered, knowing that an exorbitant amount of messages usually signaled trouble.

His first call was to Lynn at the offices of Propel. When she picked up his private line after two rings, he skipped all pleasantries.

"What's going on?" he pressed, before she had barely gotten her "hello" out.

"Mitch Douglass has been calling for you every ten minutes. Things are about to blow in Oklahoma. It seems the state legislature wants to call a committee meeting on how the proposed pipeline was approved and to review the company's submission process for leases and building permits. They are saying we paid someone off."

"We did pay someone off," Tyler roared. "Where is Mitch?"

"On the company jet to Oklahoma. He has a meeting with a state rep named Hal Askew. It seems Mr. Leesburg contacted Mr. Douglass directly when he couldn't get you last night."

"Son of a bitch." Tyler wanted to throw his cell phone against the wall. "I can't believe Gary had the audacity to go around me."

"Mr. Douglass made it sound like something needed to be handled right away," Lynn informed him, sounding worried.

"When did Mitch leave?"

"About an hour ago. Mr. Leesburg has scheduled a lunch today with Mr. Askew."

Tyler checked his watch. "I'll call Mitch and go over a game plan. Is there anything else?"

"I've got an inspector with the Feds looking to review the safety procedures again for our Gulf rigs."

"They've been breathing down everyone's necks since that BP mess." He massaged his right temple. "Where's Lloyd McDonald? That's his department."

"His wife went into labor last night. His assistant, Marc Packard, said he can handle it, but he's never dealt with a federal safety review before. Any suggestions?"

Tyler ran through a list of names in his head, and then one stood out from the rest. "Contact Trent Newbury and explain the situation. He does a lot of consulting work for us and knows the safety regs better than anybody. He can work with Marc. The last thing I need is the Feds wanting to come in and hold up production because of some screw up in paperwork."

"I'll call him. Legal needs to speak with you, as well. They want to go over some contract changes."

He closed his eyes, suddenly feeling inundated. "All right. Let me get with Mitch, and then give Gary a call. I'll get back to you after I get a handle on Oklahoma. Have legal send me an e-mail—"

"They already did," she cut in over the phone.

"I'll look it over."

"Sorry to ruin your vacation," Lynn apologized with a tinge of trepidation in her voice. "But I knew you would want to be updated on everything."

"Thanks, and you're right, I needed to know. I'll—" A muffled yelling from downstairs interrupted him. "Let me call you back, Lynn." He hung up the phone as he heard a man's voice and then Bart's continued yapping.

"What the hell?" Throwing the phone on the bed, Tyler flew to the open bedroom door. He was at the second floor landing and about to head down the stairs when he recognized the man's voice coming from below.

"Monique, you have got to listen to me," Chris Donovan shouted.

Tyler jogged down the old walnut staircase, and was making his way along the narrow hallway when he heard hushed voices coming through the partially opened door to the living room. Dashing to the door, he was about to step into the room when Bart came running out.

"Some guard dog you are," Tyler commented.

Pushing the door all the way open, he ventured inside.

"You have no right to tell me—" Monique stopped when Tyler entered the room.

Chris was standing in front of a red-bricked hearth topped by a high white mantle that was covered with mirrors and rose all the way up to the white plaster ceiling. Dressed in a long-sleeved white shirt and dark blue slacks, his blue eyes closed in on Tyler.

"He's here?" Chris angrily pointed at Tyler. "You didn't tell me he was here, Monique."

"Is there a problem?" Tyler asked, turning to Monique.

She was standing next to a contemporary white sofa covered with a number of red throw pillows. Her hands were

204

tightly wrapped together and her pink mouth was drawn back in an angry scowl. Tyler could tell by the way her eyes were scrunched together that she was about to rip into Chris.

"Yeah, there's a problem," Chris croaked, coming toward him. "You're the problem." He motioned back to Monique. "Did you tell her to write that crap?"

"It's not crap!" Monique snapped. "You kept telling me to put more sex in my books. Well, I gave you what you wanted."

"I didn't tell you to put in bondage, Monique," Chris hollered. "That's not what Donovan Books sells. You know Hunter doesn't want any erotica, but that is exactly what you gave him." He waved a hand in the air, as if signaling there would be no further discussion on the subject.

Tyler moved across the room to her side. "Chris, you need to calm down."

"She's not screwing up your business, Tyler, so don't you dare tell me to calm down!"

"I'm not screwing up anyone's business, Chris," she roared. "Did Hunter send you here? Did he read it?"

"Of course he didn't read it. I can't send it to him," Chris insisted. "You need to change it, or at least let me find another publisher to put it out under a pseudonym. We can't tarnish your reputation with your readers."

"I won't do that." Monique crossed her arms defiantly over her chest. "It is either published as is with my name, or I'll find another publisher, Chris...and another manager." She stormed out of the room, leaving Chris and Tyler gaping with surprise at the open living room door.

Tyler listened as she trotted quickly up the stairs.

"This is your fault," Chris huffed behind him.

Balling his hands into fists, Tyler slowly faced him. "I do not see how what she writes is my fault."

"I told you before...writers are like sponges, they absorb the world around them. You came back and exposed her to your deviant sexual behavior."

Tyler raised his eyebrows. "My 'deviant sexual behavior'?"

Chris pointed to the living room door. "I know you're sleeping with her. I knew the moment I started reading her book. You came back into her life and opened the door to this forbidden world, and she wrote about it. She wrote about the male character tying up his lover, and introducing her to a world of wild sexual pleasure."

"So what if she wrote about that? What difference does it make?"

"She's not that kind of writer! Don't you get it? She has a fan base...a loyal fan base that buys books they expect to go a certain way. There's a chase, some emotional yielding, kissing, and when the characters do have sex in her books, it's pretty damn tame. Not handcuffs, whips, or blindfolds."

"So she's changing." Tyler scowled at Chris. "She has the right to change as a writer."

"She would never have changed until you came along. You made her different. Suddenly, the dream man she wrote about is in her life and she has written a book that reflects that life. But her readers don't want to see that." Chris ran his hand over his curly gray hair. "If Donovan Books publishes that piece of shit, it could end her career."

"You're being a bit dramatic, Chris." Tyler turned for the door. "She'll get new readers."

"And if she doesn't? Do you want to be the one responsible for ending her writing career?"

Tyler hesitated, before answering him. "It's her career. I'm not going to tell her what to do."

"My God, you are a cold son of a bitch! How can you just waltz in here, rearrange her life, and leave? Because that's what you're going to do, isn't it?"

Tyler stifled his hankering to punch Chris's face in "You're just her manager. What happens between Moe and me is not your concern."

"To hell it isn't! What do you think she is she going to do when you leave like you did before? We both know you're not the kind to hang around. Tell me, Tyler, are you out to break her heart or just wreck her career? Because if you destroy one, you're inevitably going to destroy the other."

Unable to hold back any longer, Tyler rushed up to Chris and grabbed the collar on his shirt. "Where in the hell do you get off accusing me of hurting her?"

Chris glared into his eyes. "Do you love her?"

Tyler let him go. "I'm not using her like you."

"I never used her." Chris straightened out his shirt collar. "I love her. There's a difference, but someone like you would never understand."

"Get out," Tyler snarled.

Appearing thrilled that he had pushed Tyler to the breaking point, Chris curled his lips into a smug smirk. "After you're gone, I'll be the one left to pick up the pieces. You won't get a third chance with her; I'll make sure of it."

Chris collected his dark blue suit jacket from the back of the sofa and hurried to the living room entrance. After he had slammed the front door closed, Tyler fled from the room.

He needed a drink, now more than ever. He could deal with the bullshit from his stepfather, and the confrontation with Chris, but the sudden realization that he may have ruined Monique's writing career was more than Tyler could stomach. He was not ready to shoulder that burden of guilt.

After reaching the kitchen, Tyler threw open the pantry door and snapped up the dark bottle. Standing in the pantry doorway, he drank one long sip after another. The burn of the alcohol calmed the furor of his emotions. It made him feel empowered, and slowly, as the warmth of the liquid worked its magic, he felt his sense of control returning. Chris's dire insinuations about destroying Monique's career quickly waned, and his thoughts reverted to his life and his problems.

He took one more reassuring swig from the bottle, replaced the cap, and returned it to the pantry floor. As he gazed down at the bottle, he made up his mind. He had to go. Staying would only end up hurting both of them. At least after last night, he could walk away knowing he had experienced that moment of bliss with another that so many hope for.

"What are you doing?" Monique called from the kitchen doorway.

Tyler backed out of the pantry. "I was looking for a can of soda."

"What did Chris say to you?"

He made his way across the kitchen. "That you could ruin your career if you publish that book. Is he right?"

She went to the kitchen table and pulled out a chair. "The market is changing. Readers want racy books with more sex in them. I guess to reflect the way relationships truly are. I mean, there is still an audience for the tame stuff, like I used to write, but I really don't want to write that way anymore. I want to get edgier with my characters, but Chris has been fighting me on that." She flopped down in the chair. "I know I will lose readers who liked what I used to write, but I may pick up readers who are into the meatier stories."

Tyler sat down next to her. "Is this what you want to write?"

She slowly nodded her head. "I would never have had the courage to do it before you came back into my life." She took his hand. "You showed me how it should be between two people, and that is what I want to put into my books. Chris was just not ready for me to change."

Tyler squeezed her hand. "So what are you going to do?"

"Publish it, either with Donovan Books or with someone else. I can't write the way Chris and his brother want me to anymore. I want to write what I feel."

Tyler let her hand go and sat back in his chair, feeling like absolute shit. "Chris was right. Maybe I shouldn't have come back in your life."

"Are you kidding?" she said, half-laughing. "Your coming back has been the best thing that has happened to me."

"You're exaggerating, Moe. I could never be the best thing that ever happened to anyone."

She stood from her chair and moved closer to him. "How can you say that?" Her fingers played in the touch of gray along his right temple. "You sound like the man I knew twenty-one years ago, the one who never thought he was good enough to work with his stepfather."

He stood up. "Moe, perhaps you should reconsider the book. I don't want to be responsible for ruining your dream of being a writer. I've ruined enough lives already. I could not live with adding yours to the pile."

"You're not ruining my dream of being a writer, don't you see that? If anything, you reminded me of the kind of writer I want to be. You asked me before why I wrote about you in all my novels, and do you want to know the real reason? Because you were the one man I was too afraid to go after. You represented what I dreamed of in a guy, and I figured as long as I wrote about you, I was fulfilling that dream." She waved her hand down his body. "But now you're here, and those fantasies I wrote about were nothing compared to the reality of being with you. From that first night we were together back in Dallas, I realized that, and that is why I changed my book. I wanted it to be the reality and not the fantasy anymore."

He held her arms. "But the fantasy of being with me is inevitably going to be better than the reality. Go back to writing about the way you thought I was, Moe. Those stories are always going to read better than the lies I can give you."

Monique stared at him, her gray eyes pleading for illumination. "What lies?"

He let her go. "The big lie I've been hiding from the world about me. On the inside, I'm terrified, Moe. I'm terrified that I can't run Propel, and I will let all of our employees down. I wake up every morning and wonder, is this the day that everyone will find out what a screw up I really am?"

"Ty, everyone wakes up and thinks the same thing, every single day of their lives." She rested her hand on his arm. "I

209

wonder when people are going to figure out I can't write. Mat used to have nightmares about being in surgery and not being able to save his patient. Even Chris confided to me that he is winging it most of the time. No one is born with confidence; we just pretend to know what we are doing and pray to God no one ever figures it out."

"But I am a screw up, don't you see that?"

"That's not the Tyler Moore I remember. You could tackle any challenge that came your way."

He spun away from her, moving toward the kitchen doors. "But it's the Tyler Moore I've become."

"I believe in you, Ty," she declared behind him. "I believed in you twenty-one years ago, and I'm not about to give up on you now. Being in love means you're willing to fight for someone, or die trying."

He stopped at the doors, but did not turn to face her. "Please don't love me, Moe. I'm not worth the effort."

"You're worth it, Ty. Sometimes we only find our self-worth when it is shining back at us through the eyes of the ones we love. People come into our lives for a reason, maybe it is to show us how special and worthwhile we really are. That's what you did for me all those years ago."

"How on earth did I do that?"

"You loved me." She came up to him and placed her hand on his back. "Encouragement may be instilled with words, but it's only fortified by love."

Tyler was not sure if he should flee or hold her in his arms. He craved another shot of bourbon to bolster his caving confidence, but he knew the alcohol would not help. Years of sobriety had taught him that all of his problems could not be washed away with a bottle of booze. He could get drunk and feel like crap, but his insecurities would still be there, haunting him just like the image of a murdered victim taunts a remorseful killer.

Opting to keep his distance, he migrated closer to the door. "I have e-mails to get out," was all he could think to say before quickly departing the kitchen.

As he climbed the stairs, he was convinced of what he needed to do. He just prayed that he had the strength to do it.

Chapter 20

Spending the next hour in his room, answering e-mails and making phone calls, Tyler tried to remain focused on work, but there was not a second when he did not rehash his conversation with Chris. When he had first planned on coming to see Monique, he had never intended to hurt her or her career.

"I'm such an idiot," he muttered after he had read an e-mail from his legal department for the third time.

Reaching for his cell phone, he was startled when it rang in his hand. After checking the name on the caller ID, he eagerly took the call.

"Gary," he said into the phone speaker. "I heard. You want to tell me why you called Mitch?"

"Running a company means you are available twenty-four-seven, Tyler. You tell me, what choice did I have?"

Tyler did not say a word.

"When can you get to Oklahoma City?" Gary pressured, sounding out of breath.

"Mitch is on his way. He can see to all—"

"You're the CEO, Tyler," Gary broke in. "You need to handle this. I told Hal Askew you were going to see him, not some second-in-command. Drop what you are doing and head to Oklahoma."

"Mitch knows the pipeline project better than me, and he is the one who sealed the deal with the locals."

"He didn't seal a goddamned thing, and you know that. If Mitch had done his job in the first place, you wouldn't be fighting with the state legislature. Get your ass on a plane and get to Oklahoma." Gary coughed into the phone. "Your mother told me you're with some old flame in New Orleans, and I know how you get with your women, Tyler, but you can't blow this off for some broad."

Tyler bit his tongue, refusing to elaborate on his feelings for Monique to a man who viewed her as nothing more than a fleeting amusement for his stepson.

"I'll get a flight out in the morning," he assured him.

"You need to go today," Gary protested.

"I'll go tomorrow, Gary. That will give Mitch time to try and close the deal; if he can't, I'll be there tomorrow. That's it. You left me the company to run, and this is my decision. And if you ever go around me again, I swear I'll talk to the board about cutting you out completely."

"Why you arrogant little shit. I left you the company because your mother swore you could handle it. I've always had my doubts about you, now more than ever, and I—"

"I will handle it, Gary."

"You better not screw this up, Tyler. This company is everything to me, and I will never—"

"I don't have to answer to you anymore," Tyler barged in. "If you don't like the job I'm doing, why don't you get off your ass and come back to Propel?"

Enraged, Tyler hung up the phone. But as he sat there, listening to the beating of his heart, he also felt empowered by his refusal to cater to Gary's demands. For the first time since taking over Propel, he had acted as if he was the one who was truly in charge.

"Everything all right?" Monique asked from his open bedroom door. "I heard you shouting at someone."

Tyler sat on the edge of his bed and held up the cell phone in his hand. "Gary."

"Is there still a problem in Oklahoma?"

Tyler nodded.

She approached the bed and sat down next to him. "About what I said before, I just wanted to—"

213

He tossed the cell phone to the bed. "Forget it, Moe. I know what you were trying to say."

"I don't think you do."

His eyes swerved to the iPhone next to him as a bitter taste rose up his throat. "It doesn't matter now. Looks like I've got to head to Oklahoma in the morning."

Tension filled the air between them, and all the intimacy they had shared the night before felt as if it had happened centuries ago.

She got up from the bed. "You've got your business to run."

"And you've got your books to write."

"Attempt to write, anyway." She stood for a moment, as if she were going to say something, but then changed her mind. "I'll leave you to your phone calls. I can take you to the airport in the morning."

Ignoring the growing heaviness around his heart, he reached for the iPhone. "Thanks, Moe, but I'll get a car. I may have to leave pretty earlier."

A hint of disappointment crossed her features. "While you take care of business, I'll head to the store. Is there anything special you would like me to make for dinner?"

"Let me take you out for dinner tonight. Anywhere you want," he enthusiastically offered, trying to lift the mood in the room.

She shook her head, moving toward the door. "No, I really don't feel like going out."

"How about pizza? We can have it delivered?"

A faint smile faltered on her lips. "That sounds good, and you know how I love pizza."

"Yeah, I know."

After Moe had left his room, Tyler stared at the phone in his hand as a slew of reasons to go after her barraged his mind. There were things he should tell her, things he should explain about his life, but in the end he never got up from the bed. Disgusted, he hit his secretary's number on his call list.

"Lynn," he barked into the phone before she could get a word in. "Get me a commercial flight to Dallas from New Orleans first thing in the morning. I'll catch the company jet from there to Oklahoma."

"You're not going to let Mr. Douglass handle it?"

"No. I'm the boss, I need to be there."

An uncomfortable moment of silence passed before Lynn spoke again. "I had hoped you were learning to give up some of that precious control you guard so closely, Mr. Moore."

"I can never give up control, Lynn. As soon as I do, everything turns to hell."

***

They dined on barbeque chicken pizza and garlic cheese sticks delivered from Monique's favorite restaurant, The Sweet Note. Tyler tried to keep the conversation cheerful during dinner, sticking to subjects like the city, Monique's books, and, of course, the ever-present Bart.

"Is it my imagination or is that dog always eating?" Tyler questioned as they sat at the kitchen table after their meal.

"He is always eating." Monique watched as Bart sniffed around for crumbs beneath the table. "The vet told me to put him on a diet, but I don't have the heart to deny him what he wants."

Tyler leaned his elbows on the table as his eyes roamed over the remnants of pizza in the white cardboard box set between them. "You ever think about living with someone else besides Bart?"

She picked up the bottle of chardonnay she had opened to go with her pizza. "I don't know. Bart can be a pretty picky customer when it comes to roommates." She refilled her wine glass.

"You shouldn't be alone, Moe. You're a beautiful woman who has a lot to offer a man."

Monique put the bottle down on the table, the trepidation glistening in her eyes. "Are you trying to tell me to go out in the world and find someone else?"

He could feel the acid beginning to churn in his stomach. "You know what I do, and there will be times we want to be together and then I will have to leave, like tomorrow. Is that what you want?"

"No one said it was going to be easy." She lifted her glass of wine.

"Long distance relationships are hard to maintain."

She sat back in her chair, eyeing him thoughtfully. "You sound like you're already coming up with excuses."

"No, not excuses." He held up his hands in resignation to her. "I'm presenting the challenges this will create."

"Challenges? I thought you liked challenges." She quickly took a sip of wine.

"I do, but they can tear two people apart just as easily as they can build them up."

"I'm not made of crystal, Ty. I won't shatter into a million pieces if you don't call or come to visit regularly." She banged the wineglass down on the table. "I'm not going to put demands on you."

That awkward tension between them resurfaced, adding to his discomfort. "I just want you to know what you're getting with me."

"I already know, and I will stick by you until…." Her voice failed her. "Until you don't want me anymore."

He remembered the bourbon in the pantry and yearned for a sip. "How could I ever not want you, Moe?"

She stood from the table and carried her empty plate to the sink. "You want me; I don't doubt that. The question is if you need me in your life."

He sat back in his chair and looked over at her. "I don't understand."

She turned from the sink and stared at him for the longest time. "You don't need anyone, you never have," she finally stated. "If you ever did find yourself needing anyone or anything, I think that would equate to weakness for you. And weakness means losing control, and you never like losing control."

"A lot of people don't like losing control, Moe." He stood from his chair. "But you're right. I have to maintain control every day. I run a multi-million dollar company with hundreds of employees counting on my decisions to keep their jobs."

"This has got nothing to do with your company."

"It has everything to do with it," he insisted, moving closer. "I can't separate myself from Propel. It's a twenty-four hour job that has been hell on all of my relationships." He ran his fingers along her cheek. "And you're wrong, you know. I do need you in my life." Tyler placed his arms about her. "Would you consider relocating to Dallas?"

She squinted, as if mulling over the question. "Nah, I like it here," she eventually conceded.

He kissed her forehead as the heavy feeling encapsulating his heart spread throughout his body. "Then we make a go of this with me in Dallas and you in New Orleans. We can commute on weekends, and I can travel to your conventions."

"If I have any more conventions. It might be a while before I can get set up with another publisher."

Tyler playfully frowned, as if deep in thought. "Perhaps I should start a publishing company and then you could write whatever you wanted."

The suggestion made Monique laugh with exuberance, and Tyler savored the way her eyes disappeared behind her wide smile.

"Now that would really send Chris over the edge," she extolled as her laughter abated.

"Might be worth it. The arrogant ass."

She patted his chest. "He thought you were arrogant. He said so that day you came to the convention."

"I hope you defended me."

She shrugged, grinning. "To a point."

Tyler's hands snuck beneath Monique's T-shirt. "You'll pay for that." He began tickling her sides.

"No, not that!" Monique squealed, wiggling in his arms. "You know I can't stand to be tickled."

"I remember you were particularly ticklish right here." Tyler glided his fingertips over her flat stomach.

Monique screamed and bent over, trying to pull away from his hands. But Tyler held on to her, tickling her relentlessly up and down her sides and along her stomach. Darting away from him, she took off running out of the kitchen, giggling as she went.

Tyler pursued her with Bart trotting behind him. He finally caught her on the stairs, just as she was starting up the steps.

"I've got you," he whispered, holding her against him.

When he looked down at her face, her eyes were on fire and her cheeks were burning with color. Unable to resist, he touched his mouth to her full, pink lips and his arms instinctively tightened around her. Her kisses became overwhelming for Tyler. She tasted of wine, and her lips were so soft that he heard himself moan as she opened her mouth for him. Deciding he could not wait anymore, he pushed her down on the steps.

She laughed as he struggled to pull his T-shirt over his head. "What about the bedroom?"

He put his arms about her. "I can't wait that long. I want you now, Moe."

When he kissed her again, the passion in her lips was so intense that Tyler forgot where they were. He removed her T-shirt, and she helped him slide the heavy fabric of her baggy blue jeans down her hips. Tyler let his lips slowly travel over the contours of her breasts and stomach, relishing every inch of her sweet-smelling skin. As she reclined back on the steps, he unzipped his fly and wriggled his jeans and briefs down his hips. Kissing her gently, he threw her beige silk panties to the side, and then wrapped her legs about his waist. When he entered her, Monique's eyes were filled with such warmth and affection that he could not look away.

Tenderly, he made love to her on the stairs, taking his time to please her. Monique met his every thrust with her hips, and as that delightful heat spread through his muscles, his desire rose. He cradled her in his arms, concentrating on holding back, waiting for her pleasure to come first. When she sucked in a breath and trembled against him, Tyler let go, slamming his hips into her. As the tingle running from his loins turned into an unstoppable rush of electricity, he curled against her, grunting right at the moment of his release. She kissed his cheek and held him while the last vestiges of his climax rocked his body.

They lay on the steps for several minutes, clinging to each other, as if cherishing their last seconds together.

"We should do it that way from now on," she murmured against him. "It's never been so intense between us."

He settled against her and the peace that had pervaded his restless mind during their lovemaking was soon pushed aside by his nagging sense of guilt.

"We are just getting better together, that's all," he explained.

She made no attempt to argue, and simply ran her hands over his wavy hair. Then, the ringing of his cell phone could be heard from his room down the hall.

Her body sank back on the steps. "Do you ever get a break?"

He sat up on the step beside her, pulling up his jeans and briefs. "Not when there is a crisis brewing."

"How often does that happen?"

"Seems like every day," he sighed.

As Monique tugged her T-shirt over her head, Tyler scooped up her jeans and underwear from a lower step. He kissed her on the neck and took her hand. When she stood beside him, Tyler placed her clothes in her arms.

"Let me see who that is."

She nodded. "I'll be in the shower."

He patted her round behind. "Save some hot water for me."

After she had trotted up the stairs, Tyler bent over and retrieved his T-shirt. Shaking his head, he slowly ascended the steps, wishing that he had turned off his cell phone so they could have had a few more minutes together before his harsh world had intruded.

Cover to Covers

Chapter 21

After throwing on his jeans and fresh long-sleeved shirt, Tyler quietly maneuvered down the staircase with his overnight bag slung over his shoulder and his black suitcase in his hand. He had been very careful that morning to slip out of Monique's bed without disturbing her, wanting to let her sleep in, and also hoping to avoid a painful good-bye. He tiptoed through the darkened house to the front door. In the entranceway, he glanced up the stairs and was alarmed to see Bart staring at him from the top step.

Holding his finger to his lips, he urged Bart not to make a sound. The dog angled his head to the side as if debating whether or not to alert the household of the interloper's plans. Eventually satisfied that Bart would not betray him, Tyler headed to the front door.

He unlocked the deadbolt, and was about to open the door when he heard Bart's feet tipping on the hardwood floor next to him. Looking down, he saw the dog gazing up at him with his red tongue hanging from the side of his mouth.

"Take care of her," he whispered.

Bart sneezed and had a seat on the floor. Tyler figured that was Bart's way of saying good-bye, or perhaps good riddance, he was not sure.

When he closed the front door, Tyler let out a relieved sigh that he had been able to get away without seeing her one last time. It had been hard enough to leave her warm, lithe body beneath the sheets of her bed, but if he had to look into her eyes and say good-bye, he might not have been able to go.

Waiting on the street was a black Town Car, its headlights sending out bright beams into the dusky light enveloping the street. A very tall man, dressed in black trousers and a white shirt, stepped from the car when Tyler made his way down the porch steps.

The driver took Tyler's suitcase. "I'm Conner, Mr. Moore. Clark sends his apologies, but he had another ride this morning."

"Thank you, Conner." Tyler went to the open back passenger door and shoved his overnight bag along the back seat.

Gazing back at the house, he longed to see Monique standing on the porch or peeking out from a window, but the three-story home was dark and lifeless. With a heavy heart, he climbed into the back of the car and shut the door.

"Did you have a pleasant stay in New Orleans, Mr. Moore?" Conner inquired when he settled in behind the wheel.

Tyler smiled politely for his driver. "Yes, Conner, thank you." He peered out the window to Monique's front door. "I had the time of my life."

***

Tyler was waiting in the office of the hangar used by Propel at Love Field while the company jet went through a pre-flight check. The coffee he had been sipping was lukewarm and his patience was waning as he waited for Marty and his co-pilot, Frank, to finish up. He had changed in the hangar restroom from his casual jeans to the gray business suit Lynn had dropped off, in preparation for his flight to Oklahoma. But as the morning temperatures rose, his suit was becoming rather uncomfortable.

Beyond the wide office window, Tyler watched as smaller private planes took off from the runway between the larger jets of Southwest Airlines. Distorting ripples of heat rising from the runway almost made the solid cement appear as if it were buckling beneath the glare of the excruciating summer sun. Tyler checked his gold Italian watch again, wondering what was taking so long. He needed to get in the air soon in order to make his afternoon meeting with state representative, Hal Askew.

He was about to return to the hangar behind him to find out what the hold up was when his cell phone rang inside his jacket pocket. His heart froze when Monique's name and number appeared on the caller ID.

"Hey, Moe," he softly said, taking the call.

"You didn't wake me. I wanted to say good-bye."

He lowered his head to the faded linoleum floor. "If you had been awake, I might never have been able to say good-bye. It was hard enough leaving your naked body in that bed."

"When I woke up, I was disappointed to find Bart and not you next to me."

He pressed the toe of his black loafer into a gouge on the floor. "Yeah, well, I think Bart was glad to see me go. Now he has you all to himself again."

"Guess what I am doing right now?"

He closed his eyes and pictured her pink lips. "I have no idea."

"I'm going through a package delivered to me this morning from that picture shop we visited in the Quarter. There is just one thing. There are over twenty-five matted photos in this box, in addition to the framed one you bought me. Do you want to tell me how this happened?"

"I know how much you like those old pictures of New Orleans, so I arranged to buy the entire collection for you."

"You shouldn't have done that, Ty. This must have cost a fortune."

"You're worth it."

She giggled and Tyler ached at the sound. "Where am I going to put all of these?"

"You'll find room." He heard a door to the office shut behind him and when Tyler turned, Marty was waiting patiently for him to finish on the phone. "I've got to go. My plane is ready," he told her.

"You're not in Oklahoma yet?"

"Not yet. I'll call you later tonight, after I get settled in my hotel." He did not want to hang up, but Oklahoma was waiting. "I've got to go, Moe."

"Just call when you want to, Ty." Monique quickly hung up.

Tyler gripped his iPhone. This was turning out to be harder than he expected.

"We're ready to go, Mr. Moore," Marty reported. "Sorry about the wait."

Tyler inspected the round grease stain on Marty's white button-down shirt. "What was the problem?"

"We had trouble with the fuel gauge, but it's fixed now."

Tyler slung his overnight bag over his shoulder. "How long until we reach Oklahoma?"

"An hour, Mr. Moore."

Tyler walked purposefully for the door that led to the open hanger. "Let's get moving. I've got a full agenda for the afternoon."

"Yes, sir." Marty collected Tyler's suitcase by the office door. "It's a shame your vacation got cut short," he added.

Unhinged by his statement, Tyler wheeled around and faced his pilot. "What makes you think my vacation got cut short? Maybe I needed it to end."

Marty shifted the suitcase from one hand to the other, wrinkling his brow at Tyler. "You needed it to end? I don't understand, Mr. Moore."

Tyler realized what he had said and silently cursed his inability to reign in his emotions. Waving toward the sleek white jet standing outside of the hangar, Tyler tried to allay his pilot's concern. "Never mind, Marty. Let's just get in the air."

As Tyler proceeded toward the plane, he could feel that familiar knot in his chest returning. He had forgotten the sensation while he was with Monique in New Orleans, but now that he was back in his world his old self began to re-emerge.

He had lived out the perfect fantasy, and he did not want to destroy his illusions by scrambling schedules, meeting for trysts in hotel rooms, and generally fitting her in until she grew tired of it all; or worse, until he grew tired of her. That was what he really feared…moving ahead with her only to discover she would end up becoming just like every other woman he knew. He did not want what they had shared to become part of a long list of forgettable memories. No, it was best to put Monique behind him. He had lived his dream, now it was time to return to his reality.

***

From the moment his Embraer Phenom 100 jet landed on the runway in Oklahoma City, Tyler was on the move. After being whisked away by a limousine to the offices of the state capital, he spent the rest of the day meeting with Hal Askew, his aides, and a few of the state legislators who supported his pipeline project.

Following a rather lengthy meeting with a verbose representative from Lawton, Tyler withdrew to a corner window on the fifth floor of the government office building and surveyed the active oil rigs that dotted the landscape about the vast state capital complex.

"You get what you needed from Stan?" a deep, but winded voice asked beside him.

Tyler studied the heavyset man with a baldhead, bright blue eyes, and pasty skin standing next to him. Sporting a custom-tailored, blue-pinstripe suit, snakeskin boots, and an array of gold rings, Hal Askew reeked of power, prestige, and a hell of a lot of Oklahoma oil money.

"He guaranteed me that he would get everything out of committee by the end of the week," Tyler informed him. "As long as we funneled some needed revenue to his district," he mentioned with an arched eyebrow.

Representative Askew patted Tyler on the shoulder. "Yeah, Stan's a real whore. Sorry about that." Hal Askew went to the window and briefly basked in the golden light from the late afternoon sun. "I told Gary we could handle everything without you having to fly up here, but I'm glad you did. Having the CEO of Propel here to argue his point means a lot to these legislators. Like anyone else, they want to look into someone's eyes and ask questions, not hear it second hand from an old politician like me."

"I want to thank you again for helping us." Tyler checked his watch, and for a second wondered what Monique was doing.

"You got plans for dinner?" Hal Askew's pushy voice derailed his thoughts.

"Thanks, but I have a ton of work to catch up on. I'll probably just eat in my hotel room."

"You're welcome to join me and Emmie for dinner at our place. My wife loves to entertain. She'll cook you a great down-home meal and talk your ear off." Hal Askew chuckled lightly, making his round belly jiggle up and down. "Lord love her. I've been married twenty-five years to the woman and at times she drives me crazy, but I wouldn't be where I am without her."

"I'm sure she has been your most ardent supporter," Tyler replied, not really interested in hearing about the representative's wife.

"You should get yourself one of those."

"One of what?" Tyler questioned, unsure of what he meant.

"A wife," the large man boomed. "Get a good woman who keeps you grounded and supports everything you do. Who knows, you might even like what you do then, because if you ask me, son, you don't like what you do now."

Tyler covered his hand over his mouth, hiding his sneer. "I, ah, had two wives, and neither one of them made what I do worthwhile. In the end, my job has stuck by me, not my wives."

"Then you married the wrong women, Tyler. A good woman marries you, not your money." He waved his hand at the window in front of them. "I see all kinds here in the capital. A lot of those great-looking trophy wives on the arms of old men, like me. But those relationships seem rather sad and empty. Sure, it's probably great for the ego, but I doubt it fulfills the soul. I learned a long time ago that it's not about going to bed with a beautiful woman, it's about waking up with a friend, because only a friend will stand by you when you're old, fat, and ugly." He patted his protruding gut. "I know my Emmie loves me for who I am, Hal Askew the son of a butcher from Tulsa. She could care less about representative Askew, and if everything turned to shit one day, she would still be standing there, right beside me. That's real love, not the pretty, fake kind a lot of men my age end up with."

"Well, I think my marriage days are behind me," Tyler confided.

Hal Askew roared with laughter and the plain white-tiled hall surrounding them resonated with his mirth. "You definitely don't have the poker face for politics." He paused as his happy blue eyes scrutinized Tyler's brooding features. "Gary told me you came here from New Orleans. Said he didn't know if he could get you to leave the woman you went to see. He made it sound like she was something pretty special."

Tyler's cheeks uncharacteristically flushed with a combination of surprise and embarrassment. "My stepfather exaggerates," he returned, playing it cool.

Hal grinned. "No, he didn't. Just watching you today in all our meetings, I could tell you were somewhere else. Seeing your reaction now, I know exactly where your mind was." He took a step back from the window. "I may be just a wily old politician, but let me give you a bit of advice. If she can bring color like that to your cheeks, then she is worth her weight in gold. The good ones make a man smile; the great ones make him blush."

Tyler pushed the toe of his black loafer against an imaginary spot on the white-tiled floor. "She is…well, things are complicated between us."

Hal Askew slapped his back, making Tyler take a slight step forward. "Son, things are gonna get a whole lot more complicated, trust me. At least if she is by your side, you'll be able to face whatever storms life blows your way." His features sobered as he looked Tyler over once more. "If you change your mind about dinner, let me know."

"I appreciate that, Hal."

"When do you leave?"

"First thing in the morning, but I'm leaving Mitch Douglass behind to tie up any loose ends." Tyler held out his hand. "I want to thank you again for all that you've done."

"No problem, Tyler." Hal shook his hand. "You keep in touch."

Hal Askew strutted away, appearing unusually light on his feet for such a heavyset man.

Tyler admired the man's exuberant stride and then checked his watch again. He needed to get to his hotel and call his secretary before he could catch up on e-mails and messages. His stomach rumbled with hunger after five cups of watered down coffee and one stale ham sandwich. A vision of sitting on the levee and eating fried shrimp po-boys with Monique snuck across his mind, making his stomach protest even louder. Determined not to let her eat away at him, Tyler filed away the thought of her tiny body and soulful gray eyes deep into some forgotten chasm of his heart.

As he jogged down the front steps of the white limestone office building adjacent to the domed capital, Tyler became preoccupied with legal matters and projects that needed his immediate attention at Propel. But as his limousine driver opened the back door for him, Tyler spied the setting sun on the horizon and was reminded of how the sunlight had glistened in her hair that day in the French Quarter.

Disgusted, he climbed into the rear of the car and slumped into the soft, black leather seat. When the limousine pulled on to the road, Tyler contemplated the decanter of bourbon set out on the small bar across from him. The burning that had tormented him in New Orleans was gone and he no longer craved the taste of alcohol on his lips. But now a different kind of need was consuming him, and he feared that there would be no cure for this addiction. What he really wanted, he could never have. He just wished he could figure out a way to stop wanting her before it tore him apart.

Cover to Covers

Chapter 22

His suite at the Colcord Hotel was smaller than he was accustomed to, but the luxurious furnishings, elegant decor, and view of the city skyline made up for the lack of space. After a quick shower to wash away the grime of the backroom deals he had made at the capital, Tyler donned his complimentary white robe, got comfortable on the king-sized bed with his iPad and cell phone, and switched the television in the black walnut cabinet before him to his favorite twenty-four hour news station. He was back in his element; staying in the best hotel Oklahoma City had to offer, and about to order a gourmet dinner from room service before spending the evening juggling his multi-million dollar company. He should have been content, but he was far from satisfied.

The room was cold, the blaring news was disturbing, and the robe on his body was itchy and smelled of bleach. Before his trip to New Orleans, he had never minded such details, now he was overwhelmed by them. He yearned for the comfort of Monique's warm home, the smell of coffee in her kitchen, the sound of her old creaking stairs; hell, he even missed Bart's hideous mug.

Wiping his face in his hands, he fought his longing to reach out to her, but eventually he realized it was pointless. Exasperated, he grabbed for his cell phone and found her number.

"Hey, you settled into your hotel yet?" Her excited voice reverberated through the phone speaker.

"Yeah, I just got in, had a shower, and was about to get to a bunch of e-mails and missed calls."

"Well, that sounds a lot more interesting than what I'm doing."

He heard an odd splashing sound in the background. "What is that noise?"

"I'm bathing Bart."

He smiled, heartened by the image. "How is the ugly beast?"

"Don't call him that. He's self-conscious about his looks."

The idea that Bart would care what anyone thought of his appearance made Tyler break out into a stint of hard belly laughing.

"It's not funny," Monique implored. "He's very sensitive."

Tyler laughed even louder. By the time he regained his composure, tears had welled up in his eyes. He could not remember when he had laughed with such exuberance, or who had ever made him feel comfortable enough to let go like that.

"Christ, I miss you," he blurted without thinking. Taken off guard by his comment, he closed his eyes and silently reprimanded his lack of self-control.

"I miss you, too. How long are you going to be in Oklahoma?"

"I leave tomorrow," he affirmed, trying to sound businesslike again. "Then I fly back to Dallas for a bunch of meetings with our engineers on a major design problem we are having with some wells."

"It never ends for you, does it?"

"No, I'm always in the middle of one crisis or another." He wanted to tell her so many things, but refrained from offering too much.

"Well, as long as you are happy, Ty."

"I'm not sure if I'm ever going to be a one of those happy people."

"Being happy is not a gift; it's an innate ability that you have to fight to hold on to. It's part of you. It's the weld that holds your soul together. Ignoring it doesn't make the yearning for it go away."

He pictured her pink lips speaking those words. "You sound like a writer."

"Yeah, I get that," she added with an adorable giggle.

Wanting desperately to talk about something else, he asked, "Any news on your new book? Has Chris changed his mind?"

"He won't change his mind. He was pretty adamant. I've notified another publisher that I am shopping around for new representation. May take a few days to hear anything, but I'm hopeful."

He heard more splashing. "So you're going to leave Donovan Books."

"Not leave, but not publish my new book with them. They still own the rights to my old books, and I can't cut them off completely."

"Does Chris know you're shopping for another publisher?" Tyler thought of his last encounter with her overzealous manager. "He won't like it, Moe."

"No, he won't, but I'm sure he'll get wind of it soon enough. It's a small business and news tends to spread quickly."

"What are you going to do when he finds out?"

She was very quiet for a moment and then admitted, "Not answer the door."

Tyler wanted to tender his concerns, but then thought better of it. "Well, I'm sure you'll figure it out."

Bart's heavy breathing began in the background. "Do you know when you'll be passing my way again?"

Tyler's mind raced with plausible excuses. "I've got a lot on my plate for the next few days." He strained to keep the emotion from his voice. "Until I get this Oklahoma business straightened out, I'll be stuck in Dallas."

Silence. The effect was devastating for him. He wanted to soften the blow by offering hope for a future meeting, but that would be delaying the inevitable. Why was he doing this? But he already knew the answer. Once Monique discovered the real Tyler Moore, she would walk away, and the thought of that sickened him.

"Yeah, things are kind of out of hand for you right now." He could hear the veil of disappointment shadowing her words. "I guess you will let me know when you can fit me in."

His restraint floundered. "Moe, I want to be with you, but...you just have to be patient."

"Patient? I think I have to be a hell of a lot more than that." She paused, and the knot in Tyler's chest twisted tighter. "I found the half-empty bottle of bourbon in the pantry this afternoon. I'm not a fool, Ty. I know you were drinking when I wasn't looking. What made you feel like you needed a drink after so many years of sobriety?"

His irritation stirred at her accusatory tone. "Moe, let's not get into this right now."

"You know, in all of those books I wrote, none of my male characters ever had your fear. I left that out, thinking it had been an exaggeration of what I remembered about you, but now I know it wasn't. You drank twenty-one years ago because you were afraid of being what everyone wanted you to be...responsible, grown-up, and productive. Now you're afraid of me, and what I could do to your well-ordered life. That's it, isn't it?"

"For God's sake, Moe. You know what I am, and I'm not going to change who I am for you."

"Well, well, I'm glad to see you're still the same selfish bastard you always were. You embraced that first opportunity to be rid of me because I wouldn't fit into your life, and I can see that history is repeating itself. Tell me, Ty, how many people are you going to push away until you find yourself completely alone?"

"I'm not pushing you away." His anger kicked in. "This is the same shit we went through before. You blamed my drinking back then for keeping us apart, but I had to be everything everybody else wanted. My mother, you—everyone was pushing me in a direction I did not want to go."

"And here you are, exactly where Barbara intended, but you're miserable and too damn afraid to walk away. Is that why you went back to the bourbon, because you know I'm right? Or is this about me, and what I want for you?"

"You are reading way too much into this. I had a few sips of bourbon, so what? I haven't had a drink since I left you."

"Is that supposed to make me feel better? Why did you drink when you were here, Ty?"

"Come on, Moe. I have a life, and I have responsibilities. I can't drop everything for you, and I knew you would want…more than I can give right now."

He waited for her to speak, and then after a brief interlude she said, "Ah, there it is. I understand, Ty."

"No, you don't."

"I have to go." She abruptly hung up.

Tyler threw his iPhone on the bed and stood up. Walking to the picture window that looked out over downtown Oklahoma City, he ran his hand over his damp hair. "Shit. I shouldn't have said those things."

Rolling his head back, he gripped his hair in his hands, feeling tempted to rip it out by the roots as punishment for hurting her. Maybe this was for the best. End it now before he got in too deep. *And what was too deep?* The thought echoed through his head. The concept of spending the rest of his life with her was so comforting that it scared him to death. Could another person fill such a gaping void in him, or was he just getting old? Tyler had heard that men got softer with age, settling for women they may not have wanted in their youth, but that was not the case with Monique. He had always wanted her; the only problem was he had never believed he deserved her. He was the one who had felt inadequate, and all the bourbon in the world was never going to help that.

"I'm such an ass. I can't blow this with her. Not again. I'll never forgive myself."

236

Stomping back to the bed, he scooped up his phone and dialed Lynn Stallmaster's cell phone.

After three rings she picked up. "Yes, Mr. Moore?"

"Lynn, cancel whatever is on my agenda tomorrow. I'm flying back to New Orleans in the morning."

"You are?" She sounded more than a little shocked. "But you had me set up those meeting with the engineers, and then legal has a ton of contracts for you to sign off on."

"Just handle it, Lynn. I've got to go back…and straighten something out."

He could almost hear her smiling on the other end of the phone. "I'm glad to see there is a woman who has finally gotten through that thick hide of yours."

"What makes you think this has to do with a woman?"

"Just let me know when you plan on returning. I'll tell everyone you have food poisoning or something."

He laughed as a measure of relief coursed through his veins. "No one will believe you."

"They'll believe me, but get back as soon as you can. I can't hold off the world forever, Mr. Moore."

He pulled at his itchy robe. "If you're going to lie for me, perhaps you should start calling me Tyler."

"And ruin a perfectly good working relationship?" she scoffed. "I'll notify Marty and make sure he is ready to fly out in the morning. Do you need anything else? A dozen roses sent on ahead, perhaps, to butter her up for you?"

"What makes you think she needs that?"

Lynn's light tinkling laugh came over the phone speaker. "If she has had to put up with your BS, she'll need roses and a hell of a lot more."

Tyler shook his head at her assertion. He hated to admit it sometimes, but Lynn knew him almost as well as Monique. Almost.

"Have a nice trip, Mr. Moore." Lynn hung up, her twittering laugh still resounding in his ears.

Tyler viewed the iPad on his bed and daydreamed of Monique sprawled out naked next to it, waiting for him. Lifting the cell phone in his hand, he dialed Lynn's number again.

"Yes, Mr. Moore?"

"You'd better make it three dozen red roses."

"Where do I send them?" Lynn's reserved voice inquired.

"To Monique Delome, 2918 Prytania Street in New Orleans."

"What do I put on the card?"

Tyler grinned. "From the selfish bastard."

Lynn chuckled. "Seems there's hope for you yet, Mr. Moore."

Cover to Covers

Chapter 23

As Tyler anxiously peered out the back passenger window, the Town Car parked in front of the raised, gray and white house on Prytania Street in New Orleans. The late morning sun was rising over the top of the surrounding homes as cars and trucks rumbled up and down the busy street. When he stepped from the rear of the car, Clark came jogging up to his side.

"It was good seein' you again, Mr. Moore," Clark added as he stopped next to Tyler, holding out his hand. "I guess this is just a short stay."

Tyler shook his hand. "I'm not sure."

"Just didn't see any bags this time, so I assumed...you want me to come back later?"

"Thanks, Clark. I'll let you know." Tyler stared at the white front door and adjusted the yellow tie on his black pinstriped suit.

"Just tell her how you feel," Clark suggested behind him.

Tyler faced the tall, lanky man. "Excuse me?"

Clark's small green eyes probed Tyler's features. "It's written all over your face, Mr. Moore. Just tell her what you're feelin'. They love that stuff."

Tyler grimaced. "I wasn't aware I was being so obvious."

Clark removed a white card from his black jacket pocket. "My cell phone number is on the card. I can come right back, just in case."

"I'll keep that in mind." Tyler slipped the card into his pant's pocket.

After leaving Clark at the curb, Tyler rushed down the red-bricked walkway to Monique's front door. Before he had even arrived at the porch steps, the door opened. But it was not Monique standing in the entrance; it was Chris Donovan.

Casually dressed in blue jeans and a wrinkled button-down light blue shirt, Chris appeared slightly disheveled, as if he had just gotten out of bed.

"What are you doing here, Tyler?" Chris quickly glanced back into the house.

Tyler raced up the steps. "Why are you here?"

Chris stepped outside, quietly shutting the front door. "Get out of here. She doesn't want to see you. And don't send anymore damned roses. She dumped them all in the trash."

Tyler waved his hand down Chris's outfit. "What's going on?"

Chris folded his long arms over his chest. "She called me last night, very upset. She never said what was wrong, but I knew you had something to do with it. I caught the first flight out of Atlanta and came right over."

Tyler edged closer to him. "She doesn't need you, Chris. I'm here."

"She doesn't want you, Tyler. She's already made that very clear."

"Did Moe tell you that?"

Chris rocked back and forth on his bare feet. "She didn't have to. Last night we settled a lot of things between us."

Tyler cocked back his right arm about to punch Chris in the face when the front door opened.

"Chris, did you get the paper?" Monique froze when she saw Tyler on her doorstep. "What in the hell are you doing here?" she shouted.

Tyler spied her blue robe, mussed hair, and sleepy gray eyes. Instantly, he realized what was going on. "I'm gone for one day and you've already jumped into bed with him!"

She rushed toward him. "You self-centered, cold-blooded bastard. Where do you get off saying something like that to me?"

Tyler pointed to Chris, who was still wearing his smug grin. "You slept with him, admit it."

Chris came up next to her. "Do you want me to defend your honor?"

"Shut up," she howled at him.

"Hey." Chris held his hands up. "I think he needs to know the truth about us, Monique."

"So you did sleep with him," Tyler alleged. "Christ, Moe. Why? Was it to get back at me?"

"Is that what you think?" When she faced Tyler, her eyes were brimming with tears. "You think I slept with him because I wanted to get even with you?" She wiped her hand over her cheek just as a single tear tumbled down. "Is that the kind of person you think I am?"

"I don't know! Are you?" Tyler hollered.

The revulsion that registered in her face made Tyler want to turn away, but he kept his eyes focused on her, hoping to discover that his suspicions were not true.

"Go home, Tyler." Her voice was flat and emotionless. "You were right. I am better off without you."

Retreating into the house, she slammed the front door closed.

Chris's blue eyes shined with satisfaction. "I told you to leave. Now you've heard it from her." Snatching up the newspaper from the edge of the porch, he pointed to the black Town Car still waiting by the curb. "Don't come back, Tyler. The better man has won her."

Giving Tyler one last haughty sneer, Chris stepped inside and then slowly shut the front door.

Tyler stood gawking at the bright brass handle on the door, debating if he should force his way in and confront Monique and Chris. All the possible outcomes roared through his head like a runaway train, but in the end, Tyler did nothing. After barreling down the steps, he tore through the black iron gate at the end of the red-bricked path just as Clark opened the rear passenger door.

"Where to, Mr. Moore?"

Tyler was relieved the young man did not ask any questions. "Back to Lakefront Airport, Clark," he instructed before disappearing into the car.

Traveling down Prytania Street, Tyler felt that rock in his gut sink to the depths of his being, awakening him to a sad reality. Monique had in a very short time become embedded in his heart. Tyler thought he had been impervious, or at least hoped he had been able to keep her at a distance, but he had failed. Just like the first time, he was again thrown into a tailspin by the certainty of her never returning. But what hurt more this time around was how easily he had been replaced.

"Everythin' okay, Mr. Moore?" Clark worriedly asked as the car glided up the on ramp to the interstate.

"Fine." Tyler's heart hardened against the image of Monique's face. "Everything is just fine, Clark. Thank you for waiting back there."

"No problem, sir." Clark's eyes stayed on the road ahead. "When the other guy came out, I figured I would stay, just in case you needed a witness."

"I appreciate that."

Tyler reached in his jacket for his cell phone. He hit a number on his call list and waited.

"Marty," he snapped into the phone. "Prep the plane to return to Dallas. We'll need to get underway as soon as possible." He did not even wait for Marty to reply before hanging up.

After returning his phone to his jacket pocket, Tyler stared out the window at the high rises crowded along the side of the interstate. When the car passed the Mercedes-Benz Superdome, he wondered what in the hell people found so appealing about this city. As far as Tyler was concerned, he never wanted to set foot in New Orleans again.

"How much longer until we reach the airport?" Tyler sharply demanded.

"About ten minutes, Mr. Moore."

"Good." Tyler settled into his seat. "I need to get back to work."

Cover to Covers

Chapter 24

Tyler was standing before his wide office window, gazing out over the Dallas skyline. With his hands behind his back, he pondered the late afternoon sun glistening against the glass and steel structures. A bank of dark clouds was rolling in from the west ahead of a cool front. Fall was on the way, but he did not really care about the change in seasons. Time had been a blur for him over the past several weeks. The heat of summer had receded and soon the cold weather would take over the city. But aside from the change in temperature, Tyler noticed very little in the world. Every day was the same. He rose from bed, went to work, and stayed in his office late every evening, seeing to the plethora of paperwork that never seemed to end.

"You keep standing in front of that window like you're contemplating jumping out of it," his trusty secretary commented behind him.

Wearing a colorful peach dress with white piping, she looked every inch the part of an executive secretary. As she carried an armload of manila folders to his desk, he resumed his seat in his chair.

"I was watching the clouds roll in from that cool front. Hard to believe it's already October." He made himself comfortable and eased his chair against the desk.

She plopped the folders in front of him. "Accounting wants your approval for these budgets on the Oklahoma pipeline construction."

He took one of the manila folders and opened it. "Is there anything in here that can delay us further?"

246

"No. Now that all the permits are in hand, Mitch Douglass is antsy to get moving. These are the final numbers on all the costs. They are going to get started as soon as they have your signature."

Tyler gleaned the spreadsheet in front of him. "I'll get through them all tonight, so he can have them first thing in the morning."

"What about your mother? I thought you were going with her to Senator Adleman's cocktail party tonight?"

Tyler unbuttoned his dark brown suit jacket. "No, I need to get this done."

Lynn stood back from his desk. "Are you going to tell her or…." She winced slightly.

"Just say something came up." He removed the jacket from his shoulders.

"She won't believe me. She hates me."

Tyler felt that sharp stab in his heart as her words unlocked a memory. "Just tell her to call me if she has a problem." He tossed his jacket to a nearby chair.

Lynn hovered over his desk. "That's the seventeenth invitation you've declined in the past three months."

His dark eyes rose to her. "You're keeping track?"

"You bet. You've backed out of every party, dinner invitation, social event, benefit, and anything else that was not related to business." Her lovely green eyes weighed his features. "You've spent every night here for weeks," she motioned around the office, "doing paperwork."

He knew where this was going and redirected his eyes back to the spreadsheet. "That's because there has been a lot of paperwork to do. You know how I hate social functions."

"You never hated them before. Tolerated them, but never hated them." She paused and then added, "You're sulking."

His eyes shot to her face. "Sulking? What am I sulking about?"

"You know as well as I do, you haven't been the same since you came back from…you know where."

247

He cast his eyes to the paperwork. "I told you never to mention that to me again."

"I didn't mention it. I said you know where, not New Orleans."

He slammed his fist on the desk. "Damn it! I will not—"

"And you were never testy before, either," she cut in. "You've been spitting like a rattlesnake caught in a stampede. You jump all over anyone who tells you something you don't want to hear."

"You're exaggerating, Lynn."

"Three weeks ago you yelled at Lisa Bailey in Risk Management when she was late with her quarterly reports. You even threatened to fire her."

"I yelled because she is always late with her reports and I'm sick of it."

Lynn sashayed to the office doors. "Lisa has been late with her reports every quarter for three years. You never threatened her before."

"Maybe I should threaten to fire you," he barked, knowing she was right.

Grabbing the brass handles on the black leather-covered doors, Lynn turned to him. "You can't fire me. I know all of your dark secrets, and I would write a tell-all book about you."

Tyler cracked a smile. "You would write a book about me?"

"I wouldn't write it. I'd probably hire a writer to do it for me." She grinned. "Know any?" She quietly shut the doors.

Rolling his head back against his chair, Tyler could feel the tension rising in his chest. He let out a long breath and once again focused on the papers scattered about his desk. Wanting to fill his head with numbers and budget problems, he lost himself in his paperwork, thankful for a brief reprieve from his bittersweet recollections.

***

Darkness had fallen over the Dallas skyline as Tyler sat at his desk, poring over figures from the pipeline project in

Oklahoma. He had removed his tie and unfastened the top buttons on his shirt after Lynn had left for the day. The carton of chicken fried rice delivered from Yen's Chinese Restaurant sat off to the side of his desk as he rubbed his tired eyes.

Standing from his desk chair, he stretched out his back in desperate need of a break from the monotony of crunching numbers. He swung around to his picture window and was drawn to the twinkling stars in the night sky.

"I thought I'd find you here," a throaty voice said from the open entrance to his office.

Tyler closed his eyes, dreading the notion of confronting the owner of that distinctive voice. "Hello, Mother." Slowly, he faced her.

Flaunting a stunning light blue silk dress that showed off her sleek figure and long legs, the attractive blonde in his office doorway still had the creamy smooth skin and full curves of a forty-year-old, despite having just passed seventy. Her shoulder-length hair was coiffed around her angular features, accentuating the toned skin of her freshly lifted face. But despite the marvelous efforts of her plastic surgeon to transform her appearance, her dark brown eyes were still just as hard and soulless as Tyler remembered from his youth.

"My own son stands me up for a party," she fussed as her stiletto heels carried her across the fine, beige European rug she had insisted on when she redecorated his office several years back. "You have a real talent for pissing me off, Tyler Dane."

Rolling his eyes at his mother's use of his first and middle name—unnerving for any child—he sat back down in his chair, feeling the tension return to every molecule of his being.

"What are you doing here?" He peeked at his gold watch. "I thought you'd still be at Senator Adleman's cocktail party."

She came up to his desk, eyeing the carton of fried rice. "Why would I do that? The only reason I accepted the invitation and came all the way to Dallas was because you said you would go with me. You know how I hate going to parties alone." She motioned to the carton. "Must you eat such trash?

You need a wife to cook for you." Her hand waved over the scattering of papers on his desk. "Someone to get you away from all of this."

He ran his hand behind his neck, working out a kink. "I don't remember Gary ever getting home before eight every night when he ran the business."

She swiveled her disconcerting eyes to him. "Perhaps, but he still had me to come home to. Who do you have?"

Impatiently, he crossed his arms over his chest. "You didn't have your driver come all the way downtown at this time of night to chastise me for not taking you to a cocktail party, Mother."

She adjusted a diamond tennis bracelet on her slender wrist. "Guess who was at the party?"

He took in a fortifying breath. *Here it comes*, he mused.

"Hadley was on the arm of Beau Gaste...you remember Beau. You went to UT in Austin with him before you dropped out."

"And what did Hadley say? That's why you're here, right? To report on Hadley's bad behavior." He pushed away from the desk. "We're divorced, and I really don't care what she says or who she is seen with."

"You might care about this." Barbara approached the side of his desk. "She was going on and on about you and that New Orleans girl."

"I really wish you would stop calling her that."

Barbara flung the silver-beaded clutch in her hand on his desk. "Hadley seemed to think it was pretty serious between you two. She was telling everyone about how you were fawning all over the woman when she was in Dallas last summer."

Tyler turned back to his desk. "I wasn't fawning. We were catching up. Hadley was being nosy, as usual."

"I never did understand your infatuation with that woman. I know she is a big author now, and I can see her being of some use to you, but honestly, Tyler, she was never the most socially acceptable creature."

His temper seething, he snapped up his pen. "She wasn't like all the other social deviants you tried to set me up with. Moe was original and spoke her mind."

"Is that what you wanted?" She gave a nonchalant shrug. "I always got the impression women were more or less a hobby with you. None of them ever held your interest for very long."

"No they didn't, but Moe was different."

Barbara paused, analyzing the lines of his face. "So what happened when you went to New Orleans?"

"Nothing happened." He slammed his pen down on the desk. "We spent some time together and then I had to go to Oklahoma."

"I always could tell when you were lying to me, you know that?" She leaned over his desk, her emerald and diamond necklace scintillating in the overhead lights. "You were the easy one to figure out. Your brother was the one who always…." She waved a dismissive hand in the air.

"Why is that, Mother? Why did you make Peter your problem child and me your angel? He knew how you felt and resented the hell out of it."

She stood back from his desk, her dark eyes resonating with the blow he had landed. "I never did any such thing. Peter was my first born, my baby, until he started hanging with the wrong crowd, coming home at all hours, and then when the police began showing up, I knew he was lost to me."

"You gave up too easily. You washed your hands of him way before he left us."

"I had to protect you." She pointed her finger at him. "You were all I had left, and I had to make sure he didn't turn you into the drug fiend he was becoming."

Tyler leapt from his chair. "Peter was never into drugs!"

She squared her shoulders against his furor. "Your brother was a drug dealer and a criminal."

"What are you talking about? Peter was a great guy."

"Oh, come on, Tyler. You never knew your brother." Her voice grew louder. "You were just a child when he left and you only saw what you wanted to see with him. I could never let you know what was really going on. When he was arrested—"

"Peter was never arrested," Tyler angrily broke in.

Barbara's chilly demeanor fizzled. "I was never going to tell you." She turned away from his desk. "Peter was arrested about three years after he left us. I didn't want to say anything because you worshipped the ground he walked on, and I could not stand for you to be hurt by him anymore."

Tyler came around the desk to her side. "When did this happen?"

"I got a phone call from a prison in Arizona, right after you left for UT in Austin. He was busted for dealing heroin and cocaine."

Tyler's hand went through his thick hair. "You should have told me."

Barbara's smirk cut through his heart. "Why? It wouldn't have done you or your brother any good. Besides, I was married to Gary then and I could not afford the scandal of having a drug dealer for a son, so I kept my mouth shut. I never even told Gary."

"Christ, he was your son, not some nameless criminal." He paused and stared into her icy eyes. "What happened to him?"

She shook her head. "What difference does it make?"

He stood before her. "It matters to me, Mother. Peter has always mattered to me. I need to know where he is."

"Why? So you can have a family reunion? Catch up on old times? He was no good, Tyler. Just like his father. I could never let him influence you. I had to protect you, make sure you never became like him. So, I cut him off."

"That wasn't for you to decide!" Tyler bellowed, throwing his hands in the air.

"Of course it was. You were all I had left and you had a golden opportunity with Gary. I could never allow Peter to screw that up for you."

252

Tyler's fury burned his cheeks as he stared at the woman who bore him with all the loathing he had ever possessed. "Where is he?" he hissed.

Barbara removed her purse from his desk. "Dead," she casually replied. "About ten years ago there was a fight in the prison where he was being held. He was stabbed and died two days later. They buried him there." She waved her purse in the air. "Some place outside of Little Rock, Arkansas."

Pain ripped through his chest and for a moment it was impossible for him to breathe. When he regained his composure, Tyler screamed, "You heartless bitch! He's dead and you never told me."

"Don't you dare speak to me like that." Her voice trembled with rage. "Do you know what I have done for you? The shit I have had to endure so you could make it? I married a man I...you'd better be thankful I've done all that I have for you, Tyler. I've given up everything to secure your happiness."

Flabbergasted, Tyler backed away from her, shaking his head. "My happiness? You married a man you hate for me, is that it? You wrote off your son so I could achieve what? Glory, riches—"

"Success," she hollered. "So you could be successful and not make me look like the failure of a mother I always felt I was. So what if I married a man I never loved? He treats me well, keeps a roof over my head, and has given me everything I ever wanted. I could live with that as long as I knew you were set for life."

"I can't believe this." He pressed his hands against his head. "All this time I have been killing myself for you. I gave up my happiness so you could be proud of me. I've been trying to make it up to you for years because of Peter; only to find out you never gave a damn about him. How could you be so cold? I thought you were trying to protect yourself by saying Peter was dead, but I think you are actually thankful that he is dead."

She glowered at him, accentuating the lines around her small mouth. "You ungrateful bastard."

253

"That's right, I'm ungrateful." He went back to his desk. "You'd better leave before you tell me how you really feel."

"What is that supposed to mean? How I really feel?"

He stood behind his desk, placed his hands on the back of his chair, and gaped at her. "None of this was ever about me. It was about you. It's always been about you. If you wanted me to be happy, you would never have pushed me into this life, and away from…." He motioned to the open office doors. "Get out before I say something I'm going to regret."

She slapped her hand on his desk. "Don't you dare stand there and judge me. I did everything to make sure you ended up here."

"Yes, you did. I'm exactly where you wanted me to be, but am I where I want to be?" He turned away to the window. "Get out, Mother."

He listened as her heels thudded across his office to the open doors. After silence once again filled the room, Tyler closed his eyes against the grief in his heart.

"All these years, I thought…Jesus, Peter."

When he faced his desk, the clutter of paperwork suddenly sickened him. His office appeared different, as if it were not his anymore. The walls were closing in around him, and he felt as if he were a caged animal, frightened and confused. He had to get away.

Leaving the folders on his desk, he wrestled his jacket from a nearby chair and headed for the central elevators.

As the elevator car descended to the lobby, Tyler replayed the conversation with his mother and then sorted through all the life choices he had made because of the vain and self-centered demands of Barbara.

He knocked his head back against the elevator wall behind him. "What an idiot I have been."

Suddenly faced with a symphony of "what ifs," Tyler was besieged by his emotions. Suppressed feelings for his brother, his mother, and for Monique all came bubbling to the surface. Grabbing for the silver railing that encircled the walls of the elevator, Tyler took in several deep breaths, but it did little good.

Running from the elevator car when it hit the lobby floor, he bounded out of the building and to his car in the VIP lot. Once on the expressway heading to his home in North Dallas, he considered all the things he would have done differently in his life had he known about Peter. No matter where his thoughts strayed, all his second-guessing eventually led him back to Monique. So many things might have been different for them.

Tightly gripping his burl walnut and leather steering wheel, he cursed his mother. Then, the burning started again in his gut…the same sensation he always felt when his emotions were getting the better of him. Hitting the accelerator, he skirted along the outer lane of the expressway, eager for home.

Chapter 25

Tyler slammed the door to his four-car garage and then stood at the entrance to his gourmet kitchen, listening to the hum of the amber-colored appliances and the rapid beating of his heart. His hands were shaking as he threw his car keys on the cream and amber granite countertop. Gazing around the wide kitchen Hadley had insisted on redoing when she moved in, he went to the custom made white oak kitchen cabinet and pulled out an iced tea glass. After reaching for the carton of orange juice from the built-in refrigerator, with shelves wide enough for party platters— another of Hadley's requirements— he poured the cold juice into the tall glass. Smashing the carton down on the countertop, he struggled with that burgeoning desire to add something more substantial to his drink. But he had long ago emptied the house of any alcohol, refusing to have such a temptation under his roof. Even when Hadley and Tessa had lived with him, he had insisted there be no alcohol kept in his home. Tyler remembered how pissed Hadley had been not being able to have ready access to her favorite scotch, but she had abided by his wishes.

"That bitch never wanted to make me happy." He snatched up his glass. *But you know who did want to make you happy, don't you, Tyler? And you pushed her away.*

Memories of Monique made his need for a shot of something more satisfying all the more acute. Squeezing his hand around the glass, he waited until the insistence of his insides diminished. After releasing a long, disappointing sigh, he put his drink on the countertop and let his shoulders fall forward.

Unlike the other women in his life, Monique had never asked anything of him, except to be sober. Encouraging him to shoot for the moon, she had never tempered his desires, never wanted him to be something he was not, and had never kept secrets from him. His mother, on the other hand, had kept his brother's life from him to further her ambitions. His exes had been with him either for monetary or social achievement, but were never interested in his hopes or concerns. Of all the women he had known, the only one he felt who had truly cared for him had been Monique. Or so he thought.

For months he had been reliving that gut-wrenching confrontation with her and Chris, trying to make sense of the entire affair, but with little success. He knew he should put her behind him, but he was having a hard time letting her go. And that, more than Monique's betrayal, bothered him. Where was the cold man he used to be? For the first time since running into her at the Ritz-Carlton Hotel, he missed his old self, and his former wicked ways.

As he stood there, contemplating the indelible facets of his soul, he wondered if he could have ever had a life with Monique. She had gotten close to him, but could she have torn down the walls he had set up around his heart ever since his brother had left? Ah, but that was the true crux of his problem. No one had ever meant more to him than Peter, and since he had walked away Tyler had never let anyone wield that kind of control over him again. But now he knew the truth about his brother, and his perspective had changed.

Tyler had always blamed his mother for his brother's hasty departure, but he suddenly realized that Peter had left because he had been selfish. Instead of sharing the burdens of their unhappy home life, Peter had deserted him, and never once given any regard to his little brother's feelings. Why had he not seen that before?

Tyler pushed away from the counter, heading to the white door that led to the den. Walking through the dark-paneled room with its massive stone hearth, thick-beamed ceiling, and Texas themed décor, he made his way down a hall that lead to the master bedroom suite.

Tossing his jacket on the rustic king-sized bed with the thick wooden beamed canopy that Hadley had designed, Tyler went to the bathroom and flipped on the doublewide, Mexican-tiled, walk-in shower he had insisted on when Hadley renovated the bathroom.

Quickly stripping down, he stepped beneath the multiple jets that sprayed into the center of the shower and let the hot water soothe the tension in his back and shoulders. While stretching out his aching muscles, Tyler decided he was tired of feeling like crap. He was fed up with the constant knot in his chest, the continuous acidic aftertaste in his mouth, and feeling as if he were carrying the weight of the world on his shoulders. For so long he had been bearing the burdens of living up to everyone else's expectations, that he had forgotten his wants and desires. He needed a change; something to help put his brother, mother, and Monique behind him. Considering his options for a new start, Tyler became enthused with the prospect of living as he had always wanted. Never before had he entertained the concept of chasing dreams and not women. He had spent enough years putting his plans aside…now it was time to shake the dust free of his aspirations and start pursuing them.

"The first thing I am going to do is take over Propel," he declared, bolstering his confidence as the water beat down on him. "It's time to make that company mine."

As he turned off the water, a smattering of energy returned to his body. Perhaps a new direction for his company was exactly what he needed to put his life in order. If he could no longer drive the regrets of his past from his heart with alcohol, then he could surely do it with lots of hard work.

***

The next morning, Tyler was at his office before his devoted secretary, Lynn. Determined to implement changes he had always envisioned for the company, but had been apprehensive to start because of Gary's objections, Tyler was sitting at his desk working on a new business plan for his alternative energy division when Lynn walked into his office.

"I can't believe you're in before me." She stopped before his desk and placed her hands on her round hips. "Is something wrong?"

He spied her sleek gray pantsuit and light yellow top. "Nothing is wrong. I just decided I'm going to start that alternative energy division I've been talking about."

"But I thought Mr. Leesburg was dead set against it."

Tyler bristled at the mention of his stepfather. "Yeah, well, I run Propel now, and if Gary doesn't like it, he can give up his retirement and come back."

Lynn gave a curt nod of her head. "'Bout time."

"What is that supposed to mean?"

"Mr. Moore, you've been here for ten years and never once have you made this business yours. In my opinion, a company should be a reflection of the person who runs it. But Propel has always been Gary Leesburg's and never completely yours."

Tyler bobbed his head in understanding. "Well, that's about to change."

"Anything I can do to help?" she offered, sounding enthused.

He sat back in his leather chair. "Just be ready for a fight. If Gary goes against me on this, we may have to do some fast talking to the board to keep our jobs."

Lynn took a step closer to his desk. "I'm ready. Are you?"

"If I can't run this company the way I want, then I won't run it at all." Looking over his carved Napoleon desk, he added, "I'm through with letting other people run my life."

Lynn raised her dark eyebrows. "Are we still talking about Gary Leesburg, or is there someone else you are referring to?"

259

"I have no idea what you are talking about." He handed her some papers. "I need these typed up."

Lynn took the papers from him. "I'm not a fool, Mr. Moore. I know you haven't stopped thinking about her. I'm just wondering is this change for her or for you?"

He waved off her question. "She is in the past. I am moving on with my life."

"Moving on?" Lynn snickered. "I don't see it that way." She turned for his office doors.

Her comment ate at him. "And how do you see it, Lynn?" he finally asked.

She stopped at the doors. "I've never known you to give up on what you want. And despite what you portray, you still want her."

He pictured Monique and Chris together on her porch. "She doesn't want me. She made that very clear."

"Did she?" Then Lynn quietly closed his office doors.

***

By the end of the day, Tyler had spent hours on the phone with the accounting and legal departments, lining up contracts and setting up accounts for his new alternative energy division. It was well after six, and he was still at his desk seeing to the other paperwork that he had not gotten to earlier that day. He was taking a break and admiring the night cloaking the skyline of Dallas when his cell phone on his desk began ringing. Tyler smirked when he saw his stepfather's name flashing over the phone display.

"Gary," he said, taking the call. "What can I do for you?"

"What's this horseshit I hear about you forming an alternative energy division in my company?"

Tyler was not surprised that his stepfather had heard the news so quickly. It only confirmed his suspicions that many in his organization were still loyal to Gary.

"I'm branching out. With all the federal money that will be pouring into—"

"We do oil and gas, Tyler. Nothing more," Gary loudly interposed. "You're going to break our backs stuffing money into a market that will never fly."

"It will fly, Gary. I've done a lot of research into this and I feel we need to prepare. If we stay in just oil and gas, we may lose out on some great opportunities."

"When I left you my company to run, I told you not to change anything. It makes us money. Now you're growing balls and wanting to change what works for us?"

Tyler was unfazed by his stepfather's comment. "It's my company now, Gary. Has been for ten years, and I have run it just like you wanted, but it is time for a change."

"No changes!" Gary coughed. "I still have a vested interest and I'll demand the board of directors cut you off at the knees. I still own the majority shares and I can have you removed as CEO."

"Gary, do you want me to run this company or do you want to run it, because if you don't let me do what I think best, you might as well come back and take over."

"Maybe I should come back. You obviously can't be trusted to—"

"Fine," Tyler interrupted. "I'll leave tonight. You can fly up from Austin in the morning and take over first thing."

"Now hold on, Tyler." Gary's voice rose over the cell phone speaker. "I don't want you to leave; I just want you to do as I would have done." He took in a wheezy breath. "I know you mean well, but that market is too unsteady and untested to gamble on."

Tyler took a strategic pause, letting Gary stew for a moment. "What if I sent you some research to prove my point? I've got a guy at UT in Austin in the alternative energy research program with some exciting numbers, and a few projects that are certain to take off. All we need to do is set him up with us to develop this. Long-term, this could make us a fortune."

Gary was quiet for several seconds, making Tyler grin. He had gotten his stepfather's attention.

261

"All right, send me what you have and I will take a look at it. But if I am not impressed, you'd better be ready to pull the plug."

"Gary, with oil getting harder to drill and the lease prices going up in the Gulf, it would behoove us to find another energy prospect. I know Shell and BP created such divisions years ago. We need to keep up and fend off possible future downturns."

"Perhaps you have something there. Send me everything you've got."

Tyler felt a rush of victory in his veins. "If you don't mind my asking, how did you find out about my plans for an alternative energy division?"

"I've still got a few friends in place there. They keep me updated."

Tyler viewed the flashing lights from atop the skyscrapers outside his office window. "I can't truly be in charge until your old cronies start listening to me and not you, Gary. You gave me this company to run, so perhaps you should let me run it and stop being a backseat driver."

A low whistle echoed through the phone. "This is a side of you I've never heard before. You mind telling me what's going on? A week ago you were fine with the way things were, now you want to change everything."

"I just want what is best for Propel. If we are going to stay competitive, we need to explore the changing energy markets."

Gary chuckled, a low rumbling noise that had always reminded Tyler of cattle mooing in the field. "That's a nice line to use at board meetings, son, but it don't mean shit to me. I figure you're out to prove something to someone, am I right?"

Tyler leaned back in his chair, shaking his head. "I'm not proving anything—"

"This is about that New Orleans girl, isn't it?" Gary coughed again. "Your mother told me you would do something stupid when you found out. But an alternative energy division? I never saw that coming."

Tyler paused as a trickle of dread rose up his throat. "What are you talking about, Gary?"

"That writer you went to see in New Orleans...the one I couldn't get you to leave during that Oklahoma mess. Your mother heard from her friends at the club that she got engaged to some guy. They said it was all over the Internet. Barbara predicted you would pull some foolish stunt when you found out." Gary paused to take a breath. "Boy, was she right."

Tyler sat up in his chair. "I have to go, Gary." He hung up his cell phone as he turned to his laptop computer on the corner of his desk. Hitting the keyboard, he waited as the Google page came up. Typing Monique's name into the search engine, he pressed enter and scanned the results.

It did not take long to find her fan website with the announcement that she and Chris Donovan were getting married at the end of the year. Tyler stared at the screen for several minutes, wondering if somehow it had been a mistake. But as he absorbed the truth, he became sick with disbelief. Monique had turned to Chris for comfort and Tyler was positive her pit bull of a manger had taken advantage of the situation. But how could she have swept aside her feelings for Tyler and planned on marrying another? Had he been so wrong about her? Perhaps she had not really cared for him at all.

Overwhelmed by his rage, Tyler threw the cell phone in his hand across the room. After watching the phone bounce off the far wall and crash to the ground, he slammed his fist into the desk. The pain that shot up his arm felt good. Damn good.

"If that's what she wants, then she never truly wanted me," he thundered.

Grabbing his suit jacket from the chair behind his desk, he spotted the cell phone on the floor. He stopped, wondering about the calls he would miss without it.

"Screw it!"

Tyler marched out of his office, determined to put Monique and the past behind him. He had to believe that she was just another in a long line of women he would eventually forget. In the end, she had turned out to be just like all the others.

Heading down the hallway toward the entrance, he reasoned he was better off without Monique Delome and her silly romance novels. All he needed was another woman and he could put her out of his mind for good. Or at least he hoped he could.

Tyler stepped up to the silver elevator doors in the reception area just about convinced that he was over Monique. As the elevator doors opened, his heart grew colder. It was best not to feel anything for anyone, that way he could be spared the eventual blow of disappointment. Peter had taught him that, and now Monique Delome had only reinforced that belief.

When the silver elevator doors closed before him, Tyler felt that surge of confidence awaken in his bones. The old Tyler Moore was back, and the emotions Monique had brought to the surface were quickly drowning behind his cool disregard. He was ready to get back to the business of being a grade "A" bastard. It was time to not give a damn about anyone anymore.

Cover to Covers

Chapter 26

A cold December breeze was whipping around Tyler's head as he emerged from the back of the black limousine. He pulled at the lapel of his fitted black Armani tuxedo and then took the sleek white hand that was outstretched to him.

A very young, leggy brunette with brown, bedroom eyes rose from the car. "You look sexy in that," she cooed, admiring his tuxedo.

"Only you would accept an invitation to one of these stuffy fundraisers." Tyler slipped his arm about the waist of her barely there, beaded black dress.

The off-the-shoulder number was fitted about her slender body and cut in an uneven hem about her mid-thigh, accentuating the long, luscious curve of her legs. Tyler's eyes roamed the woman's figure while he thought ahead to festivities he had planned for her later that evening.

"You keep staring at me like that," the attractive brunette purred, "and we might not make it to the party."

Tyler looked up at the grand entrance to the Dallas mansion in front of them. The ten-foot high double oak doors had bold Texas stars carved into them, with large brass knockers shaped like cowboy boots in the center of the stars.

"Not to worry, Giselle. We'll say our hellos and get back to my place as soon as politely possible."

Giselle placed her red-painted lips next to his ear. "Just don't tie my hands so tight this time. They had to put make up on my wrists at my last photo shoot because of your little games."

He patted her small butt. "I promise this time, no bruises."

The double doors suddenly opened before them and a matronly woman, wearing a shiny silver dress that resembled something better suited for outer space, let out an ear-piercing cackle.

"There he is," she called from the doorway. "I almost thought you were going to stand me up, Tyler Moore."

Tyler's lips spread into a flirtatious grin. "Now would I ever do that to you, Lynnette? You are the best hostess this side of Fort Worth."

Another boisterous cackle shattered Tyler's eardrums. "This side of the Mississippi is more like it," Lynette admonished. She motioned to Giselle on Tyler's arm. "My word, you look wonderful, Giselle, and congrats on making the cover of Cosmo. You were fab, girl."

Tyler could not help but notice how Giselle beamed at the mention of her celebrated cover photo.

Lynette waved them up the front steps. "Well, get your gorgeous butts in here and come and meet the victims I lined up for this shindig."

Tyler escorted Giselle to the wide steps that were surrounded on either side by lush gardens.

"Who are we supporting this month, Lynette?" Tyler inquired as he came to a stop before his hostess.

Lynette waved a plump hand covered with diamonds at him. "Some art council from New Orleans looking for money to rebuild the music programs in their public schools."

Tyler halted at the doors. "New Orleans?"

Lynette came up to his side. "Yeah, Mike Guidry talked me into it. He knows quite a few of the musicians that are here tonight. Most are still living in Dallas since Katrina."

"Are only musicians coming to this thing?" he cautiously questioned.

Lynette directed her saggy brown eyes to him. "Yeah, why?"

He shrugged, trying to appear uninterested. "No particular reason."

"I love New Orleans," Giselle imparted. "I spent a weekend there so drunk I can't remember it."

Lynette let out a short snort. "Didn't we all." She motioned for them to move ahead into the house as her gaze swept over the model's figure. "Why don't you two check out the buffet?"

Tyler dipped his head to their hostess. "Thanks, Lynette."

As they made their way through an outlandish entryway with delicately painted tiles of flowers set into a marble floor and a fountain shaped like a steer built into a sidewall, Giselle turned to Tyler.

"Let's find the bar."

The entryway opened into a huge living room with twenty-foot ceilings made of rustic wooden beams anchored into white plaster. Two oversized fireplaces built out of stone sat on opposite ends of the room, while a carved wooden bar occupied the corner. An old-fashioned jukebox to the side of the bar filled the room with golden oldies from the seventies and eighties.

Giselle's eyes devoured the thick, plush white furniture, long paintings of red sunsets covering the walls, and assorted brass chandeliers hanging from the ceiling. "I want a place like this someday."

"Work hard and you'll get it," Tyler assured her.

She rubbed up against him. "Maybe there is another way to get what I want."

Tyler was all too familiar with that lusty look for his wealth and when he saw it in a woman, it was time to cut his ties. He made a mental note to get everything he wanted from the attractive Giselle, but once morning arrived, he was going to send her on her way and never see her again. She had served her usefulness, and Tyler was ready to move on.

"I was thinking that perhaps we should set up some kind of living arrangement," Giselle coyly hinted.

Tyler's eyes darted about the room. "Living arrangement?"

"With me going back and forth to New York, and you working here with Propel, it's always so hard to coordinate our schedules. Perhaps if we shared a place, we could spend more time together."

Yes, it's definitely time to move on, Tyler thought.

He nodded to the bar. "Let's get a drink and discuss it later, at my place."

Tyler quickly turned his attention to some of the other guests milling about. They were slowly making their way to the bar as Tyler identified several familiar faces amid the crowded room. He nodded to his divorce attorney, Fred Bishop, and made a mental note to stop and say hello when a petite woman with dirty-blonde hair stepped out from behind Fred.

Tyler's heart pounded and then he stopped short. She was wearing a deep burgundy dress that gathered at the waist on one side and dipped suggestively at the neck. Her hair was swept up in a fancy twist, and a simple pearl necklace hung about her slender neck.

"What is it?" Giselle implored beside him.

Tyler waited as the woman turned. When she faced him, his eyes traveled over her pale white skin, pink lips, and deep gray eyes.

Giselle seized his arm. "Tyler?"

Monique observed Tyler from across the room but her countenance remained cool and impassive. A man's hand protectively rested on Monique's arm, and when Chris Donovan appeared from behind a heavyset woman next to Monique, Tyler's wrath took over.

He choked down every impulse he had to run to her side. He tried to soothe his ire by reasoning that she had made her choice, but something in him could not accept that Chris Donovan was the man she really wanted.

"Isn't that the writer, Monique Delome?" Giselle girlishly giggled and pointed at Monique. "I just love her books."

Unable to stand it any longer, Tyler turned to Giselle. "Stay here," he ordered, and then shot across the room.

When Monique saw him coming, she scrambled for the closest exit. But Tyler was faster and more agile on his feet, and before she could get to a glass sliding door that led to the pool area outside, Tyler grasped her arm.

"Let me go," she all but shouted.

"I want to talk to you."

"Tyler, leave her alone," Chris barked, rushing up to her.

Voices could be heard going quiet around them and Monique took in the curious looks from a few of the other guests. She shook off Tyler's grip and whispered, "Not here."

Chris stepped in front of her. "You don't have to speak to him."

She placed her hand on the sleeve of Chris's black tuxedo jacket. "Just give me five minutes. We have...things to discuss."

Chris did not budge. "You don't have to tell him anything, you know that."

"Yes, I do, Chris. You know I do."

Tyler took in the entire conversation with a heady dose of discomfort. He did not like Chris Donovan hovering over her like she was some helpless woman. Monique was stronger than that, but the way she was acting was unnerving for Tyler. It was almost as if the fire he had once cherished in her had dimmed.

Chris shifted his blue eyes to Tyler. "Don't upset her."

"Chris, please." Monique pushed him out of the way of the glass door.

"All right, Monique." Chris opened the sliding door for her. "Five minutes, and then I am taking you back to the hotel."

Monique shook her head, seeming not to care. "Fine, whatever you want to do."

Once they were alone outside, Tyler stood curiously watching her adjust the folds along the front of her deep burgundy dress. The blue lights from the kidney-shaped pool gave an eerie glow to the tile-inlaid patio. About the eaves of the house, twinkling white lights were strewn, while tea lights floated in the water.

"I didn't know you would be here." She stood off to the side, wringing her hands. "If I would have known, I wouldn't have come. Chris insisted we make an appearance. Donovan Books contributes to the organization they are raising funds for."

Tyler ran his fingers back and forth over his forehead, fighting to remain calm. "Why do you let him treat you like that? Are you honestly going to stand there and tell me you want to marry that man?"

She was silent for the longest time, and he could detect the slightest hint of regret in her voice when she finally spoke. "How did you find out we were getting married?"

"My mother found out through some friends who read about it on the Internet," he replied, sounding irritated.

"I'm sure Barbara enjoyed dropping that little bombshell, didn't she?"

He waved his hand at her. "I just can't believe you brushed me aside so easily, Moe."

"You walked away, Ty, not me."

"But with Chris!" He pointed to the glass door. "You told me you never—"

"I said a lot of things, Ty. So did you. But Chris was there for me when you left."

He shoved his hands in the pockets of his tuxedo pants. "Come on, Moe. Is he really the one you want?"

She unleashed a cruel-sounding snicker that took Tyler by surprise. "Wow, you are really full of yourself. Just because he is not you, you think I don't want him, is that it, Ty?"

"That's not want I meant. I want to know if he makes you happy." Tyler's eyes then curiously hovered over the front of her dress.

She saw him staring at her body and fidgeted on her feet. "My happiness is no longer your concern. You made that clear when you left last July."

"Moe, don't do this. You don't love him."

"Yeah, well, I tried with you, and look where it got me." She rested her hand over the front folds of her dress, accentuating the slight curve of her lower belly.

Tyler could not put his finger on it, but here was something different about Monique. When his eyes followed the outline of her slightly swollen abdomen beneath the fabric of her dress, an inkling of doubt rose up from his heart.

"Moe? Are you all right? You seem—"

"I'm pregnant, Ty," she blurted out. Removing her hand from her stomach, she held her head up high. "I'm due in April."

Tyler's gut felt as if it had been kicked by some invisible force. "That's why you want to marry him, because you're pregnant?" He recalled the smug grin on Chris's face when he had returned to New Orleans and found the man staying with Monique. "Christ, Moe. Just because Chris got you pregnant, doesn't mean you have to spend the rest of your life with him."

"I never slept with Chris. You just assumed when you saw him at my house that we…." She waved her hand at him. "You're the father, Ty. There hasn't been anyone else."

Shock, that's all he felt. Never before had Tyler been confronted with the possibility of fatherhood; it was something he had always taken precautions against…except with Monique.

"But you said…the doctors told you…it was impossible for you to get pregnant," he stammered.

"Difficult, but obviously not impossible." She smirked at his panicked reaction. "I was just as shocked as you are now."

As the surprise wore off, an unusual sense of calm enveloped him. "Why didn't you call me?"

She took a step back from him. "When you thought I had slept with Chris after what we had shared…I was so angry. Then, I found out I was pregnant, and I knew I couldn't call you. Like you told me before, you've had enough women wanting you for your money. I couldn't have you thinking I was like all the rest."

"Jesus, I would never have thought that. I would have—"

"What? Taken care of me? Is that what you were going to say?" She went around him. "No thanks, Ty. I don't need your money or your pity."

He clasped his hand about her wrist. "That's not what I was going to say." He held on to her as she fought against him. "I was going to say I would have married you."

She finally pulled away. "You son of a bitch! You think marrying me just because I am pregnant is what I want?"

"No. But it's what I want." She was heading for the glass door when he professed, "I would have married you even if you weren't pregnant, Moe, but I was too damned scared."

She stopped and turned to him. "Scared? Of what…me?"

"You told me before I was afraid, and you were right. I was terrified of letting you in." He slowly came up to her side. "The last person I cared for walked out on me, and I was convinced that you were going to do the exact same thing."

"What are you talking about? Who walked out on you?"

"Peter," he confessed. "All this time I thought the real reason he left was because of my mother and her incessant nagging for him to straighten out his life. Seems there was a stronger lure. I recently learned he was convicted of drug dealing and was serving a thirty year sentence when he was killed in prison." He took in a deep breath and suddenly a weight lifted from his shoulders, as if all his burdens were falling to the wayside. "I guess I finally got the answers I needed."

Her eyes softened. "I'm sorry, Ty. I know what he meant to you."

"That's just it, Moe. I thought he meant something to me, because I meant something to him, but you don't walk out on the people you love. He was wrong to leave me, just like I was wrong to leave you. I should have packed up you and Ugly and taken you to Oklahoma with me." He slowly grinned. "How is Ugly?"

Finally, a slight smile spread across her delicate pink lips. "Snoring worse than ever."

He marveled at how the glowing blue lights from the pool reflected in her eyes. "Do you think we could start again? It will be different this time, I will be different this time, I promise. I want to be with you, Moe; with you and my baby."

Her shoulders slouched and the fight seemed to drain from her body. "It's too late for us, Ty. We had our second chance and we blew it." Her hand clutched the door handle. "I can't afford to take any more chances. Chris has always been there for me, and he will be there for my baby." She pulled the sliding glass door open. "You have your life, and I have mine. Let's keep it that way."

She walked into the house, leaving Tyler alone on the patio. He closed his eyes as the bitter taste of regret rose up from his stomach. He had missed his opportunity to be with the one woman he could never forget. The crushing disappointment tearing at his heart was more than he could stand. It felt as if he were fourteen again, standing on the porch of his old rundown childhood home, and watching Peter drive away.

"Hey, baby, you okay?" Giselle asked as she came outside.

"Yeah, fine." He took her hand and pulled her toward the glass door. "Let's get the hell out of here. I'm not in a party mood anymore."

Cover to Covers

Chapter 27

The festivities of the New Year were over, but many employees were still out on vacation, leaving Tyler to pick up the slack in several departments. He could not begrudge his employees their time off. If he had someone to be with, he was sure he would have been spending a lot more time at home, as well.

As he sat at his Napoleon desk, reading over a progress report from his newly formed alternative energy division, his mind wandered back to Monique. Tyler had revisited the image of her bulging tummy beneath her deep burgundy dress many times since leaving the party over a month ago. After contacting Fred Bishop about his legal rights, he had learned that there were many ways he could sue for custody, or demand visitation with his child, but there was no legal way to force Monique to allow him back in her life. He did not want to make things harder for both of them by filing a lawsuit, but he did not know what else he could do. Several phone calls, e-mails, and texts to Monique had gone unanswered, and a dozen letters had been returned.

Tyler put the report in his hands down on his desk, sat back in his chair, and stretched out his back. He was getting tired, very tired of his life. The day in and day out grind of the office, the empty relationships, and the nights spent worrying about Monique and the baby were wearing him down.

"I'm going out for lunch, you want anything?" Lynn inquired when she popped her head into his office.

Tyler glanced up from the report he had still not comprehended. "No, ah, thanks, Lynn. I might just step out for a quick bite. Stretch my legs."

"It's raining out. You might not be able to walk anywhere."

"Well, then I'll drive." He stood from his desk. "I need to get out of here for a while."

She leaned against the doorway. "Good idea. You look like you're somewhere else."

He picked up his suit jacket from a nearby chair. "Do I?"

"Uh huh. In fact, you've been like that for a while."

He shrugged the dark blue jacket over his wide shoulders. "I have a lot on my mind."

"Does any of it have to do with Monique Delome?"

He scowled at her. "No."

"You can't lie to your secretary, Mr. Moore. We know all."

"You don't know anything about my relationship with Monique."

"No, I don't, but I know how you've been acting ever since you came back from New Orleans, and you're not the man I have known for the past ten years." She took a step into his office. "I'm going to offer you a bit of advice. I figured someone around here should tell you what an ass you're being."

He raised his eyebrows. "I don't think I've ever heard you talk like that."

"I'm not an idiot, Mr. Moore. I sit out at my desk and hear all kinds of things. Most of which I forget as soon as I hear it, but lately I have been hearing her name come up quite a bit. And then when Fred Bishop started calling, I figured there was more going on with the two of you than just a lovers' tiff."

"It's not a tiff," he coolly insisted.

"No, it's more than that. You're in love with this woman, and I would hazard a guess to say she is in love with you, but something is holding you both back."

He patted his jacket pocket for his car keys. "It's over. She has made that very clear."

277

"Mr. Moore, you may be a whiz at business, but you are an idiot when it comes to women. If you want her, you have to prove it to her."

"What are you going on about?"

"Women need the big gesture to forgive a man. I'm not talking about jewelry or gifts. It has to be something special." She folded her arms over her chest. "My Ed dumped me once and then wanted me back, but I refused to talk to him. He sent a mariachi band to my house and they played outside of my front door for six hours before I finally called him and begged him to stop. Four months later, we were married."

"I don't think a mariachi band will work in this situation, Lynn."

"The big gesture isn't about mariachi bands and roses, Mr. Moore. It's about showing her what she means to you."

Tyler walked across his expensive beige European rug to her side. "All right. Then how do I show her that?"

Lynn's green eyes twinkled. "Be there for her, whether she wants you or not. That's how a man proves he is in it for the long haul. He puts her first."

"She has already found someone else to do that for her. She does not need me anymore."

"I'm not talking about need, Mr. Moore. I'm talking about want. Do you still want her?"

Tyler sighed but said nothing.

"Is she as stubborn as you?"

He ran his hand over his chin. "Yes."

She took a step back outside the office doors. "Then you have a problem."

"How do you propose I deal with it?"

Lynn went to her desk. Opening a drawer, she withdrew something from it and then walked over to Tyler. Holding out a paperback book to him, her face lit up with a knowing smile.

"Did you know that Monique Delome is having a book signing today at the Barnes and Nobles Book Store at SMU for her new book?"

Tyler took the book from her and when he saw the title, *A Chance with You,* printed in bold red letters across the top, he grinned.

"You can get that signed for me while you're there," Lynn added with a wink.

He held up the book to his secretary. "You read this stuff?"

"I'm a fan. Besides, there is nothing better for keeping a relationship going than reenacting the steamy scenes from a romance novel. Why do you think I've been married for twenty years?" She pointed to the book. "You should take a look at it; might give you a few pointers."

Tyler laughed out loud when he called to mind where Monique had gotten the ideas for her newest novel.

"Don't laugh, Mr. Moore. It's actually a very revealing story about a man and woman who rediscover love after many years apart."

He recollected that day in the French Quarter when he had grilled Monique about the book, hoping for a glimpse into their future. "Tell me, Lynn, how does it end?" he softly pleaded.

"The hero has to put aside his pride in order to show the woman he loves how he feels. How he really feels," Lynn declared.

"He puts aside his pride?" Tyler reflected on her words and then shook his head. "I don't understand."

"It was the only thing standing in their way. Pride can do that. It can be your biggest asset, and sometimes your greatest enemy." Lynn nodded to the hallway that led to the reception area. "You'd better get going. She'll only be there for another hour."

Tyler weighed the paperback in his hand, as if contemplating the necessity of what he was about to do.

"Go," Lynn insisted. "You need this, Tyler. You need her."

He gazed into his secretary's green eyes, somewhat amazed that she had finally called him by his first name, then Tyler turned down the hall. He moved slowly at first, but as he considered his final destination and the woman who would be

279

there, his pace quickened. Apprehensive and elated at the same time, he gripped the book in his hand and rushed across the reception area of the Propel offices to the silver elevator doors. Suddenly, it all made sense, and he realized Lynn was right. He did need Monique, more than he had ever needed anyone.

***

While his black Mercedes sped through the rainy, cold streets of Highland Park toward the campus of Southern Methodist University, Tyler occasionally peered out the driver's side window. Everywhere people were running to and fro, hoping to avoid the wet, wintry weather, but he never noticed the dreary conditions. His mind was elsewhere. When he finally parked outside the bookstore, he sat for a few minutes with the engine running, struggling to find the courage to get out of the car.

After picking up the book from the front seat, he ventured into the rain. Pulling the blue suit jacket closer around his body, he jogged toward the gleaming glass storefront. The fluorescent lights in the store cast an odd light on the gloomy sidewalk. Standing beneath a dark green canopy, Tyler peeked in the wide picture windows, searching for Monique.

She was seated at a table close to the front windows with a line of fans snaking deep into the belly of the store. Beside her sat an unfamiliar woman with flaming red hair and a pink pantsuit adorned with white flowers. Monique's protruding belly was discreetly hidden behind a demure gray dress as she greeted and talked with her fans. Her features were glowing while her gray eyes appeared sharp and playful. Her alluring pink lips made Tyler's heart skip a beat.

"Christ, what am I doing here?" he whispered, the uncertainty shaking his voice.

As she interacted with her readers, the confidence he had felt back at his office quickly fizzled. He glimpsed the book in his hand and realized that this had been a mistake. Monique was in his city, and never once had she contacted him. That was probably the way she wanted it. Lynn had been wrong; what he needed was to let her go.

Tyler turned away from the window and the dark skies above reflected his mood. Shaking his head at his stupidity, he ducked from beneath the green canopy, heading back to his car.

"Ty?"

He stopped when the airy voice registered with him. Tyler knew that voice, too well. He had dreamed of it for so many nights that he had memorized its every intonation.

When he turned around, Monique was standing at the entrance to the bookstore with her belly poking out beneath her loose-fitting, A-line dress. He wanted to rush to her side and throw his arms about her, but instead he waited in the light drizzle of rain for her to make the first move.

She stepped from beneath the canopy. "What are you doing here?"

He held up the book in his hand. "My secretary is a fan." He motioned to her. "How are you doing? I mean, is everything all right?"

She patted her round abdomen. "Everything is fine."

The light rain was beginning to leave dark spots on her gray dress, worrying Tyler. "You need to get out of this cold rain." He took her elbow and escorted her back beneath the dark green canopy.

Safely out of the rain, she looked down at the sidewalk and curled a lock of hair behind her ear. "You didn't come here for me to sign your book, did you?"

He searched the parking lot next to them, hunting for the right words. "In all those letters and e-mails I sent you I was trying to tell you...I know things haven't been good between us, but with the baby coming...I want to figure out a way to keep in touch...not keep in touch. To share...." Tyler ran his hand through his hair, feeling completely confounded.

"Are you saying you want to be a part of her life?"

Tyler's dark eyes swerved to Monique. "Her life?"

She nodded her head. "It's a girl."

The grade "A" bastard he had struggled to be over the past few weeks suddenly ceased to exist. As he stood there, imagining a home with Monique and his daughter, a lifetime of anger, hurt, and guilt drained from his soul.

"Moe, I can't stand by on the sidelines and watch you go through this without me. I have to be a part of our daughter's life."

Monique's stoic features remained unchanged. "Maybe we could work out some kind of arrangement for visitation. See how that goes, but I don't want to get any lawyers involved and go to court fighting over when and where. Just you and me, we will settle it between us. Okay?"

Tyler's body throbbed with disappointment. It was not enough. "You did not hear what I said. I want to be there for you and our baby. I'm not talking about visitation. I want the two of you to come and live with me."

Monique took a step back. "I can't do that, Ty."

"Why? Because of Chris?"

"No, that's over. I called off the engagement after the party."

"Over?" A glimmer of hope streaked across his heart. "But why did you agree to the engagement in the first place?"

"When I found out I was pregnant, I panicked," Monique began. "After I told Chris about the baby, he seemed so happy that I thought maybe something was wrong with me for being…upset about the situation. He helped me to see the joy in things. Eventually, he worked his way into my life. When he asked me to marry him, I figured why not?" She paused and uttered a long sigh. "But the whole time I could not stop thinking about you. When I saw you at the party, and could no longer keep the truth from you…I knew I had to stop pretending. I had just settled with Chris for the sake of my baby, but in the long run no one was going to be happy with that decision."

He snuck closer to her. "What about your career? Chris will still be involved."

"I found another company to publish *A Chance with You*. They have rushed the publishing process along so I could do a book tour before the baby comes. Chris wasn't happy about any of it, but I guess he figured once we were married he could fix everything. Or at least that is what he finally admitted to me after I fired him." She waved to the redheaded woman at the table just beyond the windows. "My new publisher got me a new manager."

"A woman manager?" Tyler grinned. "I like the sound of that."

She took in the contours of his face. "Thank you for coming to see me. I'm glad we can still be friends." She swerved away from him.

"Where are you going?"

Monique gestured to the front door of the bookstore. "To my signing; I have fans waiting."

"But we need to talk. Make plans. You live in New Orleans, I live in Dallas."

"We'll figure it out." She gave him one last fleeting glance and then turned back to the store entrance.

As Monique walked away, the hope that she had encouraged quickly dissolved. She wanted him, but only as a father, a helper, and a friend. Their brief interaction had left Tyler more desperate for her than ever. Unlike his former affinity for alcohol, he knew that his desire for Monique was something he would never be able to overcome.

She paused at the wide wood and glass door to the bookstore. "Do you want to have some coffee and talk when I'm finished with my signing?" Then, she held up her hand, appearing as if she regretted asking the question. "Never mind. You probably have to get back to your office. Perhaps we could get together another time?"

"No." He quickly walked toward her. "I'm in no rush to get back. The business can wait."

"Are you sure?"

"There's nowhere else I'd rather be right now." Tyler opened the heavy glass door and held it for her. "Shall we?"

"Thank you, Ty."

Tyler became lost in her magnificent gray eyes. "I should be the one thanking you, Moe."

"Me? What did I do?"

He spied the line of anxiously waiting fans. "I'll tell you later."

"And what if you leave before you tell me?"

His eyes returned to her. "I'm not going anywhere, Moe. I am never going to leave you again. I promise. I'm going to stick by you for as long as you'll have me."

"But how can I be sure it will be different this time? When things get serious, Ty, you run."

He reluctantly nodded his head. "I know, but I'm not afraid anymore, Moe. I ran away from us in the past because I was terrified of how much I needed you…of how much I love you. I will do whatever it takes to hold on to you. Like I told you before, I would rather fail a thousand times with you than never take the chance."

A gentle smile crossed her lips. "Yeah, I remember. It was a hell of a line."

"It's no line, Moe. It's how I feel. I will never give up on us."

She touched the hint of gray hair along his left temple. "I know. I guess I've always known that. "

He breathed in the scent of her lilac perfume and whispered, "Me, too."

As she moved through the doorway, Tyler's hope for the future was reignited. Their lives had come full circle. The happiness he had longed for was once again within reach, only this time he vowed to ardently grab hold of it with both hands, and never, ever, let go.

Cover to Covers

Epilogue

Tyler was sitting at his Napoleon desk across from three middle-aged gentlemen dressed in tailored dark suits with stern-looking faces. He was going through a neatly formatted report with dozens of colorful charts and graphs as he listened to one of the men speak in a rather monotone voice.

"We have new contracts coming in daily for the alternative energy division, and if that keeps on track it will be one of our fastest growing enterprises. The oil leases for sixty-eight percent of our wells are secured for the next four years, and we—"

"Bill, just give me the bottom line," Tyler inserted. "I know the P&L numbers, what I want from you guys are the projections. I need to get everything settled before I go out of town tomorrow."

"Well, Tyler, it's like we said," Bill returned. "The projections for the alternative energy division are very good and we have—"

"Where are the Oklahoma gas pipeline numbers?" Tyler leafed through the report.

"We did not include those for this year since the line won't be up and running until next year," another of the accountants replied.

"But I need to see expenditures, Harry." Tyler tossed the thick report on his desk. "We've had enough delays with all the political games and I want to be kept informed on what kind of expenses we are drawing from that project."

"Of course, Tyler. I'll get Mitch to send those to you before the day is out. I know we—"

"Dude, what are you doing?" a man's voice called from the doorway to Tyler's office.

Standing inside the doors was a thick man with wild blond hair, wearing a T-shirt with "Surfers Do It in Waves" plastered across the chest, faded blue jeans, and dingy white tennis shoes. Beneath his tanned arm was the small, white body of Bart. The dog's red tongue was hanging from the side of his mouth and dripping drool all over Tyler's expensive beige rug.

"Tyler, it's time."

Tyler looked up at him. "Time for what, Jake? And why is Bart here?"

Jake scurried up to his desk. "Mojo called me. Her water broke when she was at lunch with your mom and Gary. They are taking her to the hospital, and she wanted me to get you."

Tyler stood from his desk. "But she still has another month to go."

Jake shrugged. "I guess no one told little Eva that."

Tyler grabbed for his black suit jacket on a chair beside his desk. "I can't believe this. When I left the house, everything was fine. She was packing for our honeymoon." He checked for his keys in his jacket pocket. Then, as if remembering the men seated at his desk, he coolly announced, "Gentleman, you'll have to excuse me, it seems my wife has gone into labor."

"Good luck, Tyler," Bill voiced as Tyler jogged out of the office. "Whatever you do, just tell her to keep breathing."

When Tyler passed through his black leather-covered doors, Jake slapped his shoulder, almost knocking him to the side. "Isn't this great? I come in town for your wedding and end up getting to meet my niece, too."

"Jake, are you sure everything is all right?" Tyler begged.

"Call me and let me know how it goes," Lynn said, coming up to him.

He nodded to her. "I will."

"And, Mr. Moore? Relax, everything is going to be fine."

He took in a deep breath, trying to calm his rattled nerves. "Thank you, Lynn."

"Hurry up," Jake exuberantly yelled. "I'm double parked downstairs."

Tyler pointed to Bart. "You can't bring the dog to the hospital, Jake."

"Mojo didn't want him left alone in your big mansion," Jake admitted. "She said he would be afraid."

Tyler took the dog from under Jake's arm and handed him to Lynn. "Can you dog sit for me?"

Lynn warily examined Bart's face. "This will cost you."

Tyler grinned at his secretary. "Add it to my bill."

"We've got to go, Tyler," Jake insisted next to him.

When he reached the silver elevator doors in the reception area, Tyler hurriedly pushed the call button several times.

"Pretty exciting stuff, eh?" Jake commented beside him. "It's just like what Mojo writes about in those trashy novels of hers. A real 'happily ever after,' you know?"

"No, Jake," Tyler proclaimed as the elevator doors opened. "This isn't anything like Moe's romance novels. This 'happily ever after' is better…because it's real."

The End

Cover to Covers

Read the Next book in the Cover to Covers Series The Riding Master

About the Author

Alexandrea Weis is an advanced practice registered nurse who was born and raised in New Orleans. Having been brought up in the motion picture industry, she learned to tell stories from a different perspective and began writing at the age of eight. Infusing the rich tapestry of her hometown into her award-winning novels, she believes that creating vivid characters makes a story moving and memorable. A permitted/certified wildlife rehabber with the Louisiana Wildlife and Fisheries, Weis rescues orphaned and injured wildlife. She lives with her husband and pets in New Orleans.

To read more about Alexandrea Weis or her books, you can go to the following sites:

Website: http://www.alexandreaweis.com/

Facebook: http://www.facebook.com/authoralexandreaweis

Twitter: https://twitter.com/alexandreaweis

Goodreads: http://www.goodreads.com/author/show/1211671.Alexandrea_Weis

Pinterest: http://www.pinterest.com/apwrncs/

TSU: https://www.tsu.co/alexandreaweis

CPSIA information can be obtained at www.ICGtesting.com
Printed in the USA
LVOW06s1446200915

454944LV00004B/303/P